MW01230074

1017

ALAMO WAY

CEE BOWERMAN

BOOK

LONESTAR TERRACE SERIES

FOUR

COPYRIGHT 2024

All rights reserved. This book or parts thereof may not be reproduced in any form, stored in any retrieval system, or transmitted in any form by any means—electronic, mechanical, photocopy, recording, or otherwise—without prior written permission of the publisher, except as provided by United States of America copyright law. For permission requests, write to the publisher, at: www.ceebowermanbooks.com

This is a work of fiction. Names, characters, places, brands, media, and incidents are either the product of the author's imagination or are used fictitiously. Any resemblance to similarly named places or to persons living or deceased is unintentional.

This is a work of fiction. Names, characters, places, brands, media, and incidents are either the product of the author's imagination or are used fictitiously. Any resemblance to similarly named places or to persons living or deceased is unintentional.

Copyright© 2024 CEE BOWERMAN

Professionally edited by Chrissy Riesenberg

Please follow Cee on Facebook, Instagram, and Twitter. Also, for information on new releases and to catch up with Cee, go to www.ceebowermanbooks.com

CEE BOWERMAN MASTER BOOK LIST

The Rojo, Texas Universe

**Texas Knights MC
(completed)**

Home Forever
Forever Family
Lucky Forever
Love Forever

**Texas Kings MC
(completed)**

Kale
Sonny
Bird
Grunt
Lout
Smokey
Tucker
Kale & Terra (Novella)
John & Mattie
Bear
Daughtry
Hank
Fain
Grady
Stoffer
Luke
Clem

**Conner Brothers Construction
(completed)**

Finn
Angus
Mace
Ronan
Royal
Tavin
Chess

**Rojo, TX
(completed)**

Rason & Eliza
Atlas & Addie
Jazmyne & Luc
Kari & Levi
Noah & Tallie
Nick & Cindy
Marcus & Reagan

**The Tempests
(completed)**

Wrath
Creed
Loki
Styx
Thorn
Freya
Sin

**Lonestar Terrace
(in progress)**

1005 Alamo Way
2011 Texas Drive
2012 Texas Drive

**Rojo PD
(in progress)**

The Dark Side

**Rojo Gems
(in progress)**

Emerald

**Rojo Kings
(in progress)**

Lucky

**Texas Queens MC
(in progress)**

Lark

Cee Bowerman's Stand Alone Series

Time Served MC
(completed)

Boss
Hook
Chef
Preacher
Captain
Bug
Santa
Kitty
Rodeo
Stamp
TS in NY
Hammer
Soda

Time Served MC: Nomads
(in progress)

Sugar

The Four Families
(in progress)

Rico Romano
Zach Campana
Luca Russo - COMING JUNE 15TH, 2024!

Springblood
(in progress)

One More Day
Fly Away with Me

The Donovans
(in progress)

Drink It Up
Pull It Up
Pretty It Up
Curl It Up
Build It Up
Whip It Up

Mereu
(in progress)

Bear Witch Me

The Rojo, Texas Universe
In Chronological Reading Order

Home Forever: Texas Knights MC, Book 1

Forever Family: Texas Knights MC, Book 2

Kale: Texas Kings MC, Book 1

Sonny: Texas Kings MC, Book 2

Bird: Texas Kings MC, Book 3

Grunt: Texas Kings MC, Book 4

Lout: Texas Kings MC, Book 5

Smokey: Texas Kings MC, Book 6

Tucker: Texas Kings MC, Book 7

Finn: Conner Brothers Construction, Book 1

Kale & Terra: a Texas Kings novella

John & Mattie: Texas Kings MC, Book 8

Angus: Conner Brothers Construction, Book 2

Bear: Texas Kings MC, Book 9

Lucky Forever: Texas Knights MC, Book 3

Daughtry: Texas Kings MC, Book 10

Mace: Conner Brothers Construction, Book 3

Reading Order for the Tenillo Guardians Crossover Series

Boss: Time Served MC, Book 1

Sin's Enticement: Ares Infidels MC, Book 1 by Ciara St James

Hook: Time Served MC, Book 2

Executioner's Enthrallment: Ares Infidels MC, Book 2 by Ciara St James

Chef: Time Served MC, Book 3

Pitbull's Enslavement: Ares Infidels MC, Book 3 by Ciara St James

Preacher: Time Served MC, Book 4

Omen's Entrapment: Ares Infidels MC, Book 4 by Ciara St James

Captain: Time Served MC, Book 5

Cuffs' Enchainment: Ares Infidels MC, Book 5 by Ciara St James

Bug: Time Served MC, Book 6

Rampage's Enchantment: Ares Infidels MC, Book 6 by Ciara St James

Santa: Time Served MC, Book 7

Wrecker's Ensnarement: Ares Infidels MC, Book 7

by Ciara St James

Kitty: Time Served MC, Book 8

Trident's Enjoyment: Ares Infidels MC, Book 8 by Ciara St James

Rodeo: Time Served MC, Book 9

Fang's Enlightenment: Ares Infidels MC, Book 9 by Ciara St James

Stamp: Time Served MC, Book 10

Talon's Enamorment: Ares Infidels MC, Book 10 by Ciara St James

Time Served In New York: Time Served MC, Book 11

Ares Infidels In New York: Ares Infidels MC, Book 11 by Ciara St. James

Hammer: Time Served MC, Book 12

Phantom's Emblazonment: Ares Infidels MC, Book 12 by Ciara St. James

Soda: Time Served MC, Book 13

A NOTE FROM THE AUTHOR

Dear Reader,

Welcome back to Rojo and the lives of some of our favorite Forresters. This book centers around Ruf - Kale and Terra's oldest son - and his wild but loveable son Koda who we have gotten to know through previous second generation books.

When I was trying to decide who would be the best love interest for Ruf, I had so many options that it was hard to choose. In the end, I decided to go with a character that has been referenced before but we've never actually met. I love a good second-chance romance, and even though this couple wasn't ready for forever when they were young, they're a little older and wiser and ready to find it with each other now.

There are some sensitive topics in this book that I'd like to warn you about. Ruf and Scoot (the little girl from Ripley and Tori's book) are siblings who survived a horrible situation of child neglect. I wrote their story based on an article I read months ago, and sadly, there was a situation much like theirs more recently that ended in the death of an innocent baby. As horrible as the situation is that happened with these characters, it doesn't even touch on what can happen in the real world and the brutal effects it has on the children that experience it. As a survivor of child abuse, I know how damaging the memories of those experiences can be and understand that it might bring up emotions that some readers don't want to deal with.

Jovi's experience with long-term verbal and psychological abuse turns into physical abuse in the first chapter. It's not horribly graphic, but it might cause some readers to be uncomfortable. I didn't want to focus on exactly what happened to Jovi but more of how she managed to triumph over it and move on to a better life full of happiness and joy.

Unfortunately, child abuse happens all the time in varying degrees just like domestic violence. As a survivor of both and a person that loves a good happy ending, I wanted to show these stories from beginning to end. I think I've done that with this book.

If you or someone you know is experiencing abuse, please know that there is help out there. The National Domestic Abuse Hotline is just a phone call away and can help you connect with someone in your area you can depend on.

National Domestic Abuse Hotline

Call: 800-799-7233

Or text BEGIN to 88788

If you know someone who needs help or know of a child who is being abused and neglected, please don't hesitate to call the authorities and get that person the help they deserve. For some people who have no control and no way out, a helping hand is all they need to find their way to a better life.

As always, I hope you enjoy this story and all the ones to follow, and I can't wait for you to get to know these characters so that you can come to love them all as much as I do. Please make sure you belong to one (or all) of my Facebook groups so that we can chat about the books I write and the characters we wish were real.

Look for the Texas Queens MC Rojo TX (for all things Rojo), Covenant of Ascent (mafia genre), Springblood (paranormal), and the Tenillo Guardians (for the Time Served MC series). I'd love to chat with you there as we share our love of reading and happily ever afters.

Happy reading!

Cee

PROLOGUE

NINE YEARS AGO

RUF

"Let's take a road trip."

I looked up at my friend Lawson and asked, "When?"

"Hell, I don't know. We're free until school starts in the fall. We could take the summer."

"The whole summer?"

"Why not? We're only young once, right?" Jonas, Lawson's twin, asked.

"I've always thought it would be cool to drive up the coast," I admitted. "Just go where the wind takes you, you know?"

"East or west?" Lawson asked as he reached into his pocket and pulled out a quarter. He flipped it into the air and then caught it and slapped it onto the back of his hand. "East is heads, west is tails."

"Are we really doing this?" I asked.

"Yeah," Lawson said eagerly.

"Well?" Jonas asked. "Are you in or out?"

"I'm in," I said firmly.

Lawson lifted his hand and held his fist out for us to

look at the coin resting on it. "We're going west, gentlemen."

"Hell yeah!" Jonas said before he leaned back in his chair and took a sip of one of the beers we'd swiped from my dad's fridge in the garage. "Let's leave Monday."

"Mom's gonna shit," Lawson said with a laugh. "We could go through Colorado and see if any of the guys want to go with us as we ride over the mountains to the coast."

"This is crazy. Y'all know that, right?"

"It's not the craziest thing we've ever done," Lawson hedged.

"That's true but . . ." My voice trailed off as my phone buzzed with a text. I read the message and then stood up. "Shit. I forgot I was supposed to pick Jovi up from work!"

"We'll be here when you get back," Lawson said cheerfully as he put his foot up on the edge of the firepit. "I bet the little missus is gonna be pissed that you're taking off right before she leaves town for college."

"She'll be cool with it."

"Yeah. I'm sure she will," Jonas said sarcastically.

He laughed when I flipped him off over my shoulder and was still laughing when I fired up my bike.

"You've been drinking."

"I just had one or two, babe," I said as I pulled my bike key out of my pocket.

"You shouldn't be riding if you've been drinking."

"Do I look drunk?"

"No, but you won't look drunk when you're a bloodstain on the highway either."

"We won't even get on the highway. I'll take the back roads. Come on. The guys are waiting for us."

"Why? We're having dinner with my parents."

"Shit!"

"You forgot."

"I did. The guys are at the house and . . ."

"I'll call my sister and see if she can pick me up."

"I'll drop you off there."

"I'm not riding with you. I don't even want you to ride. I can smell the beer on your breath, Ruf."

"Jesus, Jovi. You're so uptight sometimes."

"No, I'm responsible. There's a difference."

"Well, your responsible ass is really gonna hate what I'm about to tell you."

"What?"

"I'm going on a road trip with the guys."

"When?"

"I think we're leaving on Monday."

"You think? You're not sure? When are you coming back?"

"I don't know. We're thinking of going through Colorado and getting . . ."

"You mean a *long* road trip."

"Yeah. We're gonna go down the west coast."

"Where will you be staying?"

"We'll figure it out as we go."

"How are you gonna pay for this?"

"I've been working at the garage since I was a kid. I've got some money saved up."

"I'm not gonna see you all summer? I'm leaving in August, Ruf, and we'll barely be able to see each other from then until Christmas break."

"I know, but you'll see me plenty before that. We'll figure out a few places to meet up, and you can fly out and spend the weekend or . . ."

"I can't afford a last minute plane ticket to somewhere on the west coast, Ruf, and I've got to work to save money for the fall. It doesn't make any sense to just take off like that."

"Sometimes, you've just gotta let go Jovi. Shit. Have some fucking fun."

"We're adults now. We've got to take things seriously. Our future . . ."

"Our future? You mean the one you've got planned out down to the last detail?"

"But you . . ."

"We're eighteen, not fifty. Live a little, babe."

"I am living, and I'm working toward my goals. I thought you were doing the same."

"It's just a road trip for a few months before we have to be all grown up and responsible."

"I think I'm already closer to that than you are."

The tone of Jovi's voice pissed me off and dimmed the excitement I felt about the adventure me and the guys had planned. "I guess you are. Are you riding or waiting for your sister?"

"I'll wait."

"Have it your way."

"Ruf, I won't be waiting for you when you come back."

"I'll make sure I'm home before you leave for school, Jovi."

"No. I mean I won't wait for you at all, Ruf. We want different things, and I can't . . . I just can't do this anymore."

"You're breaking up with me?"

"I think so," Jovi whispered as her eyes filled with tears. "I think you need to be free to fly when I'd rather be rooted somewhere safe."

"It's not like that, Jovi. I just . . . ."

Jovi went up on her tiptoes and touched her lips to mine. "I love you, Ruf. Take care of yourself."

"It's really over?"

"I think it has to be."

"Maybe someday . . ."

"Yeah. Someday," Jovi said before she brushed the tears off her cheeks. "Ride safe, Ruf."

I watched as the woman I'd thought I would be spending my life with turned and walked away, and as much as it hurt, I realized she was right. Right now wasn't our time, but maybe someday . . .

SIX YEARS AGO

JOVI

"This is going to be my favorite rotation," I said excitedly as I walked down the hall with my friend True Stoffer, a woman I'd known all through school and had reconnected with on the first day of clinicals a few weeks ago. "I love all the babies."

"I can hear your uterus humming from over here," True said with a wince. "I'm not ready for that at all."

"I'm not ready *yet,* but I've got plans."

"Of course you do. Let me guess - you're going to find an intelligent and steady man, buy a house, DIY everything on a budget, get a dog, buy a minivan, and then . . ."

"No minivan," I interrupted.

True didn't even pause, "Pop out two kids, and join the PTA."

"Yes. And I'm going to start that process after I've got a full year of nursing under my belt."

"Okay then. Are we shopping for Mr. Perfect yet, or is that gonna fall into line later?"

"I knew Mr. Perfect, but we had different goals. I'm waiting for Mr. Wonderful now."

True knew exactly who I was referring to and said, "I think Mr. Perfect has settled down. He's working at Kings now. We should pop in and have a drink some night and see if the spark is still there."

"There was always so much more than a spark, True. Loving Ruf was like an out of control wildfire that consumed everything with its heat. I just couldn't let it consume me."

True didn't have time to answer before we were standing in the corner of the nursery, ready to be briefed on our assignments for the day. There were only six babies in the room during the shift change checks. As soon as we completed all of their documentation with weights and measurements, they could go back to their families and start their lives out in the world.

The charge nurse thrust three charts toward me as she barked orders. Once she was finished, I walked across the room as I flipped open the first one.

"Koda Kale Forrester," I whispered in shock as I looked down at the baby in the bassinet in front of me. "Hi, little guy! I bet your gamma is beside herself to have another baby to love." I reached out and rested my hand on his tiny chest and asked, "Who are your mommy and daddy, little guy? Why didn't I hear that you were on your way?" I tilted my head when the child's full name struck me. "Kale? You're . . ." I looked back to the chart and scanned down until I saw the name of the parents and felt my heart break. Tears filled my eyes, and I sniffed to hold them at bay as I gently patted the baby boy who was starting to squirm beneath my hand. "You were supposed to be mine."

"What's wrong?" True asked from her station a few feet away. "Jovi, are you okay?"

"This is Ruf's baby."

"What?" I nodded and True's expression turned sympathetic as she whispered, "I'm sorry, Jovi."

"I'm not. A baby is a miracle, and this one is luckier than most. He's gonna have a great life."

"He will."

"I know he will. Ruf and the rest of the family will make sure of it."

FOUR YEARS AGO

RUF

"I'm Remington Forrester. I got a call that my son was brought in. How do I find him?" The nurse's serious expression showed a flicker of sadness, and before she could answer, I asked, "Is he okay? I haven't seen him since his mother took him a few days ago and . . ."

"Give me just a second, sir," the nurse said as her professional mask slipped back into place. She got up and walked through the open doorway behind her, and it took all I had not to hop over the counter and follow her. A few minutes later, she walked past that doorway and then the double doors beside me opened with a whoosh. She gestured for me to come through and said, "Follow me, please."

We went through the twisting maze of cubicles and rooms that I'd seen more than my fair share of over the years. During my childhood, road rash, a few sprains, and a couple of broken bones had brought me to this place. I knew I'd be here with my son through all of those one day, but he was much too young for anything like that quite yet.

The nurse pushed open the door, and I was surprised to see it was an office, not a patient room.

"Mr. Forrester?" a woman asked as she stood up from the round table where she'd been sitting.

"Who are you? Where's my little boy?" I glanced over and saw a cop standing against the wall on the other side of the room. "Lawson? What's going on?"

"Have a seat, Ruf. She needs to talk to you for a minute, and then we'll take you to Koda."

"What the fuck?" I asked, but now I couldn't mask the panic in my voice. I looked at my friend and asked, "Did she hurt him?"

"Sit down, brother. I called Spruce and Jewel on our way here, and they're with him right now. Let her ask you some questions, and then I'll take you to him myself."

"When was the last time you had contact with your son?"

"Cadence picked him up Friday. I'm supposed to get him from her this afternoon."

"We received a call about an hour ago from a neighbor who said she'd found two children alone in the home. She was alerted when your son broke a window and called for help."

"He's barely two! Where was Cadence?"

"The neighbors said they hadn't seen her car at the house in more than twenty-four hours. The children . . ."

24

"She left him alone?" I asked in outrage.

"Yes. From the scene, it was obvious to the officers and the paramedics that they'd been alone for at least a day, if not more."

"Oh my god," I choked out as I fought back tears. "I never . . . I didn't know. Shit."

"I think that's enough for now, ma'am. He's obviously not going anywhere. I'm going to take him back. Ripley should be here any minute, and you're gonna get the same response from him. I can guarantee it."

I looked at Lawson, and there weren't tears in my voice, only rage, when I said, "You better find her before I do."

"Yeah. I know."

ONE

"She's a bright spot in what is otherwise a very dark sky, just like you and your sister."

Ruf

RUF

"Remington Uriah Forrester! Have you lost the last threads of what little sanity you had before you became a single father to one of the wildest children on the planet? I can say that because I have comparative data after racking up countless hours of babysitting Forrester hellspawn and now I'm witnessing all of you experience the next generation of joy and psychosis in equal amounts."

"Petra, you're really not helping," I said without lifting my head from my hands.

"Is it really your job to talk him out of this?" Cadence asked.

"Do you see her sitting there with a ouija board? Did you hear her summon a demon? No to both. Shut your fucking mouth and let the grown-ups talk, Cadence," Trinity Booker snapped, her gaze so piercing that I was surprised Cadence didn't combust.

Trinity had a vested interest in whether Cadence lived or died because she'd been beside her brother Ripley along with the rest of their family and mine four years ago as we waited for the doctors to examine my son and her niece after Cadence almost killed them with her neglect.

"I've given them both the greatest gift a woman can offer a man, and you . . ."

"A gift? What the fuck is wrong with you?" Trinity yelled as she pushed up out her chair and put her knee on the table.

A split second before Trinity launched herself across the conference table towards Cadence, Roscoe wrapped his arm around her waist and yanked her back into the chair next to him.

"Let her loose. I'll represent her," Petra cheered.

I had to admit that wasn't very professional behavior from an attorney like Petra, but then again, the woman had been marching to the beat of her own drum since we were kids. Luckily, Roscoe had a better rein on his temper and cooler heads prevailed.

"You can plot her death later. Right now, Ripley and Ruf have some decisions to make. Cadence is going to be discharged in the morning, so if they do choose to go along with this plan, we need to have the birth certificate and all of the paperwork in order before then."

"Are you going to do this?" Trinity asked Ripley. "Have you even talked to Tori about what's going on yet?"

"I haven't had a chance. Ruf and I called your office before we told anyone else, and I . . ."

"I'll do it," I blurted out loudly. "I'll sign whatever I need to so she can come home with me."

"I knew you'd step up, Ruf," Cadence said cheerfully.

"I'm not doing this for you, Cadence. I'm doing this for another innocent baby that somehow sparked the tiniest grain of motherly instinct. Not enough that you've even asked about my son or his little sister, but sufficient for you to realize that being raised as far away from you as possible is the best thing you could do for her."

"Will the three of you be official witnesses to this?" Roscoe asked the two guards who were standing behind Cadence's wheelchair and the nurse that was farther down the table watching the drama unfold alongside the hospital's notary. They nodded, and Roscoe looked at me before he asked, "Are you sure this is what you want to do?"

"I'm sure, but I want you to make it airtight, and I want her to sign away her rights to not just the baby, but Koda and Scoot too."

"Will you do that?" Roscoe asked Cadence. When Cadence nodded, Roscoe flipped through the file he'd brought in with him. He pulled out a stack of papers and set them aside before he propped his phone up at the end of the table and pushed a button on the screen. I assumed this was so he could record what was about to go down. "I thought this might come up, so I took the liberty of printing off the relevant documents just in case." He set a page down in front of Cadence and looked at the guard for permission before he handed her a pen. "This document gives full legal custody of Koda Kale Forrester to his biological father, Remington Uriah Forrester, and terminates your parental rights to the child." Cadence signed the paper before Roscoe handed it over so the guards and the nurse could sign as witnesses. "By signing this, you will be testifying to the best of your knowledge that Cadence Tripp is of sound mind and under no duress."

As soon as the nurse finished, she slid the paper to the notary who signed and stamped it, then handed it back toward Roscoe. As Roscoe put it in the folder and closed the cover, I felt a weight lift from my chest. It seemed as if I could breathe easier than I had in years. Even after Cadence disappeared, leaving Koda, who was barely talking, and Celia, who hadn't even started walking yet, alone in a house for more than twenty-four hours with no air conditioning during a summer heat wave, the court still hadn't terminated her parental rights.

Koda and Celia were so dehydrated from her neglect that they had to be on IV fluids for *days* and Celia was permanently deaf from the high fever she developed, but the court system didn't take away her rights as their mother. Instead, they'd given me and Ripley full custody of the children while Cadence served a short jail sentence and then fulfilled all the requirements of the service plans that the Department of Children and Families presented to the court with the promise that when she did, they would reassess the situation. As far as I knew, she had never attempted to complete any of those requirements, but the chance that she might at some point had been hanging over our heads for years.

The uncertainty of my son's future had made it hard to resist doing something that would leave a black mark on my soul for eternity just to make sure she never took him away from me and put him in danger again.

Now I could relax a little knowing that no matter what, he'd be safe with me from now on. I could tell that Ripley felt the same way as he watched Cadence and the witnesses sign the same paper for his daughter Celia, an adorable little girl that we lovingly called Scoot.

"Now we have some paperwork to complete regarding the little girl, but we need a name for her first."

"I think we should call her . . ."

"Don't even fucking go there, Cadence. I'll take her home and make her part of *my* family. She's gonna grow up just like *my* son - without a mother, because the one that birthed her is a waste of fucking oxygen and toxic to everyone she comes into contact with," I said as I stared daggers at the woman who had almost cost my son and his little sister their lives. "You're gonna sign a piece of paper that says you give me full custody and will *never* contact any of us - me, Ripley, Koda, Celia, or this baby - ever again. If you ever step foot back in Rojo, it will be the last step you fucking take. Are we clear?"

Cadence swallowed audibly and nodded.

"Okay, let's do this," I said before I picked up the paper that Roscoe pushed my way. "I've already got a name picked out."

I looked up when I heard my son's excited voice in the hallway and chuckled when I heard my dad say, "For God's sake, boy. Turn the volume down a few notches before you wake up every baby on this floor."

The door opened slowly, and the first face I saw was my son's. I smiled at him and then laughed when his eyes got wide with shock.

"You got me a baby?"

"I did."

"From where? I've been looking all over for one!"

"You've just gotta know the right people, I guess," I said with a wry grin.

"What's going on, son?" my dad asked. "Is there something you need to tell us?"

"Congratulations! It's a girl."

"Is that your baby?" my mom asked as she tightened her grip on Dad's hand. "Where did . . . Who . . . What the hell is going on right now?"

"Ripley didn't tell you?"

Dad snorted. "He said, and I quote, 'Take Koda. Ruf's got something you're all gonna want to see.'"

I burst out laughing, and the baby in my arms jolted at the sound. I patted her butt to calm her as I said, "Ripley has never really had a way with words."

"Whose baby is this, Ruf?" Mom asked as she ran her finger over the wrinkled brow of the tiny girl.

"She's mine now, Mom."

Dad huffed and asked, "Are you sure?"

"I've got the papers to prove it."

Koda leaned closer and studied her face before he asked, "Is she happy that she's gonna be my sister?"

"She is," I answered.

"She doesn't look very happy. She looks like Grandpa Simpson." I laughed because he was right. She was a little wrinkly and looked like a caricature of an old man. "Where did you get her?"

"She's Scoot's sister too."

"You've got to be fucking kidding," I heard my mom mutter at the same time Koda asked, "Really?"

Mom looked horrified at the thought of me going back to Cadence after everything that had happened, so I hurried to explain. "You know how you and Scoot have the same mother but different dads?"

"Yeah."

"So does she."

"You're not her daddy?"

"I am now. Your mother decided that the best place for her to live was with us, so she signed some papers that said we could keep her forever."

"Oh my God," my mom said as tears filled her eyes.

"Did she live with her mother?" Koda asked. "Is that why she's in the hospital now?"

"No, son. She never met your mom. She's here because she's brand new and too little to go home with us yet. Aunt Amethyst is going to look her over, and if she says it's okay, she'll probably get to come home with us in the morning."

"And she'll always live with us? Not her mother?"

I didn't even try to analyze how he didn't refer to Cadence as his mother, and I answered, "No, son. Her mother is going to live far away, and she's not ever going to come back."

"And you did this willingly?" Dad asked.

"You taught all of us to watch out for people who couldn't take care of themselves, and I think this fits that situation."

"Shit, son. You're working really hard to try and make a grown man cry." As he reached out and took her

32

from my arms he said, "Give me my granddaughter."

As Dad held her, Mom leaned her head on his shoulder, and they stared down at the baby. With her taken care of, I gave some attention to my son, who was probably almost as confused as he was excited. I picked him up and settled him on my lap.

"What do you think, son?"

"What are we gonna call her?"

"I already picked out her name, but I'm sure she'll get a lot of nicknames like everyone in our family seems to have. I know you've got a few."

"My favorite is Spawn. I think it sounds cool."

I laughed as I hugged him tight. "You're pretty cool, so it fits."

"Gamma says it's your fault, and since she's your baby, she'll probably turn out just like me."

"As terrifying as that is, I think you might be right."

"What did you name her, Ruf?" my mom asked, never taking her eyes off the baby.

"Her name is Star."

Koda looked confused. "Star?"

"Do you want to know why I named her that?"

"Why?" Koda asked.

"Because she's a bright spot in what is otherwise a very dark sky, just like you and your sister."

"I like that."

"So do I," my mom said through a fresh round of tears. "I like that a lot."

My dad kissed my daughter on the top of her head, and in a voice thick with emotion, he said, "Welcome to the family, Star Forrester. We're glad to have you with us."

JOVI

"What's for dinner?"

"Chicken alfredo."

"Look at you, all dressed up for your man," Rodney said sarcastically as he reached over and tugged on the shoulder of my tank top. "It's one thing to change your clothes when you come home from work, but do you have to put on the raggediest shit you own?"

"When I'm home for the night, I want to be comfortable."

"I can't believe there was a family reunion at the hospital and they didn't even call me," Rodney whined as he propped his hip against the counter and crossed his arms over his chest, his tumbler of expensive whiskey held in one hand. "I had to find out from one of the nurses."

"I'm sure the gossip grapevine was on fire today," I muttered.

"Yeah, and I had to hear that my girlfriend's family was part of the drama. You know I hate that."

"Are you even going to ask what happened, or are you just going to believe what you heard?"

Rodney scoffed. "What I heard is that your brother has *another* illegitimate little rug monster." As I stared at him in shock, he laughed bitterly and said, "Maybe now that there's another one around for you to fawn over, you'll get off my ass about having a baby."

"That was shitty even for you," I said as I turned off both burners. The chicken was barely browned and nowhere near cooked through, and the noodles still had five minutes left in the boiling water, but I had no more appetite for dinner or dealing with the man standing next to me. "And just a reminder, Rodney, that I haven't mentioned children in at least six months."

"That's also about the time you stopped putting out."

"Wow. You're on a roll tonight. How many drinks have you had? You've been home for what? Half an hour?"

"Are we keeping track now?"

"Someone has to because you never do."

"Look at little Miss Booker. She woke up and chose to be a bitch today."

"Why am I here?"

"Because you're making me fucking dinner."

"Not anymore, I'm not," I retorted as I spun around to walk away.

My head jerked back as Rodney grabbed me by the hair and yanked me off my feet. Without thinking, I threw my arms out to catch my fall. It seemed like slow motion as I fell to the floor and the contents of both pans poured down over me from the stove. Oddly enough, my first thought wasn't that this was Rodney's fault - I considered that it was mine for running my mouth and turning my back on him.

35

My second thought was one I'd had before - I'm not a statistic. I'm not the kind of woman who ignores the warning signs and stays long after she should have left.

But if that was true, then why was I still here?

I tiptoed into the room and stopped next to the hospital bed. I glanced at the face of the sleeping man and tried my hardest to ignore all of the tattooed bare skin visible at the edges of the blanket covering the baby snuggled on his chest.

Just as I reached out to touch her little fist, Ruf opened his eyes and asked, "What are you doing here at this time of night?"

"Why are you awake? Don't you know that new parents are supposed to sleep when the baby sleeps?"

"I never understood that. What if the baby falls asleep while you're pushing the grocery cart through the produce section? Are you just supposed to lay down in the middle of the aisle and take a snooze or what?"

"Well, no but . . ." I laughed as I perched on the edge of the bed by Ruf's hip. I reached up and straightened the cap on the baby's head as I said, "I suppose they mean when you're home or . . ." My voice trailed off when Ruf reached up and touched the neckline of my T-shirt. He ran his finger over the tape there, and when I looked up, I saw he was frowning. I couldn't hold his gaze, so I looked back down at the baby and asked, "Did Amethyst already come check her out, or will she be here in the morning?"

"Why are you really here, Jovi?"

"I had to get treated downstairs, and I thought that I'd come by and see you before I leave." I could feel Ruf's stare on my face and couldn't resist the pull to look back up at him. "Don't say 'I told you so,' Ruf."

"That wasn't the first thing that came to mind," Ruf said gruffly as he shifted in the bed. Once his body was all the way to the other edge, he held his arm up and said, "Come here, Bonbon." I felt tears spring up in my eyes, and I stifled a sob as I slowly shook my head. "We don't have to talk. We'll just lay here until they kick us out in the morning."

"You saw it coming," I whispered as I settled down next to Ruf. I rested my head on his arm and turned to face him, remembering all the times years ago when I'd been in this position before. Ruf seemed to remember, too, and slipped his hand into the back pocket of my jeans just like he always had when we relaxed like this together.

For the longest time, the only sounds in the room were our breathing and the scratching of his work-roughened thumb moving back and forth over my hip, soothing me until I finally relaxed.

"I'm not psychic, Jovi, but I could see the signs. We all could."

"You warned me ages ago, but I didn't listen. I never listen."

"Maybe it's time for you to start." There was silence again until Ruf finally asked, "When did it start? The physical part? I've heard about the verbal shit that you didn't even seem to notice."

"Tonight was the first time. It's never been this bad."

Ruf quietly said, "All of it's bad, baby."

37

"I know, but . . . he's never actually touched me before."

"What has he done?"

"The first time it went beyond just yelling was last week," I admitted, unable to keep shame from tingeing my words. "He'd been drinking and came into my room to rant about something. It's funny, but now I don't even remember why he was mad. Hell, I'm not even sure I knew then. I got up to go into the bathroom, and he blocked the door, then when I tried to go out into the hall, he blocked that door."

"That's fucking abuse, Jovi."

"I know," I whispered.

"Tonight was the first time he laid hands on you?"

"I swear. He's never gotten physical before."

"Did he hit you?"

"No. He grabbed me and threw me down. The burns on my chest are from what I had been cooking, and when I fell . . ."

"When he threw you," Ruf corrected.

"Yeah. My arm hit the stove and the pans fell down onto me."

"And then?"

"He was sorry, of course." I laughed bitterly. "I guess he read the script."

"Did he bring you to the hospital?"

"No. I locked myself in the bathroom and called 911. He lost it when the cops got there."

"Did they take him in?"

"Yeah."

"Good."

"What's going to happen now, Ruf?"

"That depends on you, babe. What do you want to happen?"

"He's not gonna let me go."

"I can make it so that he doesn't have a choice," Ruf offered.

"Can I keep that ticket in my pocket and redeem it later if things get really bad?"

"Of course." We were both quiet for a few minutes before he asked, "You said he came into your room. Y'all don't sleep in the same room?"

"I knew it was over when he started drinking again. I just . . . I guess I didn't want to admit it to anyone." Ruf's thumb never stopped, but he pulled me even closer as my tears dripped onto his arm. "I moved into the guest room six months ago. I took all the stuff that was important to me and stored it in Rip's barn and then started boxing the rest of my stuff up gradually and stashing it around the house."

"Are you ready to admit that it's over now?"

"Yeah."

"People might not ask, but they're gonna wonder why you stayed so long, Jovi."

"I thought I could make it work, Ruf. When he's not drinking, he's a really nice guy. He said he'd get help, and he did. He was sober for almost two years. We were planning our wedding, and I even . . ." I started crying in earnest again and felt Ruf's lips on my forehead as he murmured soothing words. "I wanted the fairy tale, Ruf. The nice house in a quiet neighborhood, a baby of my own to love . . ."

"I'm sorry, Bonbon," Ruf said when my voice trailed off. "I know it's not the same, but I've got a new one here that I'd be happy to share with you until you find your fairy tale and get one of your own."

"I might take you up on that occasionally."

"I look forward to it."

T W O

"Friends don't let friends sleep in the Waffle House parking lot unless they're passed out drunk in the back seat while everyone else is inside eating their hash browns scattered, smothered, covered, chunked, diced, peppered, and capped."

Jonas

JOVI

"Jovi, can you join me in exam four?" Wren Forrester, a good friend of mine who was also the midwife on staff, asked as she walked past.

I glanced at the monitor on the wall and saw that exam four was empty since the office was closed for lunch. Wren was already walking through the door, so I hurried down the hall to follow her.

When I got inside, I realized that there wasn't a patient waiting. Instead, I found my friend True standing at the end of the exam table. Two of my other friends, Lana Tempest, the physical therapist on staff, and Amethyst Hamilton, our pediatrician, were sitting next to her.

I had known all of these women since we were kids. We'd all been friendly to each other back then even though we weren't all the same age but had become tight since we started working in the same field. Now that we worked together, we'd gotten even closer, so it was pretty normal for us to get together for a quick chat while time allowed.

"What's up, ladies?" I asked as I walked over to the corner and opened the cabinet above the sink. Out of habit, since I wasn't one to sit still even when I had the chance, I started restocking the most often-used supplies that we stored in canisters on the counter top for easy access. "Who's got the good gossip today?"

"Were you just not going to say anything to us?" Lana asked.

I stopped what I was doing but didn't turn around. Instead, I rested my hands on the counter and took a deep calming breath. I knew she had heard what happened between me and Rodney and realized that she'd also told the rest of the girls.

"So, the gossip is about me."

"It's not gossip if you're part of the conversation," Wren corrected.

"How did you find out?"

"I saw the follow-up request come through on the server this morning," Amethyst said. "I thought I got it filed in my email before anyone else saw it but . . ."

"I was looking at it at the same time," Wren interrupted. "So was True."

"I took the printout off the copier," Lana added. I heard the sound of paper crinkling and knew she had it in her hand. "What happened, Jovi?"

There was silence behind me, and I knew that they were waiting for me to say something - *anything* - but I just couldn't get the words out. I was sure that if I started talking, I may never be able to stop, and I would be crying while I did it, as it seemed like that was all I had been able to do for the last twenty-four hours or so. I was finally able to ask, "What does the report say?"

"You need a follow up for some burns, possibly a plastic surgery consult, and that you refused counseling, but the emergency room doctor thought that should be revisited," Amethyst explained.

I cleared my throat and blinked to hold back the tears that were threatening to fall, and then I turned around and leaned against the counter. The dam broke when I saw the concern on their faces. "I don't know what to say."

"Come here, honey," Wren said as she hopped off the table. "Sit down and talk to us while True does her thing. Amy can sign off on it."

"If you don't want to talk to us, I can call my sister and get you in today," Amethyst offered.

"It's not that I don't want to talk to you guys, it's just that I feel like you're gonna judge me and . . ."

"Nope. That's not what we're doing here, babe," Lana said firmly. "This is a no-judgment zone. We'll listen if you want to talk, or we'll light some torches and ride at dusk. It's your choice."

"Let's keep the torches handy, but for now, I'll just tell you what happened while True and Amy check out my chest."

"You're cute and all, but I don't really swing that way," Amethyst quipped.

"I have a request, though."

"Whatever you need," True said firmly.

43

"Don't get all worked up . . ." When they all started to argue at the same time, I raised my hand and said, "*Yet.* And don't look at me with sympathy and shit. No crying. Treat me like any other patient. Just be . . . normal."

"That's asking a lot. I'm not sure I've got that in me," Lana mumbled.

"I don't know that any of us can do normal on a good day, but we'll try for you," Amethyst assured me.

"It's gonna hurt and probably give me a twitch that won't go away until I have a beer in hand, but I can do normal for a short period of time."

"Wren's right. I can last about this long," True said, holding her hand up with her finger and thumb barely an inch apart. "Make it quick. I don't know how long I can hold the demons back because they're hungry for blood - specifically, Rodney's."

"But If one of you starts to cry, I'll cry, then we will all boohoo together. Our eyes will be red, and everybody will think we got high behind the gymnasium at lunch with the hot guys from shop class," I quipped.

"Good times," Lana said wistfully at the same time Wren whispered, "Duke Conner."

"Good gravy," Amethyst mumbled as she rolled a metal tray toward us. I noticed that it was already filled with the supplies True would need to tend to my burns. "I have to ask, Jovi - are you taking anything for the pain?"

"Tylenol."

"Girl, I know Tylenol's not gonna touch what you must be feeling. They gave you a prescription for a reason. You should be home . . ."

"You know I can't take narcotics while I'm working. Besides, I don't have a home anymore, Amy . . . just a house with my shit in it. And now that you mention it, I really need to find a way to get all of it out as soon as possible."

I took a deep breath and winced when that pulled at the burns on my chest, but I clenched my teeth against the pain while I raised my arms and pulled off my scrub top and the long-sleeved T-shirt underneath it at the same time. I heard a few of my friends take in a sharp breath but didn't open my eyes because I knew I would break down when I saw the sympathy mixed with rage on their faces.

"I guess you guys want to know how this happened, huh?"

True sniffed and then cleared her throat before she said, "Obviously."

"Before we get into that, we need to get some details out of the way," Wren said. I opened my eyes and found her standing behind True and Amethyst with her phone in hand. "You're not in any condition to move all of your stuff out of Rodney's. I vote that you let me take care of the muscle for that, and you can just stand there and look pretty while you direct traffic."

"Do you think anyone would be available this evening? I want to get it over with."

"Office closes at six. I can have a dozen men at the house waiting for us at 6:15."

"They're all gonna know . . ."

"This is not a dirty secret, Jovi," Lana said firmly. "You didn't do anything wrong."

"You are pressing charges, right?" True asked.

"Yeah. They arrested him."

"That means one or all of the Code Blue Crew know. You realize that, right?"

Lawson Dean, Brawley Dumont, Zoey Duke, and Gray Vance were a few of the people in our circle of friends who worked as officers for the Rojo Police Department. We were friends with others who worked there, too, like Esme Cardenas and her brother, Tay, but we didn't spend as much time with them.

"Lawson and Gray were the first to arrive after I called 911."

"That's good," True said firmly.

I scoffed. "How do you figure?"

"Imagine how hard it is for a woman who is at her most vulnerable - injured and afraid - then, all of a sudden, what she thought was her sanctuary is invaded by strangers who are just there to do their job."

"I guess you're right. I don't think I would have had the guts to open the bathroom door if I hadn't recognized Lawson's voice," I admitted. "On one hand, I didn't want him to see me like that, but on the other, I was glad that it was someone I knew."

"You rode in the ambulance and then stayed in the ER alone?" I nodded, and True's eyes filled with tears as she whispered, "Why didn't you call me, Jojo?"

I had to look away so I didn't start crying myself before I said, "I stayed after everyone told me I should leave."

"He pushed you to that, you know?"

"To stay?"

"No. To cut us out," True said. "Just little things. Last minute plans so you couldn't do something with one of us. He'd call with some emergency so you had to leave when we were hanging out. Stuff like that."

"I started to realize that right before I moved into the guest room." Wren's phone was buzzing constantly, so I looked over at her and asked, "Are any of the guys available to help me move out?"

"All of them are. Every fucking one, Jovi. You're that important to them. To all of us. We've got your back whether you realize it or not."

"I'm sorry I doubted you guys," I said sincerely.

Amy wiped the tears off her cheeks before she took my hands in hers and ordered, "Just don't ever do it again, okay?"

"I won't."

"Are you sure you don't want us to take any of the furniture?" Dutch asked as he stopped in front of me. He was carrying a box full of books that I had barely been able to push into the closet once I filled it, but he didn't even seem to notice its weight. "You're gonna need some furniture when you get your own place."

"I don't want anything but the stuff in my bedroom," I insisted.

"Okay, but I think you should reconsider. Couches aren't cheap."

"Let's do a sweep and make sure you didn't miss anything," Jonas said as he walked up carrying an empty box. "The girls are finishing up in the bathroom and the kitchen. The attic is clear as are the closets you pointed out. Chief and Gauge are taking your bed apart right now, and they'll carry it to the truck when they're finished."

"I think we're good," I said as I looked around the living room.

"Except for the furniture!" Dutch called as he walked out the front door to put the box he was carrying into the truck.

"Dutch is right. You're gonna need some of this . . ."

"When I find a place to call my own, I'll want stuff that hasn't touched this life," I said quietly as I walked over to the shelves and picked up a glass figurine Rodney had bought for me on a trip to Mexico last year. I set it back down and shook my head. "I'm done, Jonas. Just done."

"I get ya, babe," Jonas said before he blew out a long breath. "You can stay with me if you want."

"I'm going to talk to my brother about moving into the RV where he and Scoot used to live."

"No can do. He's got one of his guys staying there now."

"He does?"

"Yep. I talk to the guy twice a day when I go out to check the horses."

"Shit," I said with a sigh. "I'll get a room at . . ."

"My house."

"I can't do that, Jonas."

"Damn sure can," he argued. "I know you said you didn't want to stay with any of your girls because y'all work together all day and that would just get weird if you had to spend the rest of your time with them, too, but that's not a problem with me. I've got the room and I'm rarely ever home."

"I don't want to get in your way and have all of my stuff taking up your space, Jonas."

"Get in my way? At this point, all you have is ninety-three boxes of books, some kitchen shit, and a bed. I'm a bachelor and have more crap than you do. What I've also got is a spare bedroom with a shop in the back that's got plenty of room for you to store your library. As far as the kitchen stuff, if you'd like to cook now and then, I wouldn't be opposed, but that's up to you."

"That's a very generous offer, and I'll cook for you anytime you're hungry, but I'm not sure how long I'll need to stay there. I've got to figure out my finances since Rodney shut me out of the account . . ."

"Really?" Jonas asked in outrage.

"I tried to buy breakfast this morning, but my card was declined. When I called the bank they said it had been reported stolen, so they shut it off. When I asked them to reinstate it or print a new one for me, the woman hemmed and hawed until I finally got her to spit out that there was a hold on the account that said no one could do anything except Rodney."

"That motherfucker," Jonas muttered.

"Which means that the money I make in the near future is going to have to go towards an attorney and . . ."

"Petra."

"And how will I pay Petra? Installments of my good looks and charm?"

Jonas laughed before he said, "You know she hates him, Jovi. She'd do that shit for free with a smile."

"Petra handles criminal cases, Jonas."

"I could turn this into a criminal case," Brandt Tempest, Lana's brother, said as he walked past us carrying a box. "Easy peasy lemon squeezy."

"Why does he say shit like that?" Jonas muttered.

"He's just . . . I don't know," I said, but I was smiling now rather than on the verge of tears, which was probably what Brandt was aiming for.

"Listen, Jovi. Even if that trailer of your brother's was empty and you could move in there, Dr. Douchetastic is obviously unhinged, okay? Up until a few days ago, I would have said he was just an asshole, but now he's stepped up his game and become a *violent* asshole, meaning you don't need to stay by yourself in the middle of a field full of goats and horses with chickens singing backup. However, I do not live in the middle of a field. I live in a duplex next door to a raging asshole with a badge. I never thought I'd say this, but that could come in handy."

"I'll pay you rent."

"Cook for me and Lawson. Make whatever you want and leave leftovers in microwave-safe bowls. That's all I ask. Do that and your rent's paid."

"That's not fair."

"Have you seen us eat?"

"I don't know, Jonas."

"Where did you stay last night?"

"I didn't stay anywhere."

"What do you mean?"

"I sat in a booth at Waffle House and drank about three pots of coffee while I read my book between bouts of hysterical crying and moments of confusion where I wondered what the hell I have done with my life."

"You didn't sleep at all?"

"I took a nap in my car."

"Fuck it. Just fuck it. Friends don't let friends sleep in the Waffle House parking lot unless they're passed out drunk in the back seat while everyone else is inside eating their hash browns scattered, smothered, covered, chunked, diced, peppered, and capped," Jonas said as he thrust the box toward me.

"That was oddly specific," I said as I watched him walk out onto the porch.

He whistled to get everyone's attention before he yelled, "Take it all to my house. Park in the back. We'll unload everything into the shop."

"Options still open on that criminal shit, babe," Brandt said as he walked past me back down the hall. "Just let me know."

"Thanks for the offer, Brandt," I called out.

"Anytime!"

51

THREE

"First of all, if you've been shitty to her forever and then try to give her a hug, she's gonna assume you're trying to figure out how big to dig the hole."

Ruf

RUF

Once I had the humidifier turned on, the noise machine at the perfect level, and made sure the video monitor was pointed directly at Star, I walked out of my bedroom and pulled the door shut behind me.

The urge to lean against the wall and slide down it to rest in a heap in the middle of the hallway was almost too much to resist, but I had shit to do and a little boy to entertain. He needed a reminder that he was my number one guy because in the last week, his world had been turned upside down. I had no doubt that he knew I loved him and that everyone else still loved him just as much as they ever had, but I could tell that he was feeling the strain of sharing his life with a newborn.

My family had been more than helpful, but I knew to expect nothing less. They were all in, balls to the wall, eager to see the new baby and do whatever they could to help welcome her to the family. The fact that my family owned Kings, the bar I'd been managing for a few years now, also helped. Especially since any of them could easily slip into my position for a time, which made it easier for me to relax and let life flow into our new normal without having to worry about job security or the place running into the ground without me there.

They'd stopped by in groups of three or four since we got home, and I knew that there'd be more showing up today to check in and help out however they could, but none of them would appear before noon, so I had some time to spend alone with Koda. Since I'd already showered and gotten dressed, which I hadn't done in three days, I walked out into the living room to check Koda's progress in that area. I found him lying on the couch in his underwear with his feet up on the back and his head hanging upside down over the edge of the cushion. There was a Nerf gun in his hand, and he had one eye closed as if that would help with his aim.

"They only do that one eye thing on TV, bud. It doesn't help. If anything, it throws your aim off," I explained. He opened his other eye and then focused on the wall across the room. I looked over and found at least a dozen of the bright green suction cup darts stuck to family pictures hanging in a jumble that my sister Rain had arranged, so I asked, "Why are you killing everybody?"

"Not killing 'em, just using 'em as target practice."

"And why are you doing it upside down?"

"If I'm in a shootout, I probably won't be just standing there, so I need to learn how to hit what I want to in all the ways."

"All the ways, huh? I don't know that I've ever seen a shootout where the guy was hanging upside down, but the best case scenario would be to not get in a shootout in the first place."

"I need a rope."

"Are you gonna practice tying it while you're upside

down?"

"No. I want to practice tying it while I'm underwater," Koda explained in a tone of voice that let me know he couldn't understand why I didn't already realize that was on his agenda.

"Of course."

"But I need one to hang from the fan too."

"Why?"

"So you can make me swing back and forth and see if I can hit what I'm aiming at."

I looked up at the ceiling and said, "The fan won't hold you. We'll need to install a hook. There should be a beam close to it but you'll have to take the rope down when you're not using it so it won't get in the way of the fan."

"How do we find the beam?"

"You'll need the stud finder."

"The beep-beep laser?"

"That's it." Koda curled his body up and flipped over backwards. He landed on his feet and stood there weaving back and forth as he shook his head to clear it. "You should probably put a time limit on hanging upside down like that."

"Why?"

"So you don't scramble your brains like an omelet."

"I like omelets."

"Is that what you want for breakfast?"

"Yes, please."

"Bacon or sausage?"

"Both."

"I'll see what we've got while you look for the stud finder."

"I think it's in my toy box out back."

"Of course it is," I mumbled as I walked into the kitchen. I opened the freezer and stared into it as if I were trying to find the meaning of life, while in reality, I just hoped that the cold air would perk me up. This waking up every two hours was draining the life out of me, but I knew there was a light at the end of the tunnel. Somewhere. I just had to find the fucking tunnel first.

I finally came to, after having what I was almost positive was a quick, vertical power nap, and focused on the food in front of me. My cousin Lark had been at it again and had sent over all sorts of goodies for us to heat up to make quick meals. My freezer was fully stocked. The sight of the frozen food reminded me of all the good stuff my Gamma kept me stocked up with in the other freezer and that I needed to pull something out to thaw for dinner.

I walked into the laundry room where the upright freezer I'd purchased had a home and opened its door to a blast of arctic air that did a little bit more to wake me up. Coffee would help. Yeah. I should make some coffee.

Once I was back in the kitchen, I pulled the coffee maker out onto the middle of the counter and realized I hadn't cleaned it after the last pot I made. Was that last night or early this morning? Either way, the carafe was full of something that looked a lot like motor oil, so I carried it over to the sink and ran water in it before I got the machine primed and ready for the next round of magical bean juice that would hopefully kickstart my brain so I could be a productive parent who wasn't walking around in a permanent fog.

I wandered into the living room and took a look around, making a mental list of shit I needed to get done today. Laundry should be the first thing on the agenda, followed by rearranging the living room to make more space for all the things that came with a new baby. Right now, I didn't have much, but there was a party planned for tomorrow afternoon - a cookout in honor of Star where she'd be showered with more shit than anyone her size needed, all of which would help me navigate this new single-parent-of-two-kids roller coaster I had just strapped myself into.

Right now, Star had the basics - a bassinet next to my bed, some soft white shirts, socks that I couldn't manage to keep on her skinny feet, and at least a dozen of those zippered pajamas in various shades of pink.

My mom and sisters had all of that here when we got home - freshly laundered and waiting, but so far, they had resisted cleaning out the stores for more supplies because they knew the rest of our family, along with our friends, would be piling on the gifts at tomorrow's party.

Of course they would, which meant I needed to clean out the small room downstairs that was probably supposed to be an office but had become a catch-all for boxes I hadn't taken time to unpack since we moved in four months ago, clothes Koda had outgrown that needed to be donated, and a myriad of other shit I didn't know what to do with.

I walked down the hall and opened the door to the room next to mine, which would be the nursery as soon as I got the energy to transform it, and leaned against the door jamb while I stared at the jumble of shit that I needed to put away.

"Dad! I'm hungry," Koda called from the living room. "Why is there coffee all over the place? It's a flood! I need my goggles!"

"Shit!" I hissed as I spun around to clean up whatever mess Koda had discovered.

I wasn't sure how it had happened since I'd been making coffee for years . . . There must have been some sort of mechanical malfunction - which meant I needed a new fucking coffee maker, which would require me to pack up the kids and leave the house, which meant that there was no way I'd get to do the rest of the shit that seemed to be piling up onto the mountain of What the Fuck Have I Gotten Myself Into.

"It's everywhere!" Koda yelled right before Star started screaming from my bedroom.

I wasn't sure which way to turn, so I stopped in the middle of the hall and wondered what was wrong with me that I couldn't manage to get my shit straight and take care of business. What should I do first? Go take care of the baby, or make sure my son wasn't wading through hot coffee while he starved to death?

"Fuck!"

I opened my eyes when I heard women's laughter drift in through the open window and wondered again why I hadn't called in reinforcements instead of waiting for them to magically appear, which they had. I lifted my arm and checked my watch for the time and realized I'd been asleep for almost eight hours.

In a row.

For the first time in *years*. Okay, maybe not years - it had really only been a week, but it felt like much more.

The look on my mom's face when she saw the state I was in was almost comical, and when she started laughing, I understood why my dad sometimes spent hours alone in the garage - far away from her evil. That wasn't true. She wasn't really evil, just a touch diabolical with a few sprinkles of vengeful and petty thrown in for good measure. That's part of what made her so fucking awesome. Dad sometimes spent hours in the garage, not because he wanted to get away from her but because she would occasionally push him out the door as she told him to "Give me some space before I say something to you that will hurt your feelings." But he also enjoyed his own quiet time, building things and working on his bikes while he listened to music and let his mind wander.

I knew that when Mom and Dad decided to retire, it wasn't just to travel, which they did on occasion, but it was more to finally enjoy the peace and quiet of the house that had been so loud and hectic for so many years. With five kids, all with less than two years between them, life had been loud and crazy for so long that no one blamed them when they wanted to enjoy a little peace and quiet.

I only had one child of my own. . . well, that was going to be something to get used to, wasn't it? It was crazy to say, but now I have *two* children of my own. However, for the last six years, I had muddled my way through raising one with so much help from my family and friends that I never realized exactly how much taking care of an infant really entailed. I was young when Koda was born, not even old enough to drink, so it made sense that I'd move back home to live with my parents while I learned the ins and outs of parenting.

It had been pure laziness on my part that Koda and I stayed so long, and even though neither of my parents ever even hinted that it was time for me to buck up and be a responsible adult, I knew it was time. Even after we moved out, Koda was at my parents' house almost daily, staying with two of his favorite people while I worked. Since he started school, things had been different. I knew my parents had to be enjoying more alone time - even if that included Mom puttering around the house while Dad worked in the garage.

But now, Star was part of our family equation, and I had some decisions to make. I couldn't expect my parents to take care of a newborn every day, but they would if I asked them and probably expected to be doing just that. However, Koda was going to daycare now that school was out, and it would only make sense to get Star enrolled as soon as she was old enough, although the idea of making a place for her at Kings wasn't completely out of the question.

When my siblings and I were babies, we went to work with our parents - first at the bar where they had soundproofed a small office and turned it into a nursery, and later, to Mom's accounting office where she'd created the same set-up. The more I thought about it, the more the idea appealed to me - at least for the first few months while Star was sleeping more often than she was awake. The joy of being the boss was that I could lock myself in the office and take care of her when I needed to while my employees did their thing on the other side of the door.

I rolled out of bed and stretched my arms above my head, working out the kinks that such a hard nap - that really equated to a full night's sleep in the middle of the day - had created. While I was in the shower, I pondered the idea of taking Star to Kings with me, at least when I worked the day shift. On the rare occasions when I had to work at night, I'd leave her with my parents or one of my sisters or maybe even Ripley and Tori. I decided to at least get my parents' input before I made a final decision.

Once I was dressed in a loose pair of basketball shorts and one of my softest faded T-shirts, I padded barefoot out of my room to see what everyone was up to and make it up to my boy for disappearing when I really should have spent the time the girls were taking care of Star with him.

I walked into the living room and smiled when I saw a familiar sight - my dad kicked back in the recliner snoozing while a baby slept on his chest. I'd seen him do that with every baby in the family. Many times, we'd have a big get-together, and my uncles would join him in the living room to do the exact same thing. My mom had dozens of pictures that included one or all of the Forrester men napping just like that, and I realized that I had the opportunity to add to that treasure with the first pic of Star and my dad enjoying their first of many naps together.

I pulled my phone out and took a few pictures, and as I walked through the house to join the rest of the family in the yard, I forwarded them to my Gamma who I knew would love to see the sight. She and Papa hadn't been able to meet Star yet and I knew that it had to be killing them.

Star had a lot of visitors during her first day of life, and I appreciated all of their welcoming support, but the one that stood out most to me was Jovi. While we laid there in bed together, she mentioned that she hadn't planned to come upstairs and visit, but she'd felt a pull that she just couldn't resist.

Probably the same pull I felt whenever I knew she was near - not that Rojo was big by any means, but there were times I'd decline an invitation to go somewhere with friends but then change my mind when I found out there was a chance that Jovi might be there.

After all these years apart, I still couldn't resist that woman, even if all I got nowadays was a smile or two with the occasional casual conversation to catch up. I didn't need to catch up with her, though. I kept track. Of everything.

Her college career made me so proud of her, besides all the other things she'd accomplished. She graduated at the top of her class with honors. A guy with a regular brain like mine couldn't even dream of such a thing. It wasn't that I was dumb, but I didn't have the drive or dedication that Jovi had when it came to school. That was why I managed a bar and she worked to help sick people for a living. A few months ago, Ripley had mentioned that Jovi was almost finished with her latest round of schooling so that she could become a nurse practitioner, which in my head was right up there with a doctor as far as knowledge went.

That kind of job and education was way out of my league, that was for sure. But then again, Jovi had always been that step up I probably didn't deserve anyway. That didn't make it any easier to stop missing her, though. The ache every time I saw her reminded me of everything I'd lost.

"And look who decided to come out of his cave and join us," my sister Rylee teased as I walked outside.

"Feel any better, baby?" my mom asked from her lounge chair where she was enjoying a beer. I leaned down and gave her a kiss on the cheek and then sat down on the end of the chair when she moved her legs aside to give me room.

"I feel great. Thank you for coming to my rescue."

"I was waiting for you to admit you needed help, but I'll say, it took you longer to break than I thought it would. There's no shame in asking for help, though, son. I want you to remember that. You're no good to anyone, especially a brand new baby, when your nerves are frayed and you're walking around in a fog from sleep deprivation."

"I don't remember it being this hard when Koda was born."

"It was because you only had him to focus on rather than having to entertain a feral six year old while you cared for an infant at the same time."

"Speaking of Koda, where is he?"

"He fell asleep behind the garage." Rylee told me. I didn't even ask how that happened because that was Koda's way. The boy could sleep in the middle of the field during marching band practice and wake up well rested and moving a hundred miles an hour from the second his eyes opened again. "I went over there about an hour ago and doused him with bug spray but he didn't even flinch. He's got a whole construction site going on with his Tonkas and stuff."

"Your house is clean, the last load of laundry is in the dryer, and everything is folded and put away except your clothes. We didn't want to chance waking you up, so your stuff is in a basket on top of the washing machine."

"Thanks, ladies," I said with a smile. "Can I treat y'all to some pizza or something for dinner to repay you for all of your hard work?"

"With wings?" Rylee asked.

"Of course."

"I'm in," she said with a grin. "Want me to order?"

"Yeah. My card is in my wallet on the dresser in my room."

"On it!" Rylee said cheerfully as she scrolled through her phone. "I've got our last order saved on the app, so I'll just reuse that."

"Ripley and Tori stopped by with Scoot before they went out to dinner."

I looked up at Rain and said, "Tori's pretty cool. She and her friend Sadie are new in town, so they don't know anybody. I think y'all would get along really well."

"She seems really nice," Rain allowed. "I'll have to get in touch and see if they want to come over for dinner sometime. I'll have Lucky cook."

"You mean pick up takeout?" I asked.

"Exactly."

"We should make friends with her because God knows she's not gonna find one in Ripley's sisters. Maybe Trinity, but she's kind of finicky like her brother, and don't even get me started on Jovi," Rylee said, still looking down at her phone.

"What's wrong with Jovi?" I asked.

"What's *not* wrong with Jovi?" Rylee retorted.

"I thought you liked her." I glanced over at Mom, and she shrugged. "You don't like her either?"

"It's not that I dislike her," Mom hedged, which wasn't really like her at all.

I didn't have a chance to ask what she meant before Rain said, "She broke your heart, Ruf."

"That was years ago, Rain. I was upset but . . ."

"You left, Ruf. Just *poof,* and you were gone for months to get away from her," Rylee interrupted.

"That's not why . . ."

"You wouldn't even come home until after she left for college," Rain said.

"She ruined the whole summer."

"How?"

"You were supposed to take me on a road trip. We planned that whole thing with Jovi and . . ."

"Oh, shit," I whispered, vaguely remembering how excited my youngest sister had been to get out of town. "We were going to take you down to SeaWorld."

"Yeah, and then she had to go and ruin it all by ripping your heart out."

"I can't stand her," Rain said bitterly. I glanced over at Mom, and she shrugged again. "I can barely stand to be in the same room as her."

"I'm not quite that silent about it."

"What do you mean?"

"She's supposed to forget that she broke your heart? Every time she tries to be all goody goody and nice to me, she's lucky I don't break her face."

"I wouldn't go that far, Ry," Rain argued. "It was a long time ago."

"Y'all have been ugly to her all these years?" I asked.

"I've never been mean to her," Mom assured me. "Young love is just that - *young* love. It rarely ever lasts."

"But you've never stopped the girls from being mean to her, have you?"

"I didn't realize they were quite so bitter about the

whole thing," Mom admitted. "Her name hasn't come up in conversation in forever, so I was unaware. I'm friends with Charlene, so I've run into Jovi a million times. She's always seemed a little standoffish, but now I'm realizing why."

"But the two of you have been shitty." It wasn't a question because I knew them and how protective they were of me and our two brothers, Ransome and Rocky.

"I wouldn't say shitty, exactly. I just choose not to talk to her. I wasn't here when it happened, but I heard about it."

"I got to go visit Rain for a week since you were gone, and I missed my chance at SeaWorld. We went to Six Flags instead."

"And you've been . . . well, *yourself* would probably be the best explanation, this entire time?"

"I don't like her. She broke your heart and made you leave. I'm not gonna buy her flowers. Damn, Ruf, what's so hard to understand about that?"

"She broke up with me because we had plans for the summer, and I decided on a whim to take off with the guys on a road trip to the west coast. She was torn up about it, and I blew her off and said she could fly out and see me here and there."

"What?" Mom asked.

"Yeah. I didn't even think about SeaWorld or spending time with her before she left for college. One of the guys said 'road trip,' and I was all in."

"And *then* she broke up with you?"

"Yeah. She said something about we had different goals, and she didn't want to keep me from mine, so she was letting me go."

"You're kidding," Rain said.

"Nope. I don't remember the exact words, but that about sums it up."

"Oh, shit," Rylee muttered.

"Looks like you ladies owe Jovi an apology or two. Most especially you, Ry, because I know how you can be."

"Yeah, I think we all owe her an apology, including you, Ruf," Mom agreed. "She was a responsible adult before she had to be when you were out doing wild shit with the guys. You took off and had a summer full of fun with your friends, and she stayed here preparing for her future while dealing with the hardest decision she'd ever made."

"Fuck," I muttered. "I've never really thought of it like that."

"Start now."

"I've never stopped loving Jovi. I've compared every woman I've met to her and probably always will. I should be married to her right now, but I'm not because I was young and stupid."

"You're still in love with her?"

"What I feel for Jovi isn't something that ever goes away, Rylee. Not ever." I shook my head and took a deep breath before I changed the subject to one that didn't make me want to rage at the heavens or break down and cry. Well, actually, it sort of did. "I know y'all don't exactly run in the same circles, but what I do know is that word gets around like wildfire. Have you heard what happened last week?"

All three women shook their heads. "She and

66

Rodney broke up." They stared at me with blank expressions, and for some reason, that made me irrationally angry, but I was finally able to choke out, "I want y'all to be nice to her from here on out, but especially right now, okay?"

"I told you I'd apologize."

"I'm gonna give her a hug," Rain said firmly.

I ran my hand over my face and then shook my head. "Nope. No hugging. No touching." I looked pointedly at Rylee and said, "No hitting."

"What? I said I'd be nice."

"Your approach to 'nice,' and Jovi's inability to keep her mouth shut when someone says something shitty to her . . ."

"She's done a pretty good job of that every time I've talked to her in the last few years," Rylee muttered. I heard my mom exhale loudly through her nose and recognized that sound from childhood. It was what I imagined a bull sounded like right before it charged. I didn't have to look at her to know that she was staring daggers at my sister, her lips pressed into a thin line as she tried to control her temper. That was an early warning sign the three of us instantly recognized. If Rylee didn't watch her shit, Mom was gonna end up doing more than just stare, and then we'd have a problem on our hands. A very loud problem. Rylee sensed a shift in the atmosphere and looked up at me before she said, "I will apologize to her, and I will mean it. I will also make sure that my apology is presented in a way that won't be construed as anything other than sincere, and even if Jovi doesn't accept it, I will be understanding as I smile and walk away."

My mom snorted, and Rain looked at the ground while she concentrated on keeping herself from smiling.

"First of all, if you've been shitty to her forever and then go in to give her a hug, she's gonna assume you're trying to figure out how big to dig the hole."

Mom huffed again and then cleared her throat. When I looked over at her, she was staring at the tree above us as if she'd suddenly become an avid bird watcher.

"Secondly, Jovi is injured, and I don't know how long it will take her to heal. You can't touch her. You can't hug her. You can't . . . I don't even know. You just can't."

"Does her injury have something to do with her breakup?" Mom asked astutely. I looked over and found her staring at me intently. "I've heard Charlene talk about Jovi's asshat of a boyfriend but . . ." When I nodded, her eyes narrowed, and she pressed her lips together and made that terrifying sound again. After a few seconds, she muttered, "That motherfucker."

"My thoughts exactly."

FOUR

"You've done nothing wrong but live your life and try to find a flower growing from a steaming pile of shit."

Lawson

JOVI

"Alright, Jovi. This is the end of the road, sister. The ride is over, and it's time to get off," Lawson Dean, Jonas' brother, said as he stopped in front of the television.

I was interested in what the woman was about to do with the planks of wood she had reclaimed from an old pallet, so I tried to lean around him to see the TV while I asked, "What are you talking about?"

"I'm getting you out of this house."

"No."

"Didn't say I was giving you a choice."

"I'm not going anywhere, Lawson."

Lawson flopped down onto the couch, which jostled me and sent pain shooting across my chest. It wasn't as intense as it had been a week ago, but it was still there - a constant ache that assured me my skin was trying to mend itself. It wasn't horrible that first night after I'd left the hospital. More of an ache than anything, but that probably had a lot to do with the cream they'd put on it before they bandaged it. However, it gradually got worse, and by the end of day on Tuesday, I was in so much pain that Jewel noticed, and being her usual self, she waded right into the middle of my shit.

She was pissed I hadn't told her about my burns, inspected them herself, and then pronounced that I needed to take at least two weeks off to let them heal without the chance of infection that would come from working in a doctor's office around people that had everything from pink eye to strep throat and everything in between. She also ranted about something that, as a nurse, I understood very well - pushing myself while I was so stressed would only make the healing process slower and cause more complications. Added to that, the fact that I couldn't take the pain pills that were prescribed to me while I was working only exacerbated the problem because a body in pain focused only on that and not healing itself.

So, I'd been at Jonas' since I came home Tuesday evening and hadn't stepped outside since. Now it was Saturday. Luckily, I'd showered this morning, which was also something I hadn't done regularly this week because of what a pain in the ass it had been to wrap my bandages so they wouldn't get wet.

"Your body is going to fuse itself to the couch cushions, Jovi."

"No, it's not."

"It is. I saw a YouTube video about a woman who . . ."

"Ugh. I watched that. It was horrible. That poor woman."

"I know. She didn't have pushy friends who worried about her, so they sent the resident asshole over to bark

70

orders until she got her ass up, put her shoes on, and went to a party where there would be people who could take her mind off of her troubles."

"The last thing I need to go to is a party," I mumbled. "Hold on. Who is having a party?"

"It's a baby shower for Ruf."

"Oh, hell no."

"Come on. You guys get along just fine. Why wouldn't you want to go? Don't you want to see the baby?"

"I've already seen the baby."

"You did? When?"

"I went up to check on her that night after . . ."

"While you were at the hospital," Lawson finished when my voice trailed off.

"Yeah."

"It's been a week. She's probably doubled in size."

"Not quite," I said with a laugh.

"Jovi," Lawson said seriously. "You've got to get up and move around. I'm not saying you should run a fucking marathon, but you need to spend a few hours outside the house. Go hang out, let your friends see that you're not morphing into a couch cushion, and then I'll bring you home."

"I cannot go to a party for Ruf, Lawson. I don't need more burns to go with the ones I've already got."

"What are you talking about?"

71

"It's a party for Ruf. That means his sisters will be there."

"And?"

"They'll aim their laser beam death glares in my direction, and my skin will start melting off."

"Why don't you like them? I thought you, Rain, and Rylee got along fine."

"Does having a penis automatically mean that you're oblivious to the world around you?" I put my hand up and said, "Don't answer that. The penis also gets in the way of rational thought."

"Let's try to avoid mentioning my dick in the same sentence as either of Ruf's sisters because I'd like to keep it right where it is. If Ruf or one of his brothers senses that is happening, they'll appear in a cloud of smoke and beat me like I owe them money before they chop it off."

"I think you and Rylee would make a cute couple."

"Why do you hate me?"

I burst out laughing and then gasped at the sharp pain that caused. "Shit. That hurts."

"When will that stop?"

"It might be a while. There are two areas that aren't healing as well as they should, so Jewel had to . . . Nevermind. I'm not gonna tell you what Jewel had to do because you've got a weak stomach."

"It's better than it used to be, but you're probably right," Lawson admitted. "Now tell me why you won't go and what sort of problem you've got with Ruf's family."

"Not the whole family, just his sisters. His mom isn't

a big fan of mine anymore either."

"Why? What happened?"

"I broke up with Ruf."

"That was years ago."

"They hate me, Lawson."

"I can guarantee that if they really hated you, we wouldn't be having this conversation right now because you'd be fertilizing a field somewhere."

"They might not hate me, but they damn sure don't like me very much."

"Why?"

"They blame me for Ruf leaving town after graduation."

"When we took our road trip? How is that your fault?"

"They believe that I dumped him and broke his little Forrester heart which sent him into a tailspin that forced him to leave the bosom of his family for months and months, denying them his presence when they should have been there to help him during his time of need."

"That's bullshit." Lawson tilted his head and squinted at me like I was a bug he was trying to identify and asked, "Did one of them say that to you?"

"Does that sound like something they'd say?"

"Not at all."

"Well, those weren't the words they used, but that was the jist of it. What Rylee said was something along the lines of, 'You heartless fucking bitch. You broke my brother's heart, and if I have to look at you, I'm gonna break your fucking face.'"

"In Rylee's defense, she was a little . . . Rylee . . . when she was younger. That's the only description I can come up with."

"Rain blamed me for Ruf hooking up with Cadence but didn't word it exactly like that."

"Rain's a pretty chill girl, but she can have some bite to her."

"She said that even though she hated Cadence and thought she was a trashy bitch, she was still a step up for him compared to me."

"That one . . . oh, damn."

"That pretty much sums up our conversations anytime I ran into one of his sisters until I left for college. I've just tried to avoid them ever since."

"I can see that, but it's been a while and . . ."

"Do you think I'm stupid?"

"No."

"Have you ever been on the receiving end of Forrester rage? Let me just say from experience that it's downright terrifying." I thought about it for a second before I said, "Imagine getting trapped in the hyena enclosure at the Dallas zoo while wearing a gazelle costume made of fresh meat. That's what pissing off the Forrester women is like, even if it's the second generation."

"I can see that."

"And yet you want me to pull out my gazelle costume

and wear it again . . . on purpose."

"I'm sure they'll be civil, especially if you're standing there with me."

"I heard that Rylee made you cry."

"She did not!"

"You didn't say that she couldn't, just that she didn't. It's not a good idea for me to put myself in their crosshairs, even if it is for a baby shower."

"It's been years, Jovi. It's time for them to get over their shit. I can guarantee if Ruf knew that's what they thought, he'd set them straight."

"And then they'd be even more pissed at me for getting him riled up. No, sir. Not going there. Ruf and I have a good, solid friendship even if we are a little distant, and if, by chance, he got upset when I went *missing*, they'd probably have a seance and bring me back from the dead just so they could kill me again."

Lawson burst out laughing and said, "They're not that bad, Jovi. Rain can be a little testy, but Rylee's a sweetheart."

I waited for the punchline, and when it didn't come, I asked, "Are we talking about the same Rylee? Is there another one somewhere I don't know about? You say that even though everyone knows she made you cry."

"I didn't cry!" Lawson yelled. "If you'll come with me today, I'll stick right by you the whole time. We can come back whenever you're ready. That will help me out because it means I won't have to spend my entire day off at a baby shower, of all things, and it will get you out of the house *and* all of those women . . ."

"Who has been bugging you?"

"Wren called twice. I've gotten at least a dozen texts from Amy. Lana called and asked me to make you come, and when I wavered about it, she said she'd buy me donuts."

"Since when do you eat donuts?"

"She was making a cop joke."

"Shit. I get it now." I laughed and then groaned when I got another sharp pain. "That's three women, Lawson. You act like they're an angry mob."

Lawson continued like I hadn't said anything and tried to tempt me. "If you go, they'll get off your ass about getting out of the house, and I'll look like the good guy for doing what they couldn't."

"You're not going to leave me alone about this are you?"

"I'm supposed to text True if I can't convince you so she can come over here and try."

"Shit."

"For once in my life, I'm the lesser of two evils."

"I wouldn't say you're lesser than Jonas. You're equal."

"I was talking about True."

"Neither one of you can aspire to reach the level of True Stoffer, my friend. Don't even try."

"It's a good thing that half the residents of this neighborhood are related in some way because this is quite the crowd," I said as Lawson parked next to the curb. "Whose house is this?"

"I have no idea. That's Rain and Lucky's over there," Lawson said, pointing across the street.

"They moved in together?"

"Well, I'm sure you saw everything that went on online, but yeah. They're officially together now."

"Hmm. I can't say that shocks me. They always seemed . . . right."

"Yeah. I agree," Lawson said as he turned the truck off. "Are you gonna be okay walking over to the park?"

"He's hosting a baby shower at the park?"

"Well, first of all, he didn't plan this. Secondly, you know how these things go. You invite a few people, they tell a few other people who tell some more people, and the next thing you know, there are food trucks lined up along the street and teenagers trying to sneak beer from the keg."

"I remember those days," I said wistfully. "We had a lot of fun back then."

"We did, and they were never the same after you left for school."

"I wouldn't have been there anyway after me and Ruf broke up, Law. You know that."

"I've always thought I should shoulder at least some of the blame for your breakup."

"Why?"

"I was the one who suggested the road trip."

"Did you have to duck tape his mouth shut to keep him from calling for help before you hog tied him and dragged him to the coast?" I asked sarcastically.

Lawson laughed. "He was mopey for most of the trip, just so you know."

"Well, I was mopey through my freshman and sophomore years of college, so there's that."

"You up for this?" Lawson asked as he opened the door and got out of the truck.

He shut the door as I muttered, "Absolutely not." I carefully reached out and grasped the handle to open the door and realized Lawson was jogging around the hood of the truck to help me get out, so I let go a split second before he yanked it open. I gingerly turned my entire body and slid to the ground rather than just hop out like I would have before. Once I was standing on the sidewalk, I stopped to take a deep breath and get my mind right before we walked around the corner and found half the town staring at me.

Decision made about how I wanted the afternoon to go, I looked at Lawson and said, "You got me out the house. That was your mission, right?" Lawson nodded, so I stuck my hand out. "Give me the keys so I can turn on the AC. You go to the party, and I'll wait in the truck."

"That was not the deal."

"Technically, we didn't make a deal."

"Twenty minutes, Jovi. Let's say hello to a few people, make our presence known, and then we'll jet. I'll even take you to get a milkshake on the way home," he promised.

"Whataburger?"

"Is there anywhere else?"

"Twenty minutes. If you leave my side, I'll burn your house down."

"Well, my house is attached to the one you're living in, so . . ."

"Don't test me, Lawson. I'm on painkillers and don't know my own mind." Lawson burst out laughing and reached to take my hand. He gave it a squeeze and then let go before he started walking, and I fell into step beside him. We were quiet until the end of the block when we turned the corner, and I came to an abrupt stop. "Nope. Can't do it."

"Ruf's sisters will be nice. I promise."

"I've been dealing with their shit for years, Lawson. They're not the problem."

"Then what is?"

"All of these people are gonna know what happened five minutes after I walk up if they don't already."

"So? You've got nothing to be ashamed of."

"I should have known better."

"And I should have worn different underwear because it's fucking hot out here and my balls are gonna chafe. You live. You learn. Deal with it."

"You did not just compare my life to your testicles."

"I think I did."

"How has no one killed you yet?"

"I'm a work in progress."

"I volunteer as tribute," I muttered as I started walking again.

"You've done nothing wrong but live your life and try to find a flower growing from a steaming pile of shit."

"That is an excellent description of my relationship with Rodney, Lawson. Maybe I won't kill you after all."

"Good," Lawson said cheerfully. In a more sober tone, he said, "These people are friends that you've known since we were kids, Jovi. No one's gonna fault you for doing shit because you've done nothing wrong. How you handle this is on you, so put your shoulders back and own your decisions, including the one you made when you called 911 and pressed charges. That's all you can do, sweetheart."

"I don't think I'll be able to stand it if they look at me like I'm pitiful."

"Then stop being fucking pitiful."

I didn't have a response to that because Lawson was right, although I wouldn't admit it to him even if someone put a gun to my head.

For the last week, I'd shut myself in the house and refused to answer my phone. When someone came to visit me, I used the physical pain I was in as an excuse to cut the visit short because I didn't want to talk about it or the emotional pain that hurt almost as much.

When my parents came to see me Tuesday evening, they saw through my bullshit and stayed even after I outright asked them to leave. The night ended with me sobbing in my father's arms. Our awkward position sitting side by side on the couch so I didn't press against my burns made that almost impossible, yet somehow I figured out how to do it.

Mom and Dad were understanding and furious in equal measures but knew better than most what I'd been thinking and everything I'd been through because they'd both lived through much worse. My father had been a victim of domestic violence for years, and as often happened when it was a man on the receiving end of the abuse, he'd been ignored and often ridiculed. However, he was finally able to escape his abuser - my brother Ripley's mother - and start a new life. Together, he and Ripley thrived in the newfound peace they found after they got away from my dad's ex-wife, and a little while later, he met a woman who had taken her young daughter and made the same kind of escape.

After a long and careful dating journey, my parents married and made a family with Ripley and Trinity, and then I came along. My dad had joked more than once that I was the glue that cemented our family together, making his and hers children an ours and giving them another chance at parenting with a partner by their side that they could trust.

I didn't have much in common with my siblings. Ripley was thirteen when I was born, and Trinity was eleven. I didn't have many childhood memories that included my brother because he went to prison when I was six and didn't get out until after I'd already settled into my college dorm. Instead of a usual sibling relationship, I considered us acquaintances more than anything. I loved Ripley and knew without a doubt that he loved me, but that love didn't really come from shared experiences and touching memories. It was more of a love that was just there because it was supposed to be. Brothers and sisters love each other so that was what we did.

My relationship with Trinity wasn't much different. We had more in common because we were women, and I had more memories of her from my childhood, but she had already moved out of the house by the time Ripley went to prison, which left me home by myself.

Ripley and Trinity had grown up together since our parents met when they were six and four. Their lives before our mother and father got together were traumatic, and they understood each other much better than I had ever understood them because I was lucky enough to have been born into a calm and loving household and had never known anything different.

Between the different experiences and childhoods, along with the age difference, it felt as if I'd grown up as an only child.

I was lucky enough to have made some long-lasting friends during my childhood and was still close to most of them to this day. There were others, like Ruf, who I had grown apart from over the years, but the ones like True, Lana, and Wren had stayed steady even though Rodney had done his best to put a wedge between us. I felt terrible to know that I had let him do that.

But the one thing he'd never been able to break was my relationship with my niece Celia - our Scoot. I spotted her before she saw me and had a chance to watch her interacting with some of the other children, something that had gotten easier for her to do over the last few months.

While I was watching, my brother reached down and touched Scoot's shoulder and then pointed at me.

"Jovi!" she screamed in her hoarse, slightly nasal voice. She jumped up from where she'd been sitting on the grass with a group of children and took off toward me, but my brother caught her and swung her up into his arms to stop her from throwing herself into my arms for a tight hug.

He carried her over to me, and even over the crowd of people talking, I heard him say, "Remember what I told you, Scoot. She's got a bad sunburn, so you can't hug her, okay?"

Scoot nodded but smiled at me before she said my name again. I lifted my hands up from where they were hanging at my sides, making a pointed effort not to wince when the burns on the inside of my elbow and beneath my bicep shot pain all the way down to my fingertips.

As I spoke to Scoot, I signed, and she happily did the same when she responded.

"Hi, Scoot Scoot. How's my favorite girl?"

"I got a new sister and a new mama, and I rode my horse this morning!"

"Look at you! What an exciting life!" I replied. "Are you having fun with your friends?"

Scoot nodded, so I asked, "Do you want to go back and play with them?"

"I come to your house now. I sleep there."

I glanced over at my brother, and he gave me a tight smile. I heard that he was loosening the parenting reins lately, and I knew it must be hard for him to consider letting Scoot spend time at my house but understood that he'd probably be more inclined if he knew that I wasn't with Rodney anymore. He hadn't had much interaction with him while we were together, but the short spans of time that they'd been in the same room were usually filled with tension because Rodney was a judgmental prick to his core, something I'd tried very hard to ignore over the years.

"I just moved into a new house, and I'm still getting settled. Maybe you can come over and eat dinner and watch a movie soon, but I don't have a bedroom for you to sleep in yet. When I get a place of my own, I'll make sure there's a bed there for you."

"Good! Want tacos."

83

"A girl after my own heart," Lawson quipped. He looked from me to Ripley and then back again before he asked, "Why don't I walk Scoot back over to her friends while you two talk?"

Ripley gave him a nod and then set Scoot on her feet and turned to watch Lawson follow behind her when she took off running. When Ripley was sure she was settled with his girlfriend watching her, he turned back to me.

I saw him looking at my neck and then down at my hands, one of which still had a small bandage above my thumb that went all the way around my wrist, before he asked, "Are you doing okay?"

"I am. Better everyday."

"Healing up alright?"

"Yeah. What about you?" I asked.

"I don't have a lot of experience for comparison, but I have a feeling that a bullet wound probably heals a little faster and causes less pain than a burn like that."

Mom told him. Of course she did. "You think so?"

"How about we compare notes instead of trying them both on for size to figure it out for sure."

"Well, I'm not in the market to get shot, and I'm sure you're a careful cook when you're in the kitchen, so I think we're safe."

Ripley's lips didn't even twitch at my attempted joke. Instead, he said, "The man who shot me was pissed because the woman he'd been abusing finally had enough and got away."

"Yeah. I heard about that."

"You know how to protect yourself?"

"Um, I'm kind of in a unique situation where I'm living with a rough and tumble biker who thinks getting shot at for repossessing someone's car is perfectly normal and our next door neighbor is also the biker-type, but as an added bonus he's also a cop. I think I've got the protection racket covered."

"Sounds promising." Ripley stared at me intently before he said, "Call if you need me."

"I will."

"I want you to come to dinner soon. Get to know Tori."

"I'd love that."

"Jovi! You came!" True called out as she jogged across the grass toward me.

"I'll see you," Ripley said before he nodded at True and walked back across the grass toward his daughter and girlfriend.

"The Wranglers. The beard. The hat," True mumbled as she watched him go.

"The girlfriend," I said flatly.

"The shattered dreams," True said dramatically as she put her hands on her chest and sighed. Heartache forgotten, she smiled and said, "I'm so glad you came!"

I smiled back and sang, "It's not like I had much of a choice."

"You had to get out of that house, Jovi. Seriously. Even Jonas is worried about you, which is weird because Jonas doesn't usually notice anything that doesn't have boobs he wants to snuggle."

"Snuggle?"

"There are kids around," True said with a shrug. "Let's walk over here and get out of the sun. We saved a chair for you under the tree."

"Thank you," I whispered as I walked beside her toward a group of our friends. "I'm still having trouble regulating my temperature, but I didn't dare wear a short-sleeved shirt."

"Ugh. I can't imagine."

"How was work? I'm sorry I left y'all short-handed."

"You didn't have a fucking choice. First, you don't need to be there right now, and second, you know how Jewel gets if you try to cross her. I'm not that brave."

I smiled and nodded at the friends we passed. I was pleased to see that none of them were giving me that look of pity I had worried about. I finally asked, "Where are Ruf and the baby?"

"She's a little young to be out here in the heat or to be around all of these people, so he and some of his family are taking shifts staying inside with her."

"That's probably a good idea."

"Hey, lady," Lulu Marks called out as we walked by. I smiled at her, and she said, "Call me this week - I need some coffee time!"

"I'll do it," I answered.

"Do you want a drink or something?"

"Dammit," I mumbled before we made it to the shade. "I knew I shouldn't have come."

"Why? I swear, Jovi . . ."

"There's not a bathroom here, and I'm under strict doctor's orders to drink lots of water," I said with a smirk.

"Well, shit."

As if he sensed my distress, Lawson jogged our way. When he stopped next to us, he gave True an assessing smile, taking in her crop top and shorts before he let his gaze trail up to her eyes as he grinned at her.

"You're such a pig," True said in disgust.

Lawson blew her a kiss before he looked at me and said, "Our twenty minutes are up, and your carriage awaits."

"Oh, thank you, God," I said before I sighed deeply and smiled at True. "Can't stay, gotta go. See ya."

"You are not . . ."

"Gotta pee," I said with wide eyes. "I'm floating over here."

"Too much information," Lawson muttered.

"I'm coming to see you when I leave here," True said with narrowed eyes. "And I'm gonna stay awhile this time."

"Okay."

"And tomorrow . . ."

"I have an appointment with the DA at nine o'clock."

"I'll take an early lunch."

"Nope. I'm not gonna waver even if you're not

there."

"I don't give a fuck whether you press charges or not, Jovi. I just don't want you to be alone."

"I'm not. I have all of you, I have a phone, and I'm not afraid to use it."

"I'll see you in a little bit."

"Bring me a soda."

"Nope. No sugar. Drink water. I'll bring you a banana and some boiled eggs. They have all the good things you need to start healing."

"Ugh. No. Don't bring me anything."

"Are you pregnant?" Lawson asked.

"God, no."

"Bananas and eggs?" He looked at True in horror and asked, "Are *you* pregnant?"

True rolled her eyes, and I interrupted before they could start bickering like they always seemed to do. "Pee. Now."

"Shit, you're bossy," Lawson said.

"Tell everyone I said hello, but I need to go. This probably wasn't the best idea with the heat and all."

"You good?"

"I'll be fine," I assured her, although that was a lie because I didn't really need to pee at all. I did feel like I was about to throw up, though, and I couldn't imagine how horrible that would feel, so I wanted to avoid it at all costs.

"Want me to go get the truck?"

"No. I'll walk, but we should go now."

"Call me," True ordered. She looked at Lawson and narrowed her eyes again before she said, "Make sure she doesn't forget."

"Aye aye, Captain."

"Fuck off."

We were almost to the curb when I quipped, "Well, that was pleasant." Lawson frowned as he blew out a long, angry breath. "I don't understand what just happened, and I'm not sure I even have the energy to try right now."

"That makes two of us."

FIVE

"Sad hurts worse than angry."

Amethyst

JOVI

"Hmmm," Dr. Parker - Jewel, not Terran or Spruce - said as she rolled the stool back and stared at the burns on my chest.

I'd always been a naturally modest person, rarely ever wearing low-cut shirts or even revealing bathing suits. Of course, I had lived in Texas my entire life, so in the summer heat, tank tops and shorts were a must, but that was about as much skin as I was comfortable showing off. It wasn't because I was ashamed of my body, but because it wasn't in my nature. However, in the last two weeks, that modesty had gone out the window - obviously, since I was sitting on an exam table, shirtless with three women staring at my chest.

"What does 'hmmm' mean? That doesn't sound very promising."

"You're healing well-ish but . . ."

When Jewel's voice trailed off, I waited patiently for a few seconds until I asked, "What's the -ish mean? I can tell it's better. Only a few spots still hurt badly enough to make me occasionally take anything but over-the-counter meds for pain management."

"The center of the burn at the crease of your arm down along your bicep is worrisome, and there's a spot beneath your breast that has me concerned."

I sighed and said, "Worrisome and concerned. Still not much more information than the -ish."

True tilted her head and said, "You were on your back, right?" When I nodded, she pointed at my chest and then moved her finger just a tad to the right and said, "That fits. The boiling water would have pooled there for a split second longer before her reflexes had a chance to kick in and make her jump."

"I'm trying to pretend that I'm a work of art that you're admiring rather than a lab specimen you're about to dissect, but the discomfort I feel having women stare at my tits for an extended period of time is a bit *worrisome* and has me *concerned.*" I said sarcastically before I used my left arm to point to my shirt and ask, "Can I put my clothes back on yet?"

"Are you feeling feverish at all? How is your temperature regulation?" Jewel asked.

I scowled because it was obvious that they were ignoring me, but I finally answered, "Temperature regulation is still out of whack, and I feel a little achy."

Wren reached over and picked up the thermometer we used to scan a patient's forehead to check for fever. She ran it across my forehead and then held it the same distance from the burns on my arm and beneath my breast.

"That's a problem," Jewel said as she watched the digital readout change.

"What's a problem?"

"You have a fever," Wren said with an odd look.

"But . . ."

When my voice trailed off in question, Jewel explained, "The affected area has an elevated temperature which, along with your body temp, leads me to believe that there's an infection. I'm going to give you another round of antibiotics, and I want to see you again on Monday."

"I'll be here," I reminded her.

"No, Jovi. I'm not ready to release you to work yet."

"It's been two weeks, Jewel. I'm fine."

"Really? Lift your arm above your head without flinching." When I frowned at her, Jewel shook her head. "Same protocol for now, and if there's not noticeable improvement by Monday, we'll have to explore some other avenues. I'm going to make a few phone calls and see if there's something I'm missing." Jewel sighed before she frowned at me and asked, "How is your stress level? Are you sleeping at all? Have you been eating?"

"All I do is sleep," I admitted. "I can't focus enough to get into a book because I have to keep going back to reread the same section over and over. I can't get into a television show because my attention span is shit. I'm so bored that I'm going stir-crazy. The only bright spot in my life at this point is the thought of coming back to work on Monday."

"Can't happen yet, honey," Jewel said as she stood up from the stool and walked over to the sink. "I'm sorry."

"You're stressed out and depressed," Wren said as she sat down on the stool Jewel had just vacated.

"I can't imagine why."

"Well, her sarcasm supply hasn't been depleted, so there's that," True said drolly. "What's the status on the charges against Rodney? Will you have to testify?"

So far, I had managed to keep my emotions steady. I really hadn't had time to process the latest information I had received, but I knew I would probably break down as soon as I was alone. My appointment with the DA hadn't gone well at all, and I was still trying to wrap my head around the news he'd given me, so when I tried to answer True's question, nothing came out but a sob.

"Fuck. What happened?" True mumbled as she reached for my hand.

"There are no charges," I choked out. "The DA said that it's a 'he said, she said' case and they're just going to drop it since Rodney doesn't have any history of this sort of thing. He hired some attorney with a great record, so even if we went to trial, he'd get off."

"Are you fucking kidding?" True ground out. When I shook my head, she made a growling sound and then asked, "So, what happens if he does this to someone else? That gets dropped because he wasn't charged with your shit and doesn't have a record?"

"Probably."

"I want you to go see my sister," Jewel said as she pulled her phone out.

"What can she do?" I asked.

"She can get mad, which is what I think you should do," Jewel mumbled as her thumbs flew over her phone screen. I could tell by the sounds coming from the phone that whoever she was texting was replying, and I watched as a slow smile replaced her frown. "She can meet with you right after lunch, so you need to be at her office by one o'clock."

"To do what?"

"Siphon some of her anger and find your own," Jewel said as she looked up from her phone. "Maybe you should take some of that fever you've got in your burns and turn it into a purpose."

"And what purpose would that be?"

"He took an oath just like I did, and that doesn't magically disappear when he gets done with his shift at the hospital," Jewel said, her eyes glittering with rage. "You don't stop caring about people when you clock out, and neither should he."

"He's a surgeon, Jewel."

"That doesn't mean he's not a piece of shit that needs to answer for his sins. It's up to you to find a way to word the question so that happens, and my sister is the perfect one to help you do exactly that."

"Fuck yeah," Wren muttered.

"And if Petra can't make him pay, we know people who can," True said with a knowing look aimed at Wren and Jewel. Jewel and Wren smiled, but it wasn't the happy kind I was used to seeing. I knew that there was a silent conversation going on that I wasn't part of. "Now, why don't you get dressed before I'm unable to resist the urge to pull out some singles and stuff them into your waistband."

"She does have great boobs," Wren said with a frown. "I'm a little jealous."

"Inappropriate," I mumbled.

"That's part of our charm."

94

RUF

"This little girl seems healthy as can be," Amethyst pronounced as she smiled down at Star who had somehow fallen asleep during her checkup. "Her weight is right on track, and her color is excellent." As Amethyst bent Star's legs and pushed them toward her belly, she asked, "How much is she eating and how often?"

"She's taking every drop of the two-ounce bottles every two hours as if she's got an internal alarm."

"Up her to three and see if that helps delay that alarm," Amethyst suggested. "It won't hurt her to sleep an extra hour between feedings." She rested her hand on Star's belly and said, "She's doing great, Ruf. How are you?"

"Tired, but handling it."

"You've got help if you need it," she said firmly. I understood that wasn't a question because she was part of my extended family and knew that all it would take was one call or text and I'd have people lined up to take a shift with the baby. "How is sweet Koda handling big brotherhood?"

"Like a champ. He'd been talking about putting a sidecar on his dirtbike for her, but I convinced him they didn't make helmets small enough to fit her. That worked for a few days until we saw a little one in a commercial wearing one of those colorful helmets . . ."

"Helmet molding therapy," Amethyst interrupted.

"Once he saw that, all bets were off, and he went right back to yammering about all the things she could do if I bought her one."

"But he's careful around her?" she asked. At first, I'd been concerned about the same thing since my son didn't have it in him to sit still for any length of time, but over the last two weeks, I had seen a side of my wild boy that I'd never witnessed before. "He's tender with her. She's like a magical little sprite that he treats like spun glass. If I let her cry for too long while I'm getting a bottle ready, he jumps all over my ass. This morning he gave me a speech about being better prepared and threatened to call Gamma and tell her I was mistreating his Star Baby."

"And Scoot?"

Celia, Koda's younger half-sister, lived just a few doors down from us and was my son's almost constant companion. She didn't quite grasp the details of how they were related, but she knew that Star was her sister, too, and had big plans for her. "She's looking for a pony so she and Star can ride together."

"Sounds like they've got some great plans."

"Terrifying plans."

"I wonder how often your mom said that when you were little?"

"I was an angel."

"Remember when you and the Dean boys got the bright idea to try and ride the llama Aunt Nicole rescued?"

"I do."

"That was your first time in a cast, wasn't it?"

"The first of many."

"Let's hope your kids are more careful . . ." Amethyst burst out laughing and then said, "I couldn't even say that

96

with a straight face."

"Didn't you break your arm trying to sock-surf down the slide at Aunt Summer's house?"

"Well, I think we're done for today," Amethyst said primly. As she turned away to make notes on her laptop, she said, "You can go ahead and get her dressed."

"Have you talked to Jovi lately?" I asked Amethyst as I zipped Star back into her sleeper. I picked her up and snuggled her against my chest for a second as I moved the straps out of the way so I could lay her back in her car seat. When I looked over at Amy, I found her watching me with a strange expression, so I asked, "What's wrong?"

"She's . . . Fraggle Rock!" Amethyst sighed, and I bit back a laugh at the look on her face. I knew what she wanted to say, but she'd trained herself not to curse since she spent so much time with children. Dr. Amethyst Hamilton was an entirely different animal than the Amy I'd grown up with. It cracked me up when she blurted out random words instead of the profanity that the rest of us used without thinking. Suddenly, her demeanor brightened, and she said, "If I tell you that it's part of the sisterhood that I *not* tell you how she's doing, you'd understand what I'm saying, right?"

"Clear as mud," I told her with a laugh.

"Sad hurts worse than angry, Ruf."

"She's upset about the breakup or . . ."

"Even though they were still living together, she got through the stages of grief about their relationship ages ago. She was just existing until that hemorrhoid on the stinkhole of humanity forced her to do something about it and leave. She's not heartbroken that she's single, Ruf. She's heartbroken that someone she used to love could do such a thing, and she's turned inward instead of letting us help her

97

through it."

"She's always kept to herself when she's upset."

"I'm a few years older than you guys, so I didn't really know her well back then, but True said that when you and Jovi broke up, she did the same thing she's doing now - pulled away from everyone until it was hard for her to see the sunshine through the clouds. At least she had school to focus on back then. Right now, she can't work, so she doesn't have that human interaction, and she's living with Jonas who works all hours, so he's never there. She's alone, Ruf, and I'm afraid she's going to put herself in a cocoon and stay that way for a while."

"Shit."

"You're not working right now either, so you've got plenty of time on your hands." I sputtered out a laugh, but before I could remind her that the miniature dictator in the car seat between us ruled my time with an iron fist, Amy reached out and brushed her finger over Star's forehead and smiled. "And you've got this little ray of sunshine that could push away the darkest of clouds if you're willing to share her."

"We don't have that relationship anymore, Amy. We're more acquaintances than friends, I guess you could say. We talk when we see each other, but that's about it. Things haven't been the same between us since we broke up."

"They looked very comfortable while she was sleeping in your arms the other day," Amethyst said slyly, referring to her shock when she had walked in to check on Star and found Jovi and I sleeping in the hospital bed.

"That's the first time we've spent alone in years."

"And it seemed to soothe both of your souls, didn't

it?"

"Well . . . yeah, I guess it did."

"She could use another dose of that, Ruf."

"I'll see what I can do," I promised as I slung the backpack I used as a diaper bag over my shoulder and then picked up the carrier. "I've got her number. I'll give her a call when I finish running errands and see if she wants to have coffee or something."

"Thanks, Ruf. I'll let the girls know you're on the job."

"That might not be the best idea. It took years for True to talk to me again after Jovi and I broke up. I'm not sure if you realize this or not, but her bouts of silence aren't comfortable."

Amethyst started laughing and said, "I can imagine that they're not."

SIX

"It's not about the fucking money, it's about a man who put his hands on a woman in anger and needs to pay for that shit."

Petra

JOVI

"Jovi! It's good to see you!"

I smiled at Ebbie Conner, the receptionist at the law firm where my sister managed the office and Jewel's sister, Petra, was an associate. "I sent Trinity a message when I saw you walking up. She should be here in just a . . ."

"Hey, Jo. How are you feeling?" my sister interrupted as she walked around the corner. She tilted her head in question and asked, "What's up?"

"I have a meeting with Petra at one o'clock."

"You do?" Trinity asked as she leaned down to look at Ebbie's computer screen. "I don't see it on the schedule. What's going on?"

"Jewel called Petra and made the appointment."

"That explains it. She's got some free time this afternoon, so she just squeezed you in. What's the appointment about?"

"Um, Rodney . . . I guess."

"What's going on, Jovi?"

"The DA isn't pursuing any charges."

"You are fucking kidding," Trinity hissed. When I shook my head, she blew out a breath and said, "That's ridiculous."

"Jewel thinks Petra can do something about it, but I'm not sure what."

"It's amazing what Petra can do when she sets her mind to it," Trinity said reassuringly. "How are you feeling? Are you back at work?"

"Not yet. I went in for a checkup to get the all-clear this morning, and I'm not healing the way I should, so I have to take some more time off."

"I know it's not ideal, but you should enjoy the break. You've been working your ass off, either in school or at the office for years."

"I'd rather be working, though. Staying home gives me too much time to think."

"Where are you living? Did you kick Rodney out or . . ."

I shook my head. "It's his house. I'm living with Jonas Dean until I can get the bank to give me my money out of our joint account and . . ."

"So, you're homeless and broke?" Trinity asked angrily.

"Way to twist the knife," I muttered.

"Sorry. I wasn't trying to blame you for that, I was just pointing out that . . . Anyway, lesson learned, right?"

"Move the handle of the pan around so you can't knock it off the stove?" I asked sarcastically.

"Or keep your money in your own account," Trinity snapped back.

"Well, looks like I got here right on time," Petra said cheerfully as she appeared around the corner. "Come on back, Jovi."

I followed Petra down the hall, and as we walked through the door into her office, I said, "I'm not sure what Jewel thinks you can do about this situation, Petra."

Just like Jewel, I'd known Petra my entire life, but only because of my connection to her family through my relationship with True, and, of course, Ruf when he and I were dating in high school. There was a less than ten-year age gap between us, which was significant enough, but Jewel, Petra and their other siblings graduated early and started college very young which put them even further out of my league.

However, I'd interacted with Petra many times at the office, either when she came in for a medical reason or just to visit her siblings. And now that I was here in her office, I wondered what exactly Jewel thought she was doing by setting up this meeting, especially since I didn't have the money to hire Petra for some legal battle, whereas Rodney had the means to hire a legal team for anything I tried to throw at him.

"I can find you the justice that the legal system pussied out on." I laughed because that was *not* how I imagined most attorneys spoke, but then again, Jewel and her family weren't like most people. "We'll sue him in civil court."

"I don't want his money, Petra."

"You don't have to sue him for millions, babe."

"No amount of money is going to take away the pain

102

of the burns that I'm still dealing with or the way I felt when he put his hands on me."

"It's the point of the matter, Jovi." In an abrupt change of topic, Petra asked, "Are you a Swiftie?"

"Um, no."

"She was sued for defamation by a man she accused of grabbing her ass during a photo op. She countersued him for one dollar, insisting that the money didn't matter, it was about not being silenced. The trial went to a jury, and the man lost - only a dollar, mind you - but his dignity and reputation were in tatters, and the fact that she was awarded that judgment against him will follow him for the rest of his life. If he ever behaves that way against anyone else, there's a trail of evidence that will show it wasn't his first time being accused of such a thing."

"She did it just so it was on record?"

"Exactly. As it stands, Rodney will have this arrest on his record, although there are ways his attorney can have that expunged, which he's probably busily trying to do right now."

"And then no one will ever know."

"The question is, has he ever done something like this before and gotten away with it? If he assaults another woman in the future, it will be her word against his. He'll throw his money at his defense team and get it dismissed because the DA will see there's nothing on his record."

"He brags all the time that surgeons are like gods. They're untouchable because they hold people's lives in their hands."

"Has he ever written that down in a text or an email?"

I laughed bitterly. "More than once."

"Show me." As I scrolled through the texts on my phone, Petra said, "As horrible as the situation is, the fact that he is a surgeon and has enough money to hire not just a defense attorney, but a *team* of them is what got him out of the charges. The DA could have pushed it and been in litigation for years, but that's not something they're ever fond of doing, so he dropped it."

I knew exactly when Rodney had sent a text with an almost exact quote of what I'd told Petra, so it was easy to find. I leaned forward slightly, wincing when it pulled at my side, and handed the phone to her to read. Without asking, she started scrolling through the text thread and scoffed at what I assumed was Rodney's ego and fake swagger.

"What a dick," Petra said as she looked up from my phone. "Is there anything in the texts between the two of you that you'd be uncomfortable with me reading?"

"Not that I can remember. We weren't exactly exchanging nudes or anything."

"Do you mind if I download this thread?"

"No. You can do that?"

Petra winked and said, "I can't, but I know someone who can. Is the phone account in your name?"

"Yes. I've had it since before I met him."

"Okay, then it shouldn't be a problem for us to get the paperwork in order to subpoena the texts from your provider for an added layer of information. Vada Conner and I will go through them - she's our paralegal."

"I know Vada."

CEE BOWERMAN

"There's a possibility that one or more of the other members of our team will be involved in this, so they'll see the texts too. In the long run, we'll most likely be presenting these to a judge and jury."

"I don't have the money to pursue this, Petra," I said honestly. "Right now, I'm living off a savings account that I opened when I was twelve and have been putting money in to go toward my future children's college education."

"He shut down your bank account?"

"It was originally his account that he added me to a few years ago. He reported my debit card stolen and changed the access on their records to say that he's the only one that can make any changes or request a new card."

"Have you contacted him to ask that he not do that?"

"No."

Petra studied my face for a few seconds before she asked, "Why?"

"He's trying to use money as a tool to get me to talk to him and probably even to get me back. He wants me to beg, and I fucking refuse."

"Good."

"I see that there are several texts from him over the last few weeks," Petra said as she started scrolling through my phone again. "Man's a night owl, I suppose."

"If he's had a bad day at work, he drinks more than usual and stays up well into the night."

"That's called alcoholism, honey," Petra said without looking up. "It's obvious from this text here that he had been drinking. Doctors are usually working at the crack

105

of dawn, especially surgeons."

"He's always out of the house by six."

"Does he have rotating days off?"

"No. He doesn't work on weekends unless he happens to be on call."

"This text was sent at three in the morning on a Wednesday. And it's obvious from the grammar and diction that he was drunk."

"I can almost guarantee it."

"And then he went to work at six?" I sighed and leaned back in the chair before I nodded. "Huh. Interesting."

"Why does that have to do with anything?"

"Was he near you when you called 911?"

"He was outside the bathroom door screaming for me to let him in."

"That was all he said?"

"No. He kept saying it was an accident and he never meant to hurt me."

"Do you think the operator could hear him?"

"Yes. She kept asking me if I was safe and or if he could somehow get through the door."

"I'm going to get the recordings of that call."

"I don't think you understand, Petra. I don't have the money to pay you for any of this."

"No, Jovi, I don't think *you* understand," Petra said

as she leaned forward in her chair and tapped her finger on the desk. "It's not about the fucking money, it's about a man who put his hands on a woman in anger and needs to pay for that shit. I'd prefer that it be in blood, but short of that, I'll take his reputation."

"You'll do that for free? If I get anything from him out of this, you can have it all. I just want the money I put into our joint checking and savings accounts."

"I need you to sign some papers so I can get things in motion."

"What kind of papers?" I asked as she opened her laptop.

She clicked a few things and then leaned back before she said, "Giving me permission to access your medical records from the ambulance company, the hospital, and my sister's office."

"For proof of my injuries?"

"And so we can make sure he pays for all of that and then some." For the first time in weeks, I felt a spark of hope, and I could tell that Jewel saw it in my demeanor. "Jovi, I know that your life has turned upside down, but you're a strong woman. I know you are because my sister doesn't surround herself with anything other than that. She abhors weakness and stupidity almost as much as I do. She sees something in you that has lit a fire under her. When she texted me this morning, she shared that fire, and now I'm going to tend to it. If you've got the same fire inside you, we'll add to the flames and use them to roast that son of a bitch until he's screaming like the pig he is."

"I'm not a victim, Petra. I'm not a statistic either."

"Yeah, honey, you are. It's what you do now that determines whether or not you stay that way."

The next hour was a whirlwind of being peppered by questions not just from Petra, but from Marcus Hamilton, too, one of the most prominent attorneys in Rojo. He was Ruf's honorary uncle and Amethyst's actual uncle, and I'd known him forever, but only as a smiling, happy family man. The man who asked me questions and took written notes of my answers wasn't happy and wasn't smiling.

He was downright terrifying.

By the time we were done with the initial questioning and had scheduled another appointment for next week, my mind was whirling with the realization that Petra was right. I was going to be a victim until I found my backbone and fought back. Since the court wouldn't do that for me, I would have to do it for myself and anyone Rodney might hurt in the future. With Petra and Marcus Hamilton at the helm, my fighting spirit started to make me feel almost buoyant with hope. I was able to start to believe that everything was going to be okay.

I knew that I would have a fight on my hands and this would be a long, drawn-out process, but that just made me even more firm in my decision to pursue this. By the time I walked out of the office, I almost felt like my old self except for the horrific pain I was feeling at the moment. I was once again becoming the Jovi who excelled in everything she put her mind to and couldn't be stopped.

I was changing back into the Jovi I was before Rodney started chipping away pieces of me a little at a time until I barely recognized myself or what I was worth.

The traits that Rodney had professed to love about me were the same traits he'd tried to stifle - drive, ambition, knowledge, and self-confidence. And for the first time in a very long time, I felt them stirring to life again.

It was a wonderful feeling, and as I breezed out of

the office, I was walking on a cloud. That is, until I slammed into Ruf Forrester and fell to the ground in a heap of pain and tears.

It seemed like that was a pattern with us, and I'd been trying to avoid a repeat of it for years.

SEVEN

"So, have those feelings you only admit to when you're drunk faded, or are they still alive and kicking?"

Hawk

RUF

"Holy shit, she's perfect," my cousin Hawk said as he looked down at Star. She was awake now as he held her in his arms and gently rocked back and forth in his office chair. She would probably start yelling at me to get some food in her soon, but for now, she was staring up at him with her wide blue eyes and steadily making him fall head over heels in love like everyone who came into contact with her.

It was still amazing to me that I had a daughter even though she'd been with me for two weeks now. Sleep deprivation aside, the transition from father of one to father of two had gone really well. I was learning to juggle my time with Koda around the countless hours it took to care for a newborn. There was a definite learning curve, but I wouldn't change anything about my life.

The first time I laid eyes on Star, I felt something in my chest that told me this was right - not just the right thing to do, giving a home to a child who needed one, but becoming her father and making her part of our lives. The bullshit with Cadence aside, I knew that Star was somehow meant to be ours. The fact that I made sure she'd never suffer like my son or his sister had only added to the emotions I felt about taking her home that day.

I was already so in love with her that it floored me to think that Cadence hadn't even held her before she signed her away - but it didn't shock me. She'd thrown Koda away years ago and never once looked back.

"How are you guys adjusting to having all this pink in your bachelor pad?" Hawk asked with a grin as he touched the bow on the tiny cap Rain had bought Star. He glanced up at me and asked, "Has Koda already recruited her into his nefarious plans to take over the universe?"

"Of course. Didn't Griff tell you? Her initiation is scheduled for next month."

Koda and Hawk's son Griffin were thick as thieves even though they were completely different children. Griff was a little genius. Talking to him was like conversing with a miniature adult who was smarter than I could ever dream of becoming. Koda was a brilliant kid, there was no denying that, but he was also a boy of action who never sat still. He and Griff balanced each other out with Griff teaching Koda things that I would have never thought of.

For instance, just this morning, Koda had listed out all of the planets in the solar system and even gave me details about a few of them that I hadn't heard before. When I asked him how he knew all of that, he said that Griffin was teaching him so that when they built their rocket, he could help him decide which planet to visit first.

Their relationship wasn't one-sided, though. Koda taught Griffin things, too, but they were usually things that had his mother, Brighten, threatening my life. Last week's adventure included Koda and Griffin digging a hole that broke a sprinkler line and turned Brighten's backyard into a swamp. I had to admit that the hole was Koda's idea because he wanted to build a tunnel underneath all of the backyards between our house and Griffin's that had branches going across the street to their cousin Lyric's house, their friend

Ruthie's, and Scoot's.

The tunnel plan came about when I wouldn't let him walk over to visit his buddies after dusk because I worried that he'd get hit by a car.

The backyard swamp happened right about the time Brighten had finally forgiven me for Koda and Griffin's last adventure, which was brought on by my son's love of the movie Ace Ventura: Pet Detective, an old film I'd loved as a kid and then watched with my son months ago. Koda was still convinced that the raccoon he and Griffin had trapped wasn't wild, it was just misunderstood.

Of course, it was also really fucking pissed that it had been locked in Brighten's closet until they built it a house of its own. A house made of fence pickets that they scavenged off the neighbor's back fence.

I wasn't sure who was angrier about the whole affair - Brighten because of her encounter with a wild animal or Margaret, the neighbor who thought we were all wild animals.

In terms of volume, Brighten's screams won, but as for anger, Margaret was the definite champ.

"Where's Koda?"

"Your house," I said as I pulled my phone out. "I was just about to call and make sure they don't have Crow bound and gagged somewhere while they do something crazy."

"Let 'em have their fun," Hawk argued. "No sense interrupting them. Besides, if he *is* tied up, he won't be able to get to his phone anyway."

"True," I agreed as I set my phone on the desk in front of me. "Did you get the paperwork in order for everything?"

"I did," Hawk assured me as he glanced up from Star. A second later, he was staring down at her again and said, "As soon as we get finished in the office today, you can choke him out, little Star. You're in the will, and your daddy has a decent amount of savings and quite the life insurance policy." Hawk looked back up at me and asked, "Are you sure about the custody arrangement, man? It seems kind of . . . unique."

I smiled at him and agreed, "It is, but I think it would be the best option for the kids. Koda and Star need to keep their relationship with Scoot, and if something happens to me, having Ripley share custody with Rain will do exactly that."

"And they agreed to that?"

"They did. We met up at my house when Star was just a few days old and hashed it all out. They're both all in, and it makes a lot of sense because if something ever happens to Ripley he's got me and Jovi listed as Scoot's guardians."

"Jovi? Really?"

"She's great with kids, man. He knows that Trinity would do right by Scoot, but Jovi's got softer edges and would be a little more maternal."

"Speaking of Jovi, how's she doing? I heard about what that shit stain did to her."

"I think she's having a rough time and needs some attention. When I talked to Amethyst this morning, she tried to explain what's going on with her without breaking the girl code and giving away any secrets. It seems like she's just feeling alone, and when that happens, she hunkers down and won't let anyone in."

"Not good," Hawk said as she lifted the squirming baby up to his shoulder and started patting her back. "Why did Amethyst talk to you about it?"

"I guess because of our history. I'm not sure why else she would think I could help."

"I never told a soul about that night, man. I know Crow and Nix wouldn't have either."

"Neither would Jonas or Lawson. I know my secrets are safe with you guys. I never even considered that any of you might have spilled. It's all good. God knows I've had more than one night when I was swimming around in the deep end of the keg and probably said too much. We've all done that once or twice in our lives, haven't we?"

"True. So, have those feelings you only admit to when you're drunk faded, or are they still alive and kicking?"

I sighed before I said, "They've never really gone away, I'm just better at ignoring them than I used to be - as long as I don't drink too much and get sappy."

"Happens to the best of us."

Star let out a little squeak. I knew that was an early warning signal before the food siren went off, so I reached for my backpack and pulled out one of the bottles of water I'd prepared for our venture outside the house today. Once I had added the correct portion of formula, I swirled the contents of the bottle around to make sure it was mixed and asked, "Can I use your break room? I need some hot water."

"Down the hall across from the bathroom."

"I'll be right back," I assured him as I hopped up from my chair and walked to the door. I hurried down the hall and found the break room, and by the time I found something to heat the water in and pulled it out of the microwave to drop the bottle into it to warm, the early warning signal had turned into a full-on wail. I knew that if I didn't hurry, Hawk's ears would be bleeding by the time I got back.

The girl had some pipes on her, that was for sure. Even Koda had mentioned that she sure could make a whole lot of noise for such a little thing. He thought it was funny that I compared Star to him when I replied that for a person his size, he could cause a whole lot of mayhem.

As soon as the formula was warm enough, I poured the hot water down the drain and set the mug I'd been using in the drying rack and rushed back down the hall. Star's screams had reached the decibel that meant complete meltdown. If I didn't get to her soon, she'd stay fussing even through her bottle. I'd found out early on that the kid could hold a grudge even at this young age, and I really didn't want to get on her bad side.

Suddenly, Jovi appeared in front of me, and before I could veer away to avoid her, we collided. I slammed into her side, and she let out a yelp as she bounced off my chest and flew backwards to land on her butt. She'd naturally thrown her arms out to catch her fall, but the second she did that was when her scream turned from one of shock to one of pain. I watched as she folded her arms against her chest and pulled her legs up so that she could curl into a ball.

"Fuck!" I yelled as I dropped down beside her.

"What happened?" Petra asked when she appeared at the door of her office. "Is she okay?"

I held the bottle out toward her and said, "Take this to Hawk. I've got Jovi."

Petra snatched the bottle out of my hand and rushed

down the hallway, and I leaned down over Jovi and said, "Jovi, baby, tell me what I can do to help." She was doing an odd sort of breathing, quick pants followed by a deep breath, and then she'd slowly let it out before she started panting again. "I want to pick you up, but I don't know where I can touch you. Talk to me, Bonbon. Tell me what to do."

"Purse. Pill bottle. Two and some water. Call an Uber so I can get home."

"An Uber?"

"Can't drive like this. Can't drive after I take them." Jovi whimpered, and it broke my heart, but I did the only thing I could and dug through her purse to find the pill bottle she needed. By the time I shook two pills into my hand, Petra was back with a bottle of water, and I looked up to find Jovi's sister standing beside her with tears in her eyes.

Trinity kneeled on Jovi's other side and reached out to brush Jovi's hair off her face where it had stuck to her damp cheeks. "Oh, Jojo. Sweetie."

"Should I call an ambulance?" Ebbie asked from the end of the hall. I glanced up and shook my head as I realized that Star was quiet now as Hawk stood just outside his office with her in his arms as she greedily drank from her bottle.

"Here you go, Bonbon," I whispered as I held out the pills. She opened her mouth, and I dropped them in and then held the bottle of water for her to drink. "What now? Can I pick you up?"

"I'm sorry," Jovi said through a sob. "Just let me lay here for a minute, okay? I'm so sorry."

"Shut up," Petra snapped as she hesitantly patted Jovi's leg. I'd known Petra my entire life and had seen her in all sorts of situations. The woman had a huge heart but a

116

mean streak a mile wide. It seemed like those two sides of her were at war right now, but I completely understood why.

Watching Jovi writhe in pain made me want to hold her and comfort her, but at the same time, it made me want to hunt Rodney down and beat him until he was nothing more than pulp.

"I can . . . Help me up," Jovi ordered as before she took a deep breath in through her nose. "Get me off the floor. I'll sit down somewhere else. Not in the middle of the hall."

"You can stay right where you're at as long as . . ." The bell over the front door sounded, and Ebbie's voice trailed down the hall as she told someone that Petra was with a client and would be out as soon as she was available.

"People are looking at me," Jovi whispered. "Help me up."

I remembered how much Jovi had always hated to be the center of attention and knew that the only reason her embarrassment wasn't at the forefront right now was because she was in so much pain.

"I've got you, Bonbon," I murmured as I slipped my hand under her and slowly raised her up to a sitting position. "Tell me where I can touch and what I can do to help."

"I don't know," she said through another sob. "Everything hurts so bad. Just do it. Just pull me up. I'll be okay."

"Fuck," I whispered. I fished my keys out of my pocket and handed them to Trinity. "Go start my truck. Turn the air on and lay the passenger seat back."

Trinity took off toward the front door as Petra said, "I'll clear the waiting room."

"Baby's ready," Hawk called out. I glanced toward his office and found him with my backpack over his shoulder, carrying Star buckled into her carseat. "Come on. I've got the door."

"This is probably gonna hurt, so I'm just gonna go ahead and say I'm sorry," I whispered as I got to my feet and then bent down next to her. I kissed Jovi on the forehead and then scooped her up into my arms. She gasped but didn't try to move away, so I stood up and strode toward the door.

Just a few hours ago, I had promised Amethyst I'd give Jovi a call and take her out for a coffee or something, but those plans had changed. I'd be hanging out with Jovi, but it was going to be at my house. If I had my way, she'd never leave.

The strong woman that I remembered from years ago was still there, she just needed some coaxing and tender loving care to find her way out into the daylight again. Luckily, I was just the guy to help her. I'd resisted the pull for years, first because I was bitter and angry, then because I was trying to wade through single parenthood and all that entailed. By the time I found my footing, Jovi was with Rodney, and I'd missed my chance. But Rodney was gone now - not permanently, but that could easily be arranged. Every time I heard Jovi whimper in pain, the urge to make that happen surged.

Now there was nothing standing between us but doubt and fear, and I wasn't going to shy away because of either of those. I just hoped that Jovi had forgiven me for my stupidity all those years ago and was willing to give me another chance.

And right now, when she needed a friend the most, was the perfect time for me to convince her to do just that.

"You're taking her home? I don't think she should

be alone. I'll call and see if Jonas is . . ." Trinity asked.

"Call your mom and have her meet us at my house," I ordered. "We'll be there in ten."

EIGHT

**"My life is a fucking roller coaster. I just want
to get off and stand on solid ground."**

Jovi

JOVI

I woke up to that fuzzy-headed feeling I always got
after I took the narcotics Jewel had prescribed. When I tried
to swallow down the nausea that came with it, I couldn't
because my mouth was too dry.

I took a catalog of my aches and realized that I wasn't
on that razor's edge of pain. It was just a dull throb, meaning
I hadn't slept through the effects of the painkillers, so
without too much effort, I was able to roll onto my side and
sit up on the edge of the bed.

A bed that didn't feel anything like mine in a room I
didn't recognize.

I vaguely recalled Ruf picking me up and then
talking to my mom, but I honestly had no idea where I was
right now and that terrified me. I looked down and realized
that I wasn't just in an unfamiliar room, but I had also been
undressed.

My feet and legs were bare, and I had on a shirt I
didn't recognize.

"What the fuck?" I whispered.

I took a deep breath and then let my eyes drift closed

when I was assaulted by memories I'd tried very hard to keep at bay over the years.

I could smell Ruf - his favorite lotion with the faint coconut scent and the shea butter product he always used on his hair. I had always loved the smell of Ruf's hair and smiled when I remembered how he and his sisters had laughed at me the first time I tried to braid it. His mom had stepped in and scolded them for making fun of me when I was only making an effort to learn and then demonstrated again how to hold his hair between my fingers - not too loosely or the braid wouldn't be tight enough and not too tight or it would pull and be uneven.

I had been so proud of myself when I finally finished the last braid and was even more proud when Ruf bragged about my new skill to his brother and suggested he let me do his hair next. Even though the parts weren't as straight and the braids weren't nearly as good as they would have been if he'd let his sisters or his mom do his hair, Ruf wore the style until it was time to take it out and start over again and then sat patiently while I learned how to do another style before he wore that one proudly too.

Ruf had always loved my hair, too, sifting it through his fingers while we watched a movie snuggled on the couch or laid naked together and tried to catch our breath after we made love. I'd compared every man I'd known to Ruf - not that I'd been intimate with more than a couple. None of them ever measured up to how safe and cherished I'd felt in his arms.

"Fuck! I must still be high," I mumbled to myself as I rubbed my hands across my face and pushed my hair back. It wasn't often that I let myself walk down memory lane, but every time I did, I was filled with so much longing that it left an ache in my chest that took days to fade.

I heard a child's excited squeal and then adult

121

laughter and recognized my mother's voice as well as True's and Ruf's and a few I didn't recognize immediately. When I heard a noise to my left, I dropped my hands from my face and looked up.

"Oh my goodness," I whispered when I saw bright blue eyes staring back at me from the bassinet that held a tiny baby wearing white pajamas covered in bright pink Harley Davidson logos. I rolled the bassinet closer to me and smiled down at the little girl. "Hello, Star. It's a pleasure to see you again."

She blinked a few times and then squirmed before she made a funny little squeak. I couldn't resist anymore, so I reached over the side and gently picked her up. I held her in front of me and smiled as she studied my face for a few seconds before she started squirming again. I held her to my chest and propped her up on my left side where the burns had mostly healed, moving gingerly so I didn't pull at the ones on my right, and then gently patted her back as I let my eyes fall closed.

This sweet girl had my skin color and the dusting of hair on her head wasn't curly like Ruf's, but she smelled like him. It was so peaceful holding her in my arms that I didn't realize anyone had come into the room until I heard Ruf say, "Looks like she's pulled you into her web."

I opened my eyes and smiled as Ruf sat down beside me. "Just look at her. It didn't take much."

"How are you feeling, Bonbon?" My heart flipped when he called me by the nickname he'd always used and then fluttered again when he lifted my hair over my shoulder, running his fingers through the strands as he had so many times while we were together. "It's almost time for you to take your next round of meds."

"I'm really only supposed to take one at a time, but I

was feeling the need earlier. I don't take them on a schedule, just when the pain gets so bad . . ."

"Ah, there you go proving Jewel right," Ruf muttered. He ran his hands through my hair again as he said in a stronger voice, "That stops today, though, sweetheart. She said that if you're hurting, you won't heal, so we can't let that happen."

"I don't like feeling medicated. I'm afraid that something's gonna happen, and I'm not gonna know how to react," I admitted.

"Like what?"

"What if someone comes to the door and I can't stop them from getting in or . . ."

"Someone meaning Dr. Dickbrain."

"Yeah," I said in a sigh as Star started squirming in my arms. Her whole body tensed, and then she farted so loudly that it seemed to echo. When she relaxed again, I patted her on the butt and said, "Look at her, already acting like her dad." Ruf burst out laughing, and Star perked up and tried to lift her head. "She likes your laugh."

"You think that's something, you should see her reaction when I do something stupid."

"Like what?"

"This morning before dawn, I was half-asleep when I left the bedroom to go make her bottle, and I stepped on a pile of Legos Koda left in the middle of the floor. I hopped around, trying not to yell every profanity I know and then tripped and bumped into the door frame. I was walking back to my room with the bottle and stepped on the same fucking Legos and then slammed into the wall so hard that I knocked a picture frame off. I was still cussing when I came back into the bedroom, and I swear she was smiling at me."

"The picture you just painted makes me want to laugh, so I can't say that I blame her."

"Now that we've established she's a gassy maniacal genius with a wicked sense of humor at the ripe old age of two weeks old, let's get back to the subject at hand."

"Let's not."

"You're sort of a captive audience at this point, Bonbon."

"I can call an Uber," I said testily.

"You're welcome to do that, but when your mom and sister were in here with Jewel, they changed you into something more comfortable while they were checking your wounds."

"That explains why I'm wearing your shirt, but not why I can't leave."

"You can, but I'd like to know how you think you're going to get past your parents, siblings, *and* best friend to get to it."

"They're all here?"

"I believe they're trying to stage an intervention."

"I am not abusing the pain medicine, so I don't see why they think I need an intervention." Ruf laughed as he got up and walked over to the dresser, which had a changing pad on the top, and started pulling things out of the top drawer. I watched as he got out a change of clothing for Star, a diaper, and some wipes before I asked, "Why is that funny?"

"Because the only time any of them mentioned the

pain medication was to say you're not taking it like you should."

"I told you I don't like to feel weird."

"Oh, that's right. You want to be clear-headed in case Dr. Dingleberry makes an appearance."

"Kind of." Ruf stared at me with a blank expression until I admitted, "Yes."

"Has he made any move to see you yet?"

"He's been calling and texting at all hours, but as far as I know, he doesn't have any idea where I'm living right now."

"How would he find out?"

"Well, this isn't exactly a bustling metropolis, Ruf. He could spot my car while I'm out during the day and then follow me home, or he could hear someone gossiping and overhear that I live with Jonas."

"Or maybe he's tracking your cell phone and has known where you were this whole time." My heart stopped for a second and then started racing. When Star started fussing, I realized she could feel my tension, so I made a concerted effort to relax and maintain a steady rhythm as I patted her little bottom. "Did you ever think of that?"

"No. How would he do that?"

"I have no idea. I'm not a stalker. But I have taken a deep dive into true crime shows. Now I'm pretty sure everyone has a body buried under their house, trapdoors in their closet, and has stalked at least one person in their life."

"Wow."

"I'm also convinced that my house is haunted, I have

at least three terminal illnesses, and big pharma is putting mind control drugs in cough syrup. Don't even get me started on how hard it is to find the right shade of foundation and concealer for a person with skin like mine, the unnecessary ingredients in almost all of the food we eat, how much joy a flying squirrel would bring into my life, or the truth about the first lady of France."

I burst out laughing and asked, "Are we on the same algorithm?"

"I've seen a few theories about that too." Ruf came and took the baby from my arms and then snuggled her close as he walked back over to get her changed. He focused solely on her the entire time he worked, smiling and talking like they were having a full-blown conversation, and then he picked her up and gave her a kiss on the cheek before he walked toward the bedroom door. Over his shoulder, he called out, "I'll be back with some water, another pill, and a snack. Make yourself comfortable."

"Where are my clothes?"

"They're underneath the house with the bodies. You can get to them through the trapdoor in my closet."

I was searching through Ruf's dresser for a pair of sweats to put on when the door opened again, and my mom appeared with True right behind her.

"Why am I naked?" I asked them as True shut the door.

"You're wearing a shirt and have on underwear."

"Where is my bra?"

"The one that is keeping that wound from healing?" True asked. I glared at her, and she shrugged. "I'm just speaking the truth, the same truth that Jewel told you two weeks ago and then last week . . .Oh, and this morning. I heard her say that you needed to stop irritating your wound with underwires and . . ."

"I was going to take it off as soon as I got finished at the store."

"Or maybe just not wear it in the first place?" Mom asked sarcastically.

"It doesn't rub directly on the burn, it just pulls up the edge of the bandage," I explained.

"Since this happened to you, I've realized that the old saying is true - nurses make the worst patients."

"Fine. Take me home, and I promise I won't put on a bra until I get cleared by Jewel."

"No," Mom said as she sat down on the end of the bed.

"What do you mean no?"

"While you were sleeping, we went over what's going on and the messages Rodney has been sending you."

"How do you know what he's been sending me?" I asked in outrage, but I knew the answer before True even opened her mouth.

"Your sister and I opened your phone while you were sleeping," True admitted. "In our defense, we didn't even think about doing that until it kept buzzing with texts, and we could tell from your lock screen that they were from him."

I sighed. "What did they say?"

"Wow. You are mellow. I'm surprised you didn't scream at me for invading your privacy," True mused.

"You got off easy," my mom said with a confused look at True. "When she was a teenager, she ranted for three days because she thought I invaded her privacy after I opened a notebook she'd left on the coffee table."

"Please take me to my car."

"We were just discussing that while Ruf was in here talking to you."

"What's there to talk about? Rock, paper, scissors that shit, and then the winner gets to drive me home."

"We think you should stay here," Mom explained.

"Here? As in Ruf's house, here?"

"Well, she's oriented to place, so that's good."

"What the hell does that mean, True? I don't have a head injury!" I looked at my mom and shook my head. "I'm not staying with Ruf. I need to go back to Jonas' house."

"We're not sure that's the safest place for you right now," Mom said hesitantly.

"Why? I know you wanted me to move back in with you and Dad but . . ."

"Your dad and I aren't home during the day, and neither of us works close to the house, so that wouldn't be a good option either."

"What has changed since this morning?"

"One of the texts that Rodney sent was a picture of Jonas' house."

True could tell that I was shocked, and she winced. "He said he was going to sit there on the porch until you got back because he really wants to talk to you."

"So, I call the cops and tell them that he's trespassing and have them come give him a ticket."

"He called the office over and over this afternoon yelling at Connie to put you on the phone until Terran finally took the call and lost his temper." True raised her eyebrows before she said, "You know what it takes for Terran to lose his temper."

"What did Rodney say to him?"

"I have no idea, but he told me to call and let you know that you're welcome to stay at his house because he's got no problem eradicating vermin."

"Oh."

"Petra called too. She said to tell you that she was able to find a judge who was willing to give you a protective order and serve the bank papers to shut down the bank accounts until y'all can get into court." My mouth dropped open in shock, and True grinned. "And, uh, well . . ."

"What?"

"He's on foot," Mom said with a grin.

"Why? What happened to his car?"

"He must have parked illegally because he got towed."

I put my hand over my mouth and stared at True. "So, he's without a vehicle and without the money to get said vehicle out of impound?"

"He could call a friend and borrow . . ."

"He doesn't have any friends like that," I muttered. "Now he's pissed about the car, pissed about the money, and realizes that I've spoken to an attorney," I said aloud, working through everything and imagining how mad Rodney must be and very happy that I wasn't home alone right now.

"That about sums it up," True said with a grimace. "See why it's a good idea to stay here?"

"Why here?"

"Ruf's on leave from work to take care of the baby, so you'll never be alone," True explained.

"And honestly, if Rodney somehow finds out where you're staying and shows up to start trouble, there are plenty of neighbors around who would see him and could help Ruf discourage him from bothering you."

"Discourage him. That's awesome," True said as she stuck her fist out. Mom bumped her fist, and True grinned at me. "Your mom is the master of understatement."

"Your brother is usually next door or out back, which is close enough to get here quickly if he's needed. I'm in my office all day, so I'll also be nearby."

"He can't get here anyway because he doesn't have a car and doesn't have any money for an Uber."

"He can use a credit card to get the car out of impound or pay for an Uber," Mom argued.

"He doesn't have any credit cards," I told her. "His mom was horrible with money and spent every dime his dad ever made, so he's very careful about his spending and refuses to pay a single dime for interest unless it's for something tangible like the house or his car. He also doesn't carry cash. He'd rather the money stay in the bank and draw interest. He swears that if you've got cash, you'll spend it quicker than you would if you have to use a debit card."

"Besides, even if he had the money, he can't get his car out of impound."

"Why not?"

"One of the drug dogs alerted on it, so it's in line for a search by the crime lab."

"Why were there drug dogs near it?"

"I guess it's protocol for them to take a sniff when they drop a vehicle off at impound. Jonas said it's one of the routine tasks they have to keep their training fresh."

"You're kidding," I whispered. "Did Jonas set that up too?"

"How did you know Jonas towed him?"

"I'm not an idiot, True. I've been living with a tow truck driver, and my ex's car got towed. Simple math."

"Jonas was laughing about the drug dog thing, so I asked him if that was his doing. He said that Bob Ross was right - happy accidents *do* happen."

"That wasn't an answer," I argued.

"He swears he didn't have shit to do with that."

"Let me get this straight. You want me to stay with my first ex-boyfriend to avoid my most recent ex-boyfriend."

"Yes."

I looked around the room and asked, "Are we filming a reality show? I didn't sign a waiver for this."

"Cool. I'm glad you agree. I'll let Ruf know that he's going to have company for the foreseeable future," True said cheerfully as she hopped off the bed.

"Tell him? He doesn't know about this plan of yours?"

"He will in just a second!" she called over her shoulder before she left and pulled the door shut behind her.

"What the hell, Mom?"

"Honey, your dad and I are sick with worry for you. We wanted you to stay with us for a while, but you insisted you'd be okay. We both know you're not."

"I'm fine!"

"You only leave the house to go to the doctor, baby. You're hiding."

"I'm not hiding from him, I just . . ."

"You're hiding from everybody, Jovi, not just Rodney. It's not healthy."

"My life is a fucking roller coaster. I just want to get off and stand on solid ground."

"Please stay here, or even at your brother's, if you must, but don't go back to Jonas' and hole up by yourself again. It would make your dad and I feel so much better about the whole situation."

"And here comes the guilt," I whispered.

"I've been where you are, sweetheart. I can't imagine how differently my life would have been if I had had friends and family who were there to support me. Don't squander that gift. They can help carry you until you find your way."

"I can't live in a house and watch everything I used

to dream about going on around me and not lose my shit, Mom."

"It won't be forever. Do it for me, sweetie. Please?"

"I don't know, Mom. There's gotta be another option."

"I can call Kari and see if she's got an apartment open," Mom said as she stood and put her hands on her hips.

"I can't take a place that another woman who doesn't have anywhere to go could use."

"Then you'll stay here?"

"I guess I don't have a choice, do I?"

NINE

"The kittens aren't quite sure how to use their claws yet, but I'll give them a demonstration if they need one."

Jewel

JOVI

"What are we doing tomorrow?" I heard Koda ask Ruf before he grunted and then started laughing. "It almost went up my nose!"

"I'm gonna build some bookcases, and I figured you could work on your house."

"The electricity?"

"No. You're not going to do your own electrical work. We'll call Uncle John and Uncle Mattie to help with that."

"I wanna do it myself."

"Son, there are some things in this world that necessitate a good healthy dose of fear, and electricity is one of them."

"I ain't scared of nothin'."

"I know, but there's a slew of things you should at least be wary of."

"Like what?"

"Well, electricity, like I said. Fire is another pretty big one. Machinery you don't understand . . ."

"I can work on machines. An engine is a machine."

"But your urge to put sharp and pointy things into the middle of an engine concerns me greatly."

"It was that one time. Griff and I thought if we stuck the nail in there, we'd be making a nail gun like Lettuce used when he was making my clubhouse."

"And what did I tell you about using a nail gun?"

"That the world . . ." Koda started coughing, and I heard the recliner slam down with a loud thunk and then movement in the living room right before there were a few loud thumps. Finally, his voice oddly gruff, Koda said, "That one almost killed me, Dad."

"I'll stop tossing while you're talking," Ruf assured him. I heard the creak of the recliner going back again before Ruf said, "Now, remind me why you aren't allowed to use power tools."

"The world isn't ready for me to have that kind of knowledge."

"Yep."

"What's knowledge?"

"Brains. Smarts. Understanding."

"I'm smart!"

"The smartest!" There was a pause, and then Koda giggled. "Good catch. Anyway, no nail guns, power tools, or electrical work."

After at least a minute of silence, Koda asked, "How

135

many do you think I can fit in my mouth?"

I couldn't resist anymore and had to see what in the world they were doing, so I tiptoed down the hall. I peeked around the corner and found Koda reclining against the arm of the couch with a bag of mini marshmallows on his chest. Ruf was in his recliner with another bag and they were steadily tossing marshmallows at each other and catching them in their mouths.

I bit my lip to stifle a laugh when Ruf reached up to rub his eye after he got hit with one and smiled when Koda sang, "You'll shoot your eye out."

"Great movie," Ruf mumbled before he leaned to the side and caught a marshmallow. "So, are you cool with Jovi staying here for a while?"

"Yep. She's nice. I like her."

"So do I."

"Can she be our girlfriend?"

"Not sure she's up for that, bud."

"She's gonna live with us. Rip and Scoot's girlfriend lives with them now. She's gonna be Scoot's mom."

"True, but Jovi's situation is a little different than Tori's."

"Yeah." Koda giggled when a marshmallow bounced off his nose. "Tori's ex-boyfriend isn't a pompous douchebag who needs his balls ripped off."

Ruf sputtered out a laugh and said, "You've gotta quit eavesdropping, bud."

"What's a pompous?"

"It means cocky. Someone who thinks they're better than everyone else."

I found it funny that Koda didn't ask for the explanation for douchebag, just intuitively understanding it was an insult. It was also funny that Ruf didn't even flinch when the little boy talked about ripping off someone's balls.

"He hurt her."

"He did."

"On purpose?"

"Yeah."

"*Never* pick on people. Don't ever hurt someone who doesn't hurt you first. He did that?"

"Yeah, son. He did that."

"What a fucker," Koda mumbled.

"I don't disagree with you, but you know you're not supposed to say shit like that."

"Sorry."

"You were doing so good," Ruf chided. "You haven't dropped an f-bomb in *days*."

"I didn't say fuck, I called him a fucker."

"Boy . . ."

"My bad," Koda muttered, but he didn't look the least bit apologetic. "You gonna charge me?"

"I'll let you off with a warning, but next time . . ."

"Class A misdemeanor," Koda said sadly "I know the drill."

They kept tossing marshmallows, and even though I thought it was adorable, I found it a little gross that they didn't care how many times one bounced - they'd just toss it back and then eat it if they caught it in their mouth.

"Can I stay up all night?"

"Sure," Ruf agreed. "Just stay inside the house, okay?"

"I will. Griffin said that he saw our raccoon, and he's still pissed."

Ruf burst out laughing before he said, "You locked him in a closet, man. Wouldn't you be pissed?"

"He's gotta get over it sometime, but I think he's probably still plotting his revenge. Griffin said that raccoons don't eat eyeballs, but I think he's wrong."

"You think it's out there in the yard waiting to pounce?"

"If somebody locked me in a closet, I'd probably pounce," Koda said with a frown. "Maybe I should find him and say I'm sorry."

"Or maybe you should leave the wild animals alone before you end up missing fingers and foaming at the mouth."

"Like that time we put that nasty stuff in our mouth and freaked out Stache and Aunt Rainy?"

Ruf chuckled. "That was awesome. No, I'm talking about rabies. It's a disease you can get from an infected wild animal."

"Hi!" Koda said cheerfully when he spotted me in the doorway. "Want some marshmallows?"

"I think I . . . um . . ." I stammered as I walked into the living room.

"I won't throw the ones that hit the floor. I know girls don't like that."

"Okay," I said as I smiled at Ruf and then sat down on the other end of the couch from Koda.

"Ready?" Koda asked. I nodded and then held my mouth open and laughed when a marshmallow hit me on the nose. "Shit. I missed."

"Koda," Ruf said with a warning tone.

"Oops. Sorry."

I picked the marshmallow up off the couch and held it up in front of me as Koda opened his mouth wide. I tossed it his way, and he grinned when he caught it in his mouth and started chewing. I looked over at Ruf, and he was holding one ready to throw, so I opened my mouth and caught it when it flew my way.

"How was your nap?" Ruf asked as he tossed another marshmallow at Koda. It bounced off his chin, but he caught it in midair and threw it back at his dad. It went into Ruf's mouth, and he threw one at me before he asked, "Are you ready for another pill? And you should take some of those other ones Jewel brought over, too, huh?"

"Yeah, but I should have something to eat before I take the antibiotics."

"We eatin' right now," Koda said.

"She means real food."

Koda looked at his dad as if he were crazy and then held a marshmallow up and squished it between his fingers before he popped it into his mouth. "This is real. It only *tastes* like magic."

"I'm not much of a cook, and I forgot to get anything out of the freezer, so we're just making do with what we've got on hand." I raised my eyebrows in question, and Ruf shrugged. "If you think you can do better, be my guest."

"Do you mind if I look around your kitchen?"

"You're living here now, so it's your kitchen too," Koda said with a shrug. "You cookin' something good? We're allergic to green stuff."

I smiled at him before I asked, "Do you present with hives, eczema, or anaphylaxis?"

"I don't like to eat any of those either. Or broccoli."

I looked over at Ruf, and he was smiling, so I asked, "Are you allergic too?"

"I've got no shame. I'll eat anything you put in front of me, and so will he if there's enough ketchup on it."

"Or ranch! I like that."

"Let me see what you've got to work with." I walked into the kitchen with very low expectations, considering Ruf was the epitome of bachelorhood even though he was raising two kids. If I had any doubts about that, the engine parts, tool boxes, and neon signs strewn all over the dining room would have given me a hint.

I took stock of the pantry and cabinets and found a few things to work with and was pleasantly surprised when I discovered the upright freezer in the laundry room had a freezer bag of pre-cooked sausage and another of bacon. I also found a bag of frozen veggies that I thought I might be able to use. The refrigerator had a treasure trove of condiments, four gallons of milk, two sticks of butter, a selection of cheese that was almost awe-inspiring, and a few dozen eggs. This was going to work out just fine.

I put the breakfast meat in the microwave to thaw while I searched for cookware. Within just a few minutes, I had a frittata baking and was getting to work on a pan of oatmeal to put in the oven so we'd have something to eat for breakfast tomorrow morning.

"I smell bacon," Koda said as he walked into the kitchen. He opened the refrigerator door and stood in front of it, peering inside like he was waiting for something magical to appear while he stood there and scratched his belly. He looked so much like Ruf in that moment that I fell even more in love with him and pitied his mother for missing out on such a wonderful little boy. He looked over at me and smiled as he let the door close and asked, "Whatcha making?"

"Baked oatmeal."

"Hmm. Dad makes that in the microwave. I don't like it when it's lumpy."

"I make mine like a cake and eat it for breakfast."

Koda's eyes got wide as asked, "You eat cake for breakfast?"

I pulled a glass out of the cabinet and drained the juice out of the can of peaches I had just opened. I handed the glass to Koda and said, "You eat donuts for breakfast sometimes, I'm sure."

"I do," Koda said as he studied the liquid in the glass. "What's this?"

"Peach juice. Try it."

He took a hesitant sip, and then his eyes lit up. "That's good."

"Donuts are a lot like cake, so why *not* eat cake for breakfast?"

"I like you, Jovi," Koda said sincerely before he took another sip. "I like you a lot."

"Well, I'm glad you like me since I'll be staying here for a little while."

"Are you gonna cook all the time?"

"She's not staying here to be our personal chef, bud," Ruf said as he walked into the kitchen with Star in his arms. He pulled a bottle out of the refrigerator and then walked over to the sink and turned the water on before he said, "She needs to rest and get better, and she can't do that if she's in here standing at the stove."

"I can scoot a chair over here," Koda offered.

I burst out laughing and then said, "I like to cook."

"I like to eat. We could make a good team if we practice."

"And by practice, you mean me cooking for you all the time." Koda nodded eagerly, and I laughed. "You'll have to take me to the grocery store first because I'll need some supplies."

"Gonna need your card, Dad," Koda said before he took another sip of his juice. "She made me juice."

"Where'd you get the stuff to make juice?" Ruf asked as he filled a bowl with hot water and then set the bottle in it to warm.

"It's just the juice from the can of peaches. I figured

that amount of sugar wouldn't really make much of a difference since you were planning to have marshmallows for dinner." I realized what Ruf was doing and asked, "You don't have a bottle warmer?"

"I haven't really had a chance to go shopping yet," Ruf admitted. "We had the party and got a lot of things for Star, but that wasn't one of them."

"I should introduce you to my friend Amazon," I muttered. In a regular voice, I offered, "I can pick one up when I go to the store tomorrow."

"When *we* go to the store tomorrow," Ruf corrected.

"You don't have to go with . . . I still don't have my car, do I?"

Ruf shook his head and said, "I have to go anyway. I've got a list of shit I need to pick up and a few items I need to exchange, so we can do all of that at once."

"We're gonna paint tomorrow. You wanna help?" Koda asked.

"What are you painting?"

"Star's bedroom."

"Would you mind helping us figure out how to decorate it? It's pretty boring, so I thought I'd let Koda paint one of the walls."

"What color?" Ruf raised his eyebrows and gave me a questioning look. I laughed before I said, "Oh, right. I forgot you're color blind."

"No one really knew what to buy for Star, so a lot of people gave me money at the shower. I thought I'd get her nursery outfitted with that since I'll probably never have to buy her clothes."

"You won't?"

"Every time a woman in my family walks through the door, they're carrying a bag with something for her to wear in it."

"It's adorable! Look at this! I just love that bow!" Koda said in a high-pitched voice. "Isn't she the sweetest? Oh my goodness, she's gonna look so cute in this!"

"And they say something along those lines every time."

I burst out laughing and asked Koda, "Can I tell your grandma and your aunts how much you sound like them when you . . ."

"No!" Koda barked, completely horrified at the thought. "Snitches get stitches!"

"Good point," I conceded. "Alright, your secret's safe with me. I don't talk to them very much anyway, so I think I can manage to keep it to myself."

"About that . . ." When I turned my gaze to Ruf, he winced and took a step back. "Maybe we should discuss this later."

"Yeah, when I'm not listening because I heard Aunt Rainy and Aunt Rylee talking about you one time, and it was *not* pretty."

"Koda!"

"But you like me anyway?" I asked.

"You didn't break my heart and make me run away from home," Koda said with a shrug. "You're not gonna do that, right?"

"Nope. I won't break your heart, but I will feed you. How does that sound?" I asked.

"I like you already!"

JOVI

"Thanks for cooking dinner," Ruf said as I walked into the kitchen. He shut the dishwasher and then pushed a few buttons before he looked up at me and smiled. "Good job on sneaking those veggies in there."

"I learned that trick by watching Mom try to get Scoot to eat," I admitted. "My brother is the 'eat three bites and stop bitching about it' kind of parent, but my mom avoids that battle and just hides vegetables in everything."

"It's actually not that hard to get him to eat, especially when it's pretty outside. All you have to say is, 'You can't go out and play until you eat that.' He'll do everything but lick the plate to get back outside."

"Sounds like you."

"He's very much like me. Okay, scratch that. He's *exactly* like me, which is why when he pulls some outrageous shit, my mom laughs until she can't breathe and my dad gets that evil smile. He's even flustered Gamma a few times and . . . well, I just didn't think that was possible after all she's been through."

When he worded it like that, an outsider might think he meant a traumatic life event - an illness, an unexpected death, or maybe even just a long stroke of bad luck. However, anyone who spent a significant amount of time with *any* of the Forresters, from the original four brothers down to each of their children and now grandchildren, understood that it took a certain kind of woman to wrangle all that craziness and come out on the other side with her sanity intact.

She had *definitely* been through some shit in her life, but if you broke it down to where it all began, a person might be inclined to believe that she was the one that started it since she did raise the original four. But anyone with two brain cells to rub together wouldn't dare say that out loud - or the approximately three million people who loved her might get a slight bit testy.

I'd seen a few things over the years and heard about many more that happened to people who crossed a Forrester, especially their queen, and I didn't want to be part of that crowd. I enjoyed being able to chew my food, wipe my own ass, and breathe without mechanical intervention too much to utter a word against Martha Forrester, or any of her spawn, for that matter. That was why I hadn't ever gone toe-to-toe with Ruf's sisters.

I might not be the brightest bulb on the string, but I did have a modicum of self-preservation. Even so, it took every ounce of willpower in my body not to snap back when Rain, or especially Rylee, got her claws out and started swiping.

Which reminded me that I needed to speak to Ruf about his sisters before I got too settled in at his house.

"Do your sisters know that I'm staying here?"

"No."

"Do me a favor, okay? Give them a call tonight and tell them that it wasn't my idea, I promise to behave myself and leave everybody's hearts just the way I found them when I arrived, and I'll get out of your orbit just as soon as I'm able."

"Shit. They did a number on you, didn't they?"

"Rain is partially to blame for me getting fired from my job after you left town."

"How?"

"She came into the ice cream shop and said something shitty to me. I snapped back. My boss heard it, realized who I was going toe-to-toe with, and couldn't boot my ass out of the employee exit fast enough."

"Fuck, Bonbon. I'm sorry."

"I almost didn't apply for the job I have now because I knew that all of the staff was either part of your family or might as well be. When I had my interview with Jewel, I told her that Rain and Rylee hate me and might cause problems."

"What did she say?"

I smiled at the memory and quoted, "The kittens aren't quite sure how to use their claws yet, but I'll give them a demonstration if I need to. You start on Monday."

Ruf burst out laughing, and I smiled because I knew he was right when he sputtered, "I can hear her saying that. Holy shit."

"Now every time one of your sisters comes to the office, Jewel *always* finds a way to get close to me and hiss like a cat. Usually, no one else hears her, but the last time Rylee came in, True asked Jewel if she had a sore throat because it sounded like she was about to cough up a hairball."

Ruf was gasping for air now, and I couldn't help but

laugh along with him even though it really hurt the spot beneath my breast. I realized that I hadn't ever taken the antibiotic or the next round of pain pills, so I walked over and opened the cabinet.

Ruf managed to compose himself as I shook the pills out into my hand and then moved aside so I could get a glass of water.

"Are you hurting again?"

"Not much more than usual, but it gave me a sharp pain when I laughed."

"How bad are your burns, Bonbon?"

"Bad enough that Jewel won't release me to go back to work, and she's getting consultations from plastic surgeons and a burn specialist."

"Oh, Jovi," Ruf whispered.

"I'm lucky that it barely splashed on my face. It's really just around my collarbone, down my side beneath my breast, my bicep, and inside of my elbow that's the problem. The rest is almost healed, but the burns went deeper in some places. I was wearing a tank top when it happened, and the boiling water that didn't slide off my shoulder onto the floor with the noodles went down my shirt and pooled next to my arm."

"What did Dickbrain do when you were on the floor?"

"I guess he didn't realize I was injured until after I got up and ran to the bathroom. As I went past, he was sipping his drink. It wasn't until a few minutes that he started trying to get me to open the door and talk to him. The first officers that arrived were dealing with him at the front door when Gray and Lawson came in to find me."

"And the fucking DA isn't going to prosecute him?"

"No, but I have a feeling that Petra is going to do much worse than the DA ever could have, or at least whatever she does is going to be longer lasting."

"She's such a darlin'."

I sputtered out a laugh and asked, "Since when? She used to terrify you."

"Oh, she still does. I'm fully convinced that a government agency is gonna swoop in any day now and take her away because they've finally realized that she's an alien who is here to take over the planet."

"I've wondered the same thing about Jewel a few times," I admitted. "And Terran . . . Well, let's just say that Terran is quirky. And grumpy. He's just . . ."

Ruf shrugged one shoulder, "He's Terran."

"He is giving me some guidance on finishing my degree. He's been very helpful."

"Rip mentioned that, but you're already a nurse."

"I'm going to be a nurse practitioner. They do the same things as doctors but get paid less."

"Why don't you just become a doctor?"

"I'd love to. Can I borrow a quarter of a million dollars?"

"Sure. I'll have to sneak through that trapdoor in the closet. I've got my mother lode of cash hidden down there."

"With the bodies?"

"You guessed it." There was an uncomfortable

silence for a few seconds, so I turned to sweep some crumbs off the counter and looked around for something to wipe them down with, but Ruf stopped me by putting his hand on my arm. "My sisters want to talk to you, Bonbon."

"I'm good, thanks."

"I had no idea that they'd always thought the reason I left that summer was because we broke up."

"Water under the bridge."

"The only reason I don't wish I could go back in time and not have those beers with the guys and make an impulsive decision to go on that trip is because if I hadn't gone, I wouldn't have the life I have now."

"You're right. I don't think I would have mine either, even as fucked up as it is right now."

"No, Bonbon. You were always meant to be a nurse. You had that set in your sights for years, and you got it done because you're driven and strong. You're so smart. So much smarter than I am, and I always. . ."

"You're smart, too, Ruf. You may not be able to treat a patient, but you can do a million other things that I can't. And I understand why you wouldn't want to change your life because it's wonderful. Koda is a happy little boy because he's got you for a dad. Star is going to be just as happy for the same reason. I've fulfilled half of my dream, but you've got the other." The tender look on his face and his rough hand on my arm, the thumb rubbing back and forth like he always did when we touched, was almost my undoing. I knew that I needed to escape before I embarrassed myself even more than what I'd just admitted. "I'm tired. I'll see you in the morning."

"Bonbon . . . hey, come back," Ruf said as I walked out of the kitchen.

I didn't turn around because I didn't want him to see the tears on my face. As I rushed up the stairs I tried to sweep them away, but they just kept coming, an endless stream of heartbreak because what I'd said was true - Ruf was living my dream. He had everything I'd ever wanted and exactly what we'd talked about having together so many times. The house, the family, and the future that was meant to be ours.

Unfortunately, I wasn't part of it.

RUF

I couldn't stand it anymore. I'd been standing in the hallway of my own home for fifteen minutes listening to the most heartbreaking sound I'd ever heard. At first, I was sure that I should just leave Jovi alone - she had never been one to want attention when she was upset. Instead, she'd rather go off by herself until she could get her emotions under control.

But, dammit, I couldn't just let her barricade herself in the bedroom and cry.

Even the strongest person needed someone to lean on - I'd witnessed that between my parents, grandparents, and the rest of the couples in my family for years. If something upset Mom, she was much better after my dad put his arms around her, even if it was for just a minute or two until that first wave of emotion passed. With my father, it was much the same - when he was on edge, whether it was from anger or heartbreak, holding my mom close helped him get centered again.

It was like there was an invisible string pulling them together, and that's what it felt like right now,

I turned the doorknob and then slowly pushed the door open until the light from the hall pierced the darkness of Jovi's bedroom. I could see her laying on the bed, curled on her side. It broke my heart when I realized she was holding a shirt or something in front of her face to muffle her sobs. Without even thinking about it, I walked in and crawled into bed behind her.

Her entire body tensed, but I didn't let that deter me. I fit myself against her naturally, like I'd done a million times before, and carefully put my hand over her hip, against her belly where I knew there weren't any burns I might hurt. I slid my other arm beneath her pillow and nuzzled my face into her hair as I waited for her to calm herself.

After a few seconds, she let go and relaxed against me. I could tell by her breathing that she was trying very hard to stop crying.

"I've got you, Bonbon," I whispered against her hair. "Let it all out."

When Jovi sobbed again, it was hard to catch my breath because there were tears clogging my throat, but instead of letting them flow, I kissed her again and settled in for the duration. I would hold her until she fell asleep in my arms, just like I used to and wanted to for the rest of our lives.

TEN

"I'm not up for your snarky bullshit today and not quite sure I'll be able to control my mouth if you start running yours."

Jovi

RUF

"I'm not ever eating lumpy oatmeal again," Koda said before he took another bite of the cake he was holding - his third piece so far. He saw me watching him in the rearview mirror and gave me a thumbs up as he tried to smile, but his mouth was so full he couldn't do anything but chew.

"Your breakfast cake was a hit. Now, if only I could get him to eat something for breakfast that's not just sugar and carbs."

Jovi gave me a hesitant smile, just like she'd done more than a few times since she woke up this morning. Last night, I'd stayed in bed with her long after she cried herself to sleep, only leaving when I heard Star crying downstairs.

Neither of us had mentioned our conversation last night or the fact that I joined her in bed, but things felt different between us this morning. I wasn't sure what she was thinking, but the idea that was rolling through my mind couldn't be contained.

"There's barely any sugar in that other than some honey. The sweetness mostly comes from the canned fruit, which isn't the best I know, but it's better than a cup of white sugar. And the vanilla flavor is from the protein powder I put in it along with a shit ton of eggs, so in reality it's not the *healthiest* thing he could be eating, but it's a lot better than Krispy Kreme."

"Holy shit," I muttered as I remembered the delicious creation she'd fed us this morning. "Usually I just feed him the stuff in the packets." Out of the corner of my eye, I saw Jovi scanning the area, even twisting around in her seat to scope out cars behind us. "Are you worried that we're being followed?"

"No. Sort of. Yes."

"You hit all the bases with that one. Why are you worried? Did something happen that I don't know about?"

"Petra had him served with papers at work."

"Already?"

"Apparently, things happen faster than they normally would when she's highly motivated."

"So, he knows you're suing him."

"Yeah, and he's not the kind of person who would take that lying down. Since there's really nothing he can do about it with it being the weekend, he'll be sitting at home stewing over the whole thing."

"Do you miss him?"

"I quit missing him months ago."

"Why did you stay?" I felt Jovi's eyes on me and glanced over at her once I came to a stop behind a car at a red light. "It's an honest question, babe."

"We talked about this."

154

"Tell me again."

"I don't like to quit. Anything. I can always find a way if I work hard enough. At one point, we were happy together. I wanted to find that again."

"Were you really happy, Bonbon?" I asked without thinking.

"I tried to be," she said so quietly that I almost didn't hear her. "I tried very hard to be."

"At least you put the wedding off."

"You knew about that?"

"I've been keeping track," I admitted.

"Of me?"

"Yeah."

"Why?"

"Because even when you weren't my Jovi, you were still my Bonbon."

"Why do you call her Bonbon?" Koda asked from the back seat.

The light turned green, and I started to accelerate as Jovi answered, "There's a band that my mom really likes, and she . . ."

"Bon Jovi?"

"Yeah. You know them?"

"Ooooh! We're halfway there - ooooh!"

"Holy shit, your kid is freaking awesome!" Jovi said

155

through her laughter as Koda kept singing. "How does he know that song?"

"My dad listens to that music all the time," Koda explained.

"You do?"

"It reminds me of you," I confessed. I could feel Jovi staring at me again and made it a point not to look her way. I hadn't been pining away for her for the last nine years by any means. I'd dated a few women and had a few serious relationships, but I'd never put my entire heart into any of them because it was no longer mine to give.

I had never seriously considered a future with any of the women I'd dated since Jovi. Each relationship inevitably ended because I couldn't imagine my future without Jovi in it, which was insane because she was committed to another man. Granted, it was a man I couldn't stand, and I didn't know anybody that really could, but he was her choice. I had fucked up, and my pennance was living without her. I wanted her to be happy regardless.

But in the last few weeks, it had begun to seem like a future with Jovi might actually be possible. However, I had to play my cards right. Jovi was dealing with a lot right now, and the last thing she needed was me confusing the issue by blurting out my feelings.

I realized now that we were way too young back then to make such decisions, but we'd talked about our future to great lengths and even planned for it. As soon as she graduated from nursing school, we'd get married, and three years after that, we'd start our family. By then, we'd be well into our twenties with steady incomes and able to afford a home together.

At the time, I just thought of that as something that

would happen down the road. At eighteen, the passage of time seemed to crawl and a decade was too far in the distance to take seriously, at least it was for me. Jovi, on the other hand, was a planner. She always had been.

Jovi was a very careful person but also very driven. She weighed her options, made her decision, and then stuck to it. Unfortunately, I was the opposite and liked to do things on a whim. Today was a perfect example - I was about to let my six-year-old choose the paint color for the nursery. If it were Jovi's house, she would have taken time to consider all the things she'd talked about last night while she and Koda were discussing the color scheme - what kind of art would be on the walls, what color the bedding would be now and then later when Star was a toddler and a young girl, and how different colors affected a person's mood.

She had talked Koda off the ledge about any neon or glow-in-the-dark shades, thank God, and veered him toward more muted colors like lavender or mint green since those apparently fit the aesthetic of nurseries they had looked at online. Koda understood, and that was all that mattered since he'd be the one who had to look at it until Star was old enough to notice.

While I watched them huddled together at the table in front of Jovi's laptop, I wondered if I might be able to convince her to stay around longer than just this little stint for her own protection. Koda had an almost instant rapport with her, and even though it was rare that he found someone he didn't instantly like, his nature wasn't exactly conducive to most adults getting to know him.

As a matter of fact, the only people who didn't stare at him like he was a lab specimen or future statistic half the time were related to me - either by blood or choice. Most outsiders, even people in the grocery store who heard him talking, thought it was their business to tell me I needed to get a handle on his craziness, and some even had the balls to say he needed medication.

He'd been pretty tame for the last twenty-four hours since Jovi had been here, but I knew that reprieve wouldn't last. The new would wear off, and he'd be his old self again soon, most likely while we were in the store today where there were so many buttons, lights, colors, and sounds to entice him.

As I turned into the parking lot, I glanced at Jovi and found her still watching me. I gave her a tight smile and was happy when she smiled back, but then her face suddenly changed, and she looked alarmed.

"Why are we going to Walmart? I thought we were going to get paint and groceries."

"We are. They have those things here along with all the baby stuff I need to pick up."

Jovi let out a frustrated growl and muttered, "We're in and out. Nothing extra."

"What?"

"When I said I wanted to go to the store, I meant the grocery store."

"And how are we going to get paint and shit for the nursery at the grocery store?"

"We'd have to go to the hardware store and then . . . I didn't think about all the nursery stuff but . . ." Jovi sighed. "I didn't think this through."

"What's the problem, Bonbon? We're just getting a couple of things."

"That's how it starts. You say, 'I won't be long. I'm just gonna get what I need.' Then, next thing you know, it's five hours later, you've spent four hundred dollars, are now the proud owner of a kitchen gadget you probably won't use more than once, picked up a ton of supplies for a craft you're never gonna master but want to try, a pack of ready-to-bake sugar cookies that taste like sawdust and have colored icing and sprinkles to match whichever holiday is coming up, six candles that all smell mostly the same, cat toys even though you don't own one, four throw pillows that don't even match the couch, and *another* sign that says 'Live, Laugh, Love.'"

"Uh . . . I don't have a sign that says . . ."

"I get ten feet inside and black out, Ruf. I think they're spraying something through the vents above the door - you walk in and next thing you know, the back seat is full of shit you don't need, you're broke, and your left eye is twitching." I burst out laughing at Jovi's stress, and she glared at me. "It's your dime, Forrester. Don't say I didn't warn you."

"Why couldn't we bring my Star? This store is fun!" Koda said excitedly. "I love this place!"

"Star's a little young to be around a bunch of strangers, and Emerald wanted to hang out with her for a little while."

"Emerald's house is fun, but sometimes she watches me like I'm a bug."

"I can't imagine why," I said with a grin.

"She thinks I'm interesting," Koda explained to Jovi. "She said I'm federal and it's easier than finding a kid like Mowgli."

"Feral, bud," I corrected.

"Yeah. That too."

Jovi started laughing and said, "I think you're uniquely adorable, Koda. Don't ever let anyone dim your light."

"You say that now," I mumbled as I pulled into a parking spot. "Koda, we're about to go into the store and . . ."

"Stay close enough for you to thump me, use my inside voice, don't cuss because that makes people think you're a bad dad, and keep my fingers off of buttons or the alarms might go off again."

"Again?" Jovi asked in shock.

I nodded and then added, "Make a list of stuff you need and pick it up as we go through."

"Toothpaste, rope, duck tape, a big hook for the ceiling, and lemonade."

"Have you ever seen those posts online asking what three things you could buy that would make the cashier think you're nuts?"

"His list is usually longer and sounds a lot scarier."

"Oh! I almost forgot!" Koda said as he popped up between the seats and smiled at me. "I need body armor and paint balls!"

"Like that."

Jovi burst out laughing before she turned and kissed Koda on the cheek. As she opened the door to get out, she said, "Koda, you're the coolest kid I've ever met."

"Did you see that?" Koda whispered as he put his hand over his cheek. "She kissed me!"

"She did," I said as Jovi shut the door.

"I think we should marry her, Dad."

"You think so? Not sure she's on board for that, bud."

"Not yet, but don't worry. I'll help you."

The thought of that outcome didn't scare me at all. If anything, it made me excited. I wasn't sure if his offer was a threat or a promise. With Koda involved, it could go either way, but one thing I knew for sure - it would be one hell of an adventure.

JOVI

"Which do you like more?" I asked as I held up a blanket in each hand.

After thirty minutes of bickering with Koda about the nursery theme, we'd narrowed it down to woodland creatures or florals. I'd finally talked him out of Lego furniture by telling him that it was likely the baby could choke if a piece of her crib accidentally popped off. That led us to the argument about using a mini trampoline as her mattress and installing a shower in the corner of the room so Ruf could "spray off the nasty baby grossness" that Koda seemed to take as a personal offense.

"I like whichever one you put in the basket so we can go."

"That's not helpful, Ruf. Pick one."

"Which one do you like?"

"I like both of them equally."

"Now who isn't being helpful?" Ruf asked. He looked down into the cart where Koda was laying and put his left hand out flat and fisted his right on top. "Best out of three, you're flowers."

He and Koda played Rock, Paper, Scissors, and then Koda cheered, "I win!"

Ruf took the floral blanket out of my hand, tossed it into the cart, and said, "Next!"

"That makes things much easier," I said before I turned back to the shelf and started pulling things down that would match. Just to be funny, I started tossing items over my shoulder and smiled when I heard Ruf grunting as he maneuvered around to catch each one and put it in the cart.

"She got you right in the face!" Koda crowed from his perch as I chose sheets and other necessary items that coordinated. "Two points for Jovi!"

"I thought I heard my sweetheart," a woman's voice said from the end of the aisle.

"Stache!" Koda squealed. He was up and out in the next second , sprinting down the aisle before I could turn and see who was there.

I bit back a sigh when I saw that Terra Forrester was with Ruf's sister Rylee. Before I could turn back to the shelf, I saw Rain appear around the corner behind them. I smiled their way and then grabbed a pack of cloth diapers Ruf could use as burp rags and tossed them into the cart before I began sorting the things Ruf had tossed into the basket.

"Hi, Jovi," Terra said pleasantly.

"Mrs. Forrester," I greeted with a nod.

"We're back to Mrs. Forrester?" she asked. "Call me Terra."

"Yes, ma'am."

"I'm glad you're helping him with the nursery," Terra said as she walked toward me. "I had resigned myself to Star being surrounded by motorcycles and dinosaurs, but I love what you've chosen."

"The guys chose the final pattern. I'm just getting things that coordinate," I said quietly. I hadn't spoken directly to Ruf's mom in years, which sucked because I absolutely adored her when we were dating. However, with the tension so high between me and his sisters, I had avoided all things Forrester as much as I could. "This will make it easier to narrow down a paint color too."

"He gave up on the neon green?" Terra whispered. When I nodded, she rolled her eyes and sighed, "Thank God."

"I had him convinced that lavender or mint would be better, but I was actually thinking this beige color for the walls with some sage green accents might be nice," I told her as I picked up my favorite blanket out of the selection and pointed out the colors I was talking about in the floral print. "What do you think?"

"I think you're much better at this than I am. Luckily, I had Martha and the girls to help me. We would have already done the same for Ruf, but things have been very hectic since he got Star."

"I can imagine."

"Hi, Jovi," Rain said as she walked over and stopped on the other side of the cart.

I gave her a tight smile and said, "Hello."

"Thanks for helping Ruf out," Rain said pleasantly. "God knows he could use it. I'm sure you've noticed his decorating style is a mixture of spare parts and motor oil."

"The dining room is . . . unique," I said hesitantly.

"He and Koda would probably be content to sleep on mattresses on the floor, but the girls and I found some furniture and didn't give him much choice but to put it in the house, if for no other reason than we need a place to sit when we come over," Terra explained.

"Originally his living room decor was camp chairs he borrowed from the clubhouse," Rain added.

"Did he get the picnic table there too?" I blurted. Rain and Terra laughed and nodded. "That's quite a different spin on the latest kitchen decor trends."

"Koda suggested that they put up half walls around the breakfast nook and turn that into a ball pit," Rain told me. "Thankfully, Ruf nixed that idea before we had to wade into the mix."

"We'll be back," Ruf called out as he walked away with Koda. "Pick whatever works. We've gotta go find a snack."

I was screaming at Ruf telepathically, begging him to stay and threatening his life if he left me alone with these women, but he didn't seem to notice. However, Terra could tell that I was uncomfortable, especially when Rylee walked up and stood next to Rain. She put her hands on the basket and gave me an uncomfortable smile before she said, "Hi, Jovi."

I cleared my throat and said, "Hello."

"This is not exactly the place to do this, but I've gotta say . . ."

I put my finger up to stop Rylee and interrupted, "I told your brother I'd get this done, and I will, but I didn't agree to let you run all over my ass while I do it. I'm not up for your snarky bullshit today and not quite sure I'll be able to control my mouth if you start running yours."

"I deserved that," Rylee said with a slow nod. "But what I was going to say is that I'm sorry for the way I've treated you since you and Ruf broke up." I stared at her with a shocked expression, and she laughed uncomfortably. "I know it's not an excuse, but I was an asshole teenager who didn't have all the information because . . . well, it really wasn't my business anyway. I held a grudge about something that wasn't even my place to get involved in. I've been a horrible bitch to you, and I apologize." It took a second for me to realize there wasn't a punchline coming. Rylee cleared her throat before she said, "I understand that it's gonna take a little time - or maybe you won't ever be able to forgive me - but I would like for you to know that I'm sorry. I'd really like to try and start with a fresh slate if you can."

"Uh . . . wow. I didn't expect that, but thank you?"

Rylee laughed and said, "So, even if we can't be friends, can we at least be . . . I don't know what I'm trying to say." She shrugged and added, "Maybe we can just stop being enemies?"

"I owe you an apology too," Rain said sincerely. "I've been a bitch. Maybe not as big of a bitch as Ry, but I can hold my own. I'm sorry I've been shitty, Jovi. Please forgive me."

"Sure. Yeah. Um . . . thank you for that, and I . . .

Wow. I don't even know what to say because . . . Well . . ."
I stammered. I took the olive branches that they extended
and asked, "Want to help me spend your brother's money?
I'm going to decorate Star's nursery before he hangs up a
neon beer sign as a nightlight and lets Koda make the
furniture out of Legos."

Apparently, that was the ticket because I spent the
next two hours shopping with the Forrester women, or at
least part of them.

ELEVEN

"If parenting doesn't terrify you, then you're doing it wrong."

Kale

RUF

"I thought you came to help us paint the nursery," I said as I sat down on the lounge chair next to the one where my father was stretched out.

"Watching the baby is helping," he muttered before he patted her on the back and then closed his eyes again. "What are you doing out here? Shouldn't you be working?"

"It's awfully loud in my house."

"That's what Koda said before he threatened to run away."

"I guess you were able to convince him to stay?"

"Sort of. We went over to see Bright Eyes, and I left him there."

"If I remember correctly, she volunteered to watch Star too."

"No sense in her stretching herself too thin. Koda and Griff together is more than enough for one person to take on at a time."

"She still tried to keep her, though, didn't she?"

"She did," my dad grumbled. He patted Star again before he said, "She acts like I don't know how to care for a baby when I distinctly remember taking care of her smartass."

I burst out laughing and said, "You're at the top of my list of sitters, Pop."

"Better be."

"I guess Mom and the girls made peace with Jovi."

"Sounds like it. They used to cackle like that when they were younger, and I heard your mom laughing right along with them." After a few seconds' pause, he asked, "Have you figured out how to make things stick this time, son?"

"I'm working on it."

"You're smarter now. More mature too. Your mom and I worried back then, but you've got your shit together now. Hopefully, Jovi will recognize that and give your dumbass another chance."

"She's pretty skittish right now, but I know that doesn't have anything to do with me."

"We gonna hunt that fucker down or let him keep breathing?"

"Let him keep breathing . . . for now anyway. Petra's gonna grab him by the balls and ruin his fucking life. She'll start out by taking his money, then she'll take his reputation."

"She's always been such a sweet girl."

I burst out laughing because only my father would ever describe Petra Parker as sweet. Dad's friend Grunt,

Petra's father, had once described her as a "rabid, ball busting, vindictive harpy," but we all knew he meant that in the most loving way. Obviously, my dad and his friends appreciated different qualities than most men, and I understood that because I mostly felt the same.

"What do you think about Jovi?" I blurted.

"Smart. Funny. Driven. Loyal. She was always a sweet girl, and back then, I realized she was probably a little too good for you. You were a shit, Ruf, but she put up with you for quite a while. I always respected the fact that she let you be you and didn't try to change you while not giving up her own dreams."

"She's accomplished almost everything she planned."

"What's she lacking?"

"If I remember correctly, at this point in her life - the life she had planned for us together - she wanted to have a house where she could make a home and have a baby."

"Well, lookie here. You've got both of those things."

"Koda's a lot for a woman to take in, Dad. You've gotta admit that."

"What have I always told you, son?"

"Never admit to anything even if the proof is on the table right in front of you."

"I will say that in this instance, you're right. Koda is a handful, but if she opens her heart even a little, he'll burrow in and never leave."

"He does have that effect on people. That's why I

haven't sold him to a traveling circus yet."

"Shit. Sell him to the government. He could be their secret weapon against our enemies. They could drop him behind enemy lines and then sweep in a week later after he's razed half the countryside. He'll come in all smiling and cute and decimate shit before anyone even thinks to raise an eyebrow."

"She's already commented about how much he reminds her of me several times."

"Yep. Your gamma used to say that she hoped me and your uncles would have kids who were just like us, and we did. Then we put that curse on y'all, and here we are." Dad laughed, and when Star started to squirm, he quieted and gave her a few more pats before he adjusted the light blanket up over her shoulders. "The only reason your mama didn't return you to Walmart was because you reminded her of me. Odd that was your saving grace as a child, but you're still here, so it worked. Might help you win back your woman too."

"Pretty full of yourself, aren't you, old man?"

"This old man can still whip your ass," my dad said with a sly grin.

I didn't have any doubt about that. Even though he was older now, he was still in the prime of his life. Mom had retired recently, following Dad a year or more ago. They were enjoying themselves now that they didn't have any kids at home or responsibilities to tend to every day.

It wasn't unusual to wake up to a text from my mom letting us know that she and Dad had taken an impromptu trip on the bike and weren't quite sure when they'd get home. We'd sort out taking care of the animals on the text and then keep in touch that way - always making sure to send proof

170

of life pictures and videos so my dad wouldn't worry about the birds and the rest of their menagerie. They always came back eventually.

Our mom had spent too many years in prison for a crime she didn't deserve to be punished for, and after raising all of us heathens, she deserved time away exploring all the things she'd missed out on before. Dad had been in prison, too, but his sentence wasn't nearly as long. Since he met my mom, he'd made it his mission to do whatever it took to make her smile - not that gassing up the motorcycle and hitting the road would ever be considered a chore.

I had always been close to my parents. Koda being born was probably the only thing that saved me. When Cadence left him with me for an overnight stay and then disappeared from the face of the earth, I had no idea what to do. I didn't have a sitter arranged, I didn't have the supplies I needed to keep him long-term, and I was living in an apartment with one of my cousins and his girlfriend, which was *not* the best environment for a newborn. When Cadence reappeared a few months later and tried to take Koda with her, she found herself in a direct confrontation with my mother and barely escaped with her heart still beating - especially since my mom had explained in vivid detail *exactly* how she was going to remove it from her chest if she started any more shit and tried to take Koda from his home.

The roller coaster of sharing a child with Cadence smoothed out, and she visited him regularly but never took him with her. I didn't stand in the way of her cultivating a relationship with our son, and after a while, I even let her keep him overnight here and there. I knew that she had another child, but since Cadence never brought her around, I assumed the little girl's father was raising her.

And that was how it went until the weekend I agreed

to let Cadence keep Koda for more than just one night - which ended with my son and his sister in the hospital. During Koda's hospital stay and his recovery afterward, I made friends with Ripley Booker, a man I had known when I was very young before he went to prison for killing a man. I had heard about him while I dated Jovi, but she'd never been close to him because of their age difference and the fact that he was incarcerated, so I never interacted with him while we were together. As a matter of fact, I had no idea that Ripley was the father of Cadence's other child until we saw each other at the hospital that day. Ripley and I leaned on each other during that time and made a pact that we'd let Koda and Celia grow up together and encourage their relationship.

Like always, my family pulled Ripley and Celia into the fold, and now they were family to all of us - not just Koda. We made sure that the kids spent as much time together as possible, and all of us learned sign language right along with Ripley so we could communicate with Scoot as she got older.

Of course, being around Ripley meant that I encountered Jovi now and then, which was always difficult. I loved to see her, but it hurt to see her with someone else.

But now, that wasn't the case. That someone else had done the unthinkable and hurt my Bonbon, which he would pay for dearly in more ways than one, but that meant she was single again. I had the chance to get back what I'd lost years ago.

"How can I show her that I'm the kind of man she needs, Pop?"

"She doesn't *need* you son. She's a strong woman who can take care of herself. What she *needs* is someone who will stand beside her while she conquers the world, help hold her up when she feels like she can't take anymore, and

172

realizes that he's the one who was given a gift every time she smiles at him." My dad chuckled before he said, "We're the ones who *need* them, Ruf, whether we're willing to admit it or not. Without your mom, I'd be a grunting caveman who hated the world and just existed day to day. She's everything that's good and makes the world around her better than it was before, just like she did for me."

"I'm not sure if she'll give me another chance."

"Well, it's up to you to show her why she should. You've got more to consider than just yourself now, son. She'll realize that, too, and weigh her decision based on what she's willing to take on."

"Parenting is terrifying, Pop."

"Don't I fucking know. I've got you caring for the wildest Forrester in history and taking on a baby girl who melts my heart every time I look at her, your sister falling in love with a goddamn rockstar, Ransome and Rocky who think I'm too fucking stupid to know that both of them are about three inches from crazy, and Rylee who is so much like me that I just want to shake her until her teeth rattle. Yeah, it's hard as hell and fucking terrifying when they're tiny. Don't let anyone lie to you and tell you it gets easier or any less scary. The kids get bigger as do the problems they face. You know in your heart you need to let them go to deal with all of that shit on their own, which is a whole lot harder to do than you'd think. I say if parenting doesn't terrify you, then you're doing it wrong."

"Wow. Thanks for the pep talk. I feel so much better about things now," I said sarcastically.

"Glad I could be of help. Now, go in there and wow that girl with your charming wit and sparkling personality. I've got a baby to nap with and your yapping is interrupting my good mood."

"How has Mom not killed you yet?"

"Where the fuck do you think you got that charming wit and personality from, my boy?" Dad asked as he settled back in for the duration. "Go do good work, son. Let me know if you need another pep talk."

JOVI

"Why are we doing this?" I glanced over at Koda and smiled when I saw him studying the dresser in front of us. I had to fight back a laugh when he rolled his eyes and shook his head. "It looked good, and then you made it ugly. You painted it, and now you want to make it ugly again."

"It's a technique called distressing, Koda."

"I've heard that word before," Koda said as he glanced over at the engine parts I'd had to move aside to lay out the tarp where I was going to set the dresser in his "workshop."

"Probably when someone was describing you," Ruf said from the recliner.

I looked over my shoulder and saw that he had Star laying on his chest and smiled as she lifted her head and tried to look around. In the week that I'd been staying with Ruf and his little family, Star had changed so much that it amazed me. Every time I held her, which was as often as possible because that sweet baby had become an addiction, she did something new. She was sleeping for longer stretches but also staying awake more, too, and seemed to be aware of her surroundings and who was holding her.

Of course, Ruf was her favorite with his father Kale coming in a very close second, but she perked up when she heard my voice too. Every time that happened, my heart did a funny little flutter that took my breath away.

I'd been having that problem often in the last week - the breathless feeling that stopped me in my tracks, and it wasn't just because of Star. No, Koda had gotten in on the deal, too, and would surprise me with what could only be described as a love attack. The boy would randomly throw his arms around me and squeeze me tightly. I'd seen him do the same thing to Ruf, and it just melted my heart when Ruf would stop what he was doing and pick his son up for a big hug as he told him how much he loved him.

And then there was how Ruf had been acting over the last week. The man must really enjoy keeping me off-kilter because he seemed to have made that his mission in life. You'd think that the house was tiny just because of how close he seemed to get when we were walking past each other in the hallway or working together in the kitchen. It seemed like he took great pleasure in putting his body up against mine for the simplest things.

He hadn't come back into my bedroom since that night a week ago when he held me while I cried, but just this morning, I had been walking down the hall with my arms full of laundry, and rather than wait for me to pass, he put his hands on my hips and slid behind me - his body touching mine for what seemed way too long. Last night while I was making dinner, he stepped up behind me and then rested his chin on my shoulder to look at what I was cooking on the stove rather than standing beside me to look into the pot.

But what *really* kept my heart racing was the fact that Ruf seemed to have forgotten he owned any shirts. For the last few days, he'd worn nothing but basketball shorts that hung low on his hips, giving me a delectable view of all that tattooed skin with the dips and ripples in all the right places.

I had taken note of all of the tattoos he'd gotten since we were together years ago. We broke up soon after we were eighteen, so when I knew him, he only had one - the bright red heart on his bicep pronouncing his love for his mom. Since then, he'd covered almost his entire chest, most of his back, and sleeved both arms down to the wrist with ink. The work was excellent and flowed together seamlessly even though the images would seem random if seen separately.

When he showed up to get me after my appointment with Jewel yesterday afternoon, he had a new tattoo - this one on the webbing between his thumb and finger - a perfect nautical star that was the same vivid blue as his daughter's eyes with brown accents that perfectly matched her hair.

The explanation for that tattoo was easy to figure out, but some of the others I'd noticed gave me pause. For instance, the one on the inside of his left wrist that was a lip print in a dark wine color that complimented his skin tone. For some reason, the sight of that one made me insanely jealous. I would like to think it was a random drawing, but I knew Ruf well enough to know that he'd never mark his body with an image that didn't have some special meaning. Knowing that, I had to wonder whose lips adorned his body forever now.

I had no reason to be jealous, but that didn't lessen the feeling. Ruf and I had split up eight years ago, and in that time, he could have been with countless women. I hadn't been celibate, although I could count the number of sexual partners I'd had in that time on one hand and still have a finger left over.

But one glance at Ruf and I knew he'd have no problem finding a woman to warm his bed. I was surprised he didn't have women lined up out front vying for his attention when you added the fact that he was charming and funny to his stunning good looks.

"I just don't get you, Jovi," Koda said as he shook his head with a concerned expression. "It's pretty like this, and you're gonna jack it all up."

"Trust the process, bud."

I smiled at Ruf and said, "Thanks for your support."

"Hey, you do it however you want. The room looks great already, but it'll be even better when you put that in there."

"Do you want to work on the drawers instead of helping me with this?" I asked.

"I want to go outside," Koda said grumpily.

I glanced over at the window and saw that it was still pouring rain, and on a whim suggested, "Let's do it."

"Do what?"

"Go play in the rain."

"Will you dance with me?"

"You want me to dance with you?" I asked.

"Yeah. Lettuce always drags Stache out into the rain and dances around the yard. She laughs, and then they kiss a lot."

"Aww. That sounds sweet."

"I don't really want to kiss you, but I think we should dance."

I put the sanding block that I'd been holding on top of the dresser and then held my hand out toward him. "I'd love to dance in the rain with you, Koda."

"Dad, will you dance in the rain with Jovi?"

Ruf looked concerned for a few seconds as he stared at Koda. It seemed like they were having an unspoken conversation, but the second Ruf nodded, Koda let out a loud whoop and started jumping up and down. He grabbed my hand and pulled me toward the door, and before I knew it, I was in the front yard with Koda smiling up at me as he held one of my hands in his and rested the other on my hip.

We were drenched within seconds, but I didn't mind. The joy on Koda's face made the moment one I would never forget. After a few minutes laughing as Koda tried to spin me around, Ruf slowly walked down the steps and across the grass toward us. Koda took a step back and put the hand he was holding into Ruf's before he jumped up and down again with an excited squeal. He darted onto the porch to take shelter from the rain but stood just under the eaves and watched as Ruf pulled me into his arms.

"I don't know why this was so important to him, but I think it is absolutely the sweetest thing I've ever experienced."

"When my mother was in prison, she missed the rain more than anything else. She told my dad about it in the letters they exchanged, and he promised to dance with her in the rain every chance he got. They named my sister Rain because it was an important part of their relationship."

"That's so sweet," I whispered as I choked back tears.

"One of Mom's fondest memories of her parents is watching her father dance around with her mother and then dip her back and give her a kiss. My dad does that with my mom every chance he gets, but most especially when they're dancing in the rain - no music needed."

The thought of Kale Forrester, so gruff and grumpy, making time for Terra just to give her some happy memories made me so emotional that I couldn't stop the tears. I just let them fall and get washed away by the rain that was falling on us.

"My mom's entire family was murdered when she was sixteen, so I never met them, but I'm named after her father and brother."

"I didn't know that," I whispered. "That's horrible."

"She moved here when she got out of prison and became part of my dad's family, but she still remembers how much her mom loved her dad and made sure that we grew up watching our parents love each other the same way." Ruf spun me around, and then I had to grab his bare shoulders when he dipped me back and held me there, his face above mine shielding me from the rain. "Now every time it rains, I'll remember this moment."

"So will I," I admitted, knowing in my heart that I'd never forget it. Especially when Ruf leaned down and touched his lips to mine to give me the sweetest kiss I'd ever experienced. When he pulled away, it took me a second, but I finally asked, "What was that, Ruf?"

"That was inevitable, Bonbon, and something I've been dying to do for years."

Ruf lifted me up and then spun me around before he pulled me to his chest again and then let me go. He left me standing in the rain as he walked back onto the porch where Koda was practically vibrating with excitement. The adorable boy bounded down the stairs and threw his arms around my waist for a hug. I felt like I was missing something important, but I was too flustered to analyze what that might be after that kiss.

"I love you, Jovi!"

I looked down at Koda as his hand went to my hip and he held his other up for me to take so we could start dancing again. I meant it when I said, "I love you, too, Koda."

TWELVE

"The early morning sky is always beautiful, but it's even more special today because the sun just rose on the first day of my dream come true."

Jovi

JOVI

"Jovi!" I heard a whispered voice say frantically. "Jovi! Something's wrong."

"What is it, Koda? Are you okay?"

"Star Baby won't hush, and Dad said he doesn't know what's wrong with her."

I could hear the baby crying now and was sure the only reason I'd slept through the noise was because my door was shut and I had the fan on. Since Koda had left my door open to come inside and wake me up, Star's wails echoed through the room. It was obvious she was in distress, and from the look on the little boy's face, so was he.

"I think she's broken. She hasn't ever made that much noise. Can you fix her?" he asked worriedly.

"Let me see what I can do," I said as I rolled over to get out of bed. Koda took my hand and tried to help me up, but he was really just in my way, so I urged, "Why don't you sleep in my bed? I'll shut the door so she won't keep you awake anymore."

"'Kay. Come get me if you need help."

"I'll do that," I assured him as I walked through the door. When I turned to close it behind me, I saw him snuggling down under the covers and smiled when he waved at me. The baby was not just crying at this point, she was beside herself. She sounded so distressed that I couldn't take time to appreciate the muscular tattooed forearm holding her legs close to the hard planes of Ruf's chest or the strong hand that gently patted her back. Instead, I asked, "Do you want me to take her for a minute and see what I can do?"

"Will you stay here with Koda?"

"Where are you going?"

"I think I should take her to the emergency room. No. I should call Amethyst. She'll come over. Or she'll meet me there."

"Let me have the baby, Ruf," I said gently as I reached for Star. "Go out on the porch, take a few deep breaths. Calm yourself down, and let me have a minute with her."

"What can you do that I haven't tried for the last hour?" Ruf asked grumpily.

"Probably nothing, but taking a moment for a breath of fresh air might give you time to think of new ideas."

Rug sighed as he walked toward the front door. "Good plan. I'll be back."

I snuggled the screaming baby close to my chest as I walked down the hall toward Ruf's bedroom. I hadn't been inside his room since the first day when I woke up here, and just like it had that day, the smell of Ruf enveloped me as I stepped through the door.

I took a deep breath and flipped on the light before I sat down on the bed and laid Star down beside me. I'd spent plenty of time in the nursery ward at the hospital and then helped with hundreds of babies during my work with Amethyst, so I fell back on those skills as I inspected Star to make sure there weren't any exterior issues making her cranky before I focused on something internal.

She most likely just had gas or an upset tummy, but it wouldn't hurt to rule out everything else first. I was surprised when I took her pajamas off and found a long-sleeved onesie underneath along with a pair of socks. It only took me a minute to get her stripped down to her diaper. She was still screaming as I rolled her over to check her back for rashes or any spots that might be bothering her. I took a second to change her diaper and made sure she didn't have a diaper rash. Once her new diaper was on, I moved her legs the way I'd seen Amethyst do to babies her size and then smiled when Star farted so loud that it startled both of us. Her cries got softer, although she was still worked up, so I kept moving her legs to try and relieve more pressure. When that didn't work, I picked her up and laid her over my arm with her legs dangling down on either side of my hand and bounced her gently as I patted her back.

As I held her, I spoke softly, just gibberish really as I tried to soothe her. After just a few minutes, she tooted again and then her cries tapered off. Once she was quiet, I laid her back on the mattress and smiled down at her. She was still wide awake, but at least she wasn't screaming, so while I put her zippered pajamas back on, I talked to her as if I expected her to answer me.

I picked Star up and snuggled her against my chest and then closed my eyes as I slowly swayed and patted her back. It felt so right having her in my arms that it was difficult not to think of things I shouldn't - namely the dreams I used to have about holding a baby of my own.

When I first started staying with Ruf, I tried very hard to keep my distance from Star because baby fever was real, and it had been burning me up for almost a year now. I let myself start considering the possibility of having children when things were going okay with Rodney, but I knew they could be better. He was still going to meetings and even seeing a counselor about his alcoholism, and I was very proud of the progress he was making, but I knew it would be a long road, and he would have to keep at it to maintain his sobriety.

Knowing that, I had been hesitant to bring a child into the world and didn't follow my original plan to get pregnant soon after I was twenty-six so I could have my first child by the time I was twenty-eight. Somehow, I knew that pushing our wedding date and then completely ignoring the fact that there was even supposed to be one meant that Rodney and I were over. I lost all hope of having children when that happened. For as long as I could remember, finishing college, establishing a career, getting married, and then having children had been my plan.

Well, at first it had been "our" plan . . . with "our" being Ruf and I.

God willing, we would have four children - each approximately two years apart, the last one born when I was about thirty-four so they would all be grown and living their own lives by the time we retired. Then we would be able to turn our focus to being grandparents and enjoying a life of leisure after working so hard our entire lives.

Now Ruf was halfway there without me, and the sweet baby in my arms was part of his equation.

It was so hard to sit in his room, surrounded by his scent and all of his things while holding the little girl who was now part of him, without thinking about how right it all felt. I had dreamed of being here, just not in this scenario, and the longer I held this baby, the more those dreams came rushing back.

"I like seeing you there," Ruf said from the doorway. I swallowed hard and tried to tamp down those memories before I looked at him. I felt like he read my mind when he said, "When Koda was a baby, I would imagine what you would look like holding him, and now I am standing here watching you with Star. It's like all those dreams we had when we were younger are coming true."

"You remember?"

"How could I ever forget, Bonbon? We had our lives mapped out."

"No, not we . . . I did. I had everything planned out, but you weren't ready for all of that. I understand that now."

"But you didn't then."

"Not really."

"I'm glad you broke up with me." When I just stared at him in shock, he said, "I would have let you down eventually, Jovi. Lucky for us, it happened before we did anything permanent. You and I were so different, and that would have become insurmountable at the time. But the differences are less harsh now. There's a sort of middle ground. We're both where we're supposed to be as far as our careers go, even though I didn't follow the path that we set out. College wasn't for me. I would have been miserable."

I nodded before I said, "I realize now that the only reason you were even going to go was to get me to shut up."

"No. I was going to go to school because that's what you do when you graduate, right? Go to college, find a career, follow that path until you get a little older and find the one to spend the rest of your life with, have a couple of kids and take them to Disneyland . . . all that shit. But I was never as focused on that first part as you were. I just wanted to hang around until we got to the good part."

I burst out laughing and said, "College wasn't just hanging around. It was a lot of hard work."

"I can imagine that it was. I saw how hard my sister worked to get her degree, and a lot of my cousins did the same. Not me. I wasn't cut out for high school, let alone college, but I always knew I was cut out to be your husband and the father of your children."

I smiled and said, "We did have some big dreams back then, didn't we?"

"They've changed, but they never really went away - at least for me. I was young and immature when we were together. I'm not exactly an old fart now, but I've matured over the years. Raising Koda helped me do that pretty quickly, whereas if I'd gone to college and done the usual thing, it probably would have taken a lot more time."

"You've got your family now," I said as I stood and walked over to the bassinet. Now that Star had relieved some of her pressure, she'd relaxed and fallen asleep on my chest, so I gently laid her down and patted her stomach when she started to squirm. Once she was content and sleeping, I walked around the bed toward where Ruf was still standing in the doorway. "You might not want to dress her in layers. She seemed a little too warm, and that might have been part of why she was so cranky. I think the main problem was just gas, though. Once she deflated a little bit, she felt better."

"Koda has been a little oven since he was born. As a

186

matter of fact, he was gassy too. Still is."

I smiled before I motioned toward the living room and said, "Well, she's content now. Can I scoot past you?"

Ruf didn't move out of the way, but he turned his body enough so that I could barely squeeze through the gap between him and the doorframe. When I was right in front of him, he put his hand on my arm and said, "Thanks, Bonbon."

I sighed but didn't say anything. He let me go so I could walk away. I glanced out the front window and saw that the sky was showing the earliest rays of dawn, so I walked into the kitchen instead of going back upstairs. I could hear Ruf behind me, so I turned my head and found him following me across the living room.

"Aren't you going back to sleep?"

"Nah. Star has finally started sleeping in longer spurts, so I got four uninterrupted hours, and now my body doesn't know how to react."

"You're still not going to do that 'sleep when the baby sleeps' thing?"

"No," Ruf chuckled. "Want some coffee?"

"Do you still make sludge?"

"I think I've gotten a little better," Ruf told me with a smile. "I'll make a pot and let you decide."

I walked over to the table and sat down. I rested my chin in my hand as I stared out at the morning sky. It was streaked with an array of pinks that even someone like me who wasn't the least bit artistic could admire. "The sky is beautiful this morning."

"Usually is. It's nice being on the edge of town where we can admire the sunrise. At night, I can go out back onto Ripley's property and see all the stars."

"I'll have to do that."

"You two still aren't very close."

He didn't pose that as a question because he knew my brother better than I did at this point. Ruf and Ripley had been thrown together after Child Services intervened when Cadence neglected the children so horribly and had become good friends since. I didn't know Ripley well and usually only interacted with him at family events, so I was surprised when Ruf said, "He worries about you, Bonbon."

"He does?"

"Yeah. Obviously, he's not gonna come right out and say it, but I can tell." When I hummed in response, he explained, "Whenever your name comes up, he's always interested to hear what's going on. Let me just say that he's been a member of the Rodney Haters Club since the beginning."

"He's never really been rude to him, but I could tell. Rodney knew instantly that Rip wasn't ever going to be his biggest fan. I think that's why he always talked down about him."

"No. He did that because he's a pompous asshole. We're all beneath him because we're uneducated."

"How do you know what Rodney's like?"

"He was the surgeon who took out Mom's gallbladder a year or so ago. Total prick. She didn't meet him until her follow-up, but she didn't like him any more than we did."

"When did you deal with him?"

"He came out into the waiting room to talk to us and said, 'She's fine. She's in recovery. You can see her when she gets out.' When my dad asked him for more information, he said, 'She doesn't have a gallbladder anymore. Is that difficult for you to understand?'" I gasped in shock, and Ruf gave me a tight grin. "Yeah. That went over well."

"Surgeons are notorious for being harsh and abrupt, but I'm surprised he's still breathing. Your dad is a sweetheart, but I wouldn't push him."

"He still thinks you're the best thing that has ever happened to me."

"Well, obviously," I joked.

"He asked me if I was going to use this togetherness we've got going on to get my shit together."

"What does that mean?"

"Well, he and I think alike most of the time, so it's easy for me to explain. You're here. You're single. I'm still head over heels for you, and I want to see if I can remind you how much you used to love me and rekindle that wildfire that burned between us once." I was stunned silent, but Ruf didn't seem to notice. He pulled two mugs out of the cabinet and filled them from the carafe before bringing them over to the table. He walked over to the pantry and dug around for a minute before he pulled out a bag of brown sugar and then shook it with a grimace. He got the milk out of the refrigerator and then opened the drawer for a spoon before he brought those over too. "We're out of that creamer you like, so you'll have to go old school and take it like you did when we were younger. I'm not sure if this will work, but I guess you can try."

I picked up the lump of brown sugar and asked, "How long has this been in your pantry? It's a brick."

Ruf took it out of my hand and smacked it on the table a few times before he passed it back and sat in the chair across from me. "Now it's rocks."

I busied myself opening the package and then dropped a hunk into my coffee before I added a liberal splash of milk. I could feel his gaze on me as I stirred it but didn't look his way. Instead, I picked up my mug and turned back toward the window as I blew over the top to cool it.

"Are you not even going to comment on what I said?"

"I'm stunned that you remember how I used to like my coffee."

"I remember everything, Jovi, but that's not what I'm talking about."

"What's there to say?"

"You could tell me if I'm wasting my time or if there might be an ember or two I can tend."

"It took me almost two years to get over you, Ruf. Even then . . ."

When my voice trailed off, he asked, "And everything you felt just went away?"

"We were young and . . ."

"That's not an answer, Bonbon."

"Why do you keep calling me that?" I asked in exasperation.

"Because in my mind, that's who you'll always be. To everyone else, you're Jovi. A nurse. James and Charlene's daughter. Ripley and Trinity's sister. But you're my Bonbon."

"I don't know what to say, Ruf."

"Do you want me to back off?"

"I'm living in your house. I won't be here forever but . . ."

"You could be."

"Ruf. Seriously. Is that what that kiss was about? We broke up ages ago, and you expect me to believe that you've been carrying a torch for me this whole time?"

"Obviously, I haven't been celibate the entire time we've been apart. I'll be the first to admit that I've tried everything I could to get over you, but my feelings haven't faded."

"We were different then, Ruf. We were kids."

"We loved each other. You can at least admit that, can't you?"

"I loved you so much," I admitted in a whisper. "It tore me up to let you go."

"It was the best thing for both of us at the time. But like you said - we're different now. I'm not that irresponsible little shit who's looking for the next fun adventure, and you're where you want to be in life and thriving with your career. I've always supported what you want to do, and I always will - that includes whatever you want to happen with us."

"I just broke up with Rodney."

"From what you said before, you gave up on him a long time ago; you were just too stubborn to do anything about it."

"Harsh, but true," I admitted. In what might be the bravest, most idiotic thing I'd ever done, I met Ruf's eyes and said, "I never gave up on you."

"I still love you, Bonbon. Always have, and I always will," Ruf said with a shy smile. His smile got bigger when he added, "Obviously, I've got some attachments I didn't have the first go-round but . . ."

"It wouldn't be hard to fall in love with them." I cleared my throat and then admitted, "It's not like I haven't already, but Koda and Star pose a problem in a way you probably haven't considered."

"No. That's where you're wrong. Koda has been my life for six years, and now Star is taking her place right beside him. I was an impulsive kid when you knew me before, Bonbon. I don't have that luxury now. I'm a dad, and they have to be first in everything I do. I know you'll love them like they're your own, of that I have no doubt. I know that even if this didn't work out, you'd never hurt them intentionally. I've already thought long and hard about what bringing you into our lives will mean."

"You have?"

"It's not just our hearts on the line, Jovi. I want you in my life, and that means I want you in Koda's life. Star's so young right now that she won't know the difference if you walk away, but that will change soon. So, I have to know that if you still love me and will let me be part of your life that you know you'll be part of theirs. If you're in, you're all the way in, and that means if you leave, it won't just be my heart that's broken but theirs too."

"I've never dated anyone with children for that exact reason."

"Does that mean you're not willing to consider giving me another chance?"

"No, Ruf, that means I don't take that lightly. For the last few years, I've done everything I can to stay as far away from you as possible because it still hurts to see you. I know that's because I never stopped loving you. I'd love Koda and Star for no other reason than they're yours, and I'd never do anything to hurt them."

"I think you're saying that I have a chance here, but I need to hear the words, Bonbon."

"I'm terrified, Ruf."

"Why? You know I'd never hurt you, Jovi."

"You did, though. You never put me first but I know you're different now because you put Koda first in everything."

"Losing you taught me what was important."

"It's more than that. You're a good dad. I can see the love in your eyes even when Koda is making you crazy, and your worry about Star tonight cemented what I already knew about what kind of man you've become."

"Is that a man you want to know again?"

I took a deep breath and blew it out slowly as I picked up my coffee and stared out the window at the beautiful sunrise. Ruf seemed to understand that I needed a moment to collect my thoughts, so he sipped his coffee in silence.

193

After a few minutes, I turned back to him and said, "I've got a lot of healing to do - physical and otherwise. Are you willing to give me time to do that?"

"I've been waiting for you for years, Bonbon. A little longer won't kill me."

"You'll take things slow?"

"Your pace. Whatever you need, babe."

I took a sip of my coffee and then looked back to the window before I said, "From now on, every time I see those colors in the sky, I'll think of this moment."

"I'd like to say the same but . . ."

I laughed softly, "Believe me. It's beautiful."

"I'll take your word for it."

"The early morning sky is always beautiful, but it's even more special today because the sun just rose on the first day of my dream come true."

"It's our dream, Bonbon."

"Yeah," I agreed before I smiled at him. "Now we just have to figure out where to go from here."

"Well, you're already living with me, so that hurdle is out of the way." I burst out laughing, but Ruf stopped me when he said, "That doesn't mean I'm not gonna work, though."

"At what?"

"Making sure you never want to leave."

THIRTEEN

> "He's the best man I know. I learned everything from him, and I try to be at least half the father he is every day."
>
> Ruf

RUF

"That has to be the weirdest thing I've ever seen."

"You look in the mirror every morning, but seeing me with a baby strapped to my chest is weird to you?" I asked.

"It's like the scene from that movie with the lawyer."

Elizabeth rolled her eyes. "Michael, sometimes I wonder who you get to tie your shoes every morning."

"I wear boots," Michael said with a shrug before he walked toward the stockroom.

"And he's the assistant manager," Elizabeth said with a sigh.

"I offered that spot to you," I reminded her. "He wasn't my first choice. He didn't get it just because he's family, and he knows that."

"You know I spend way too much time with the dogs to give the position enough attention, Ruf. Besides, I don't have a problem with Michael being in charge when you're not here, I'm just saying that his elevator rarely goes up to the top floor, and when it does, it's empty."

I burst out laughing before I said, "He's a smart guy, just a little . . . Well, he's Michael."

Elizabeth laughed before she said, "He does have a point. It's like the scene from that movie where she says, 'You've got a baby . . . in a bar.'"

"My sister loves that movie." I looked down and leaned my head to the side so I could see Star's face. She was sleeping peacefully, snuggled into the carrier I'd borrowed from my friend Pearl when I went to get my tattoo last week. "She doesn't care where she is, and I don't feel right taking any more time off. It's been almost a month."

"You've been in and out, Ruf. It's not like you abandoned us. I know I've called you at least a dozen times for some simple stuff I should have been able to take care of on my own. Michael too."

"Well, she's getting more mobile now, so I can come back to work and take care of the simple stuff along with all the other bullshit that rolls in every day."

"So, you'll take the day shift, Michael will do evenings, and I'll take two nights a week?"

"Are you okay with that?"

"You do realize that you're my boss and you can just tell me that's how it's gonna be, right?"

"That would make me an asshole, and I strive very hard to keep that tiger on its chain."

"You remind me a lot of your uncle," Elizabeth said with a smile.

"Gotta be more specific," I teased.

"All of 'em rolled into one."

"That's almost terrifying."

"Speaking of terrifying," Elizabeth said as she looked over my shoulder. "Who poked the bear?"

I turned to the side and followed Elizabeth's gaze only to find my father stomping toward me with a frown on his face. My mom wasn't far behind him, and she was trying very hard not to smile.

"What are you doing?" my dad asked as he stepped way too close to me and peered down into the carrier at Star.

"I'm working. What are you doing?"

"It's nap time, Ruf."

I looked down at Star and then back up at my dad and said, "Obviously."

"You know how toddlers get when they miss their nap," Mom said as she walked around the bar and pulled a bottle of water out of the cooler. "He did everything but stomp his feet when we got to your house and you weren't there."

"I told you yesterday that I was coming back to work."

"Sweetheart, toddlers don't give a shit about your work schedule if it interrupts their chicken nuggies and nap."

"Stop calling me a toddler," my dad growled.

"Stop acting like a toddler," my mom retorted.

"You drove all the way over here to bitch at me because Star wasn't at my house for your nap?" I asked incredulously.

"I've been making time to nap with the babies in this family ever since we got Bright Eyes."

"You mean since Zeke and Lisa got Brighten."

My dad's eyes narrowed, and Mom burst out laughing. I glanced at Elizabeth and saw that she had her lips pulled in between her teeth, but her eyes were twinkling. She was probably going to lose it soon, which wouldn't help my predicament at all.

"There's a way to do things, and there's a way to fuck things up. You keep to a schedule, Ruf, and at ten o'clock, I'm scheduled to have Star time, just like I did with Koda."

Just to be a dick, I said, "But Uncle Dot called and said he was going to start . . ."

"Like hell he is," Dad barked as he reached down into the carrier and carefully pulled Star out. He nestled her against his chest, and when his beard tickled her face and made her squirm, he patted her back gently. "He can get his own, dammit. I'll be in the office."

As I watched him walk off, I said, "He does realize that . . ."

"He doesn't care," my mom interrupted.

"But I've gotta work, and when she starts staying up more during the day, I'm gonna have to take her to daycare."

"Well, they better buy a recliner," Mom said drolly.

Elizabeth burst out laughing and said, "I don't envy Merida at all. I'm going to run to the store for lemons and limes. Do we need anything else?"

"That's all as far as I can tell."

"I'll be back. Terra, it was good to see you," Elizabeth said with a wave aimed at my mom.

Mom said goodbye as I sat down on the stool next to her. "Dad's gonna have to get over this whole nap thing at some point."

"Not happening." I stared at my mom until she smiled and said, "Sweetheart, when my water broke with Rocky, your father was napping in the recliner with you and Rain. Wanna know what I did?"

"Woke his ass up and made him take you to the hospital?"

"No. I did not. I took a shower, braided my hair, called Summer to see if we could drop you and your sister off at her house on our way to the hospital, and then made the two of you lunch."

"All so you didn't interrupt his nap time?" I asked incredulously. "That's crazy."

The abrupt change of subject shocked me when Mom said, "Ages ago, when your father was in prison, he saw a shrink."

"I can't imagine why."

"The doctor said that he believed the reason your father is . . . well, the way he is might well be because his parents didn't spend enough quality time with him when he was an infant."

"Obviously, I never knew his birth mother, but I can't imagine that Papa ignored or neglected him."

"You can tell by the relationship that Papa Smokey has with his sons that he was a good father, but back when your dad and I were kids, things were different than they are today. Honestly, Koda's growing up the way we did - wild and free, and there's *nothing* wrong with that."

"I show him love just like Dad always showed us."

"I know you do."

"That's why Dad has always gone out of his way to be close to the babies in the family?"

"The doctor insisted that if he'd been shown more tenderness in infancy and early childhood that he'd be a totally different man. He snuggles them and gives them all the love in the hopes that they won't turn out to be like him."

"But I *want* to be like him," I argued. "He's the best man I know. I learned everything from him and try to be at least half the father he is every day."

"He doesn't see that he's a good man, Ruf. We are all able to see and appreciate it, but he just doesn't feel like he's good enough, so he strives to make sure that every baby around him gets one-on-one time to try and right the wrongs." Mom smiled and said, "That's not the only reason, though. He loves that babies are so innocent and have no agenda. When most people look at your father, they only see the scowl and tattoos. Babies don't give a shit about any of that. They want a full belly, a dry butt, and a warm place to snuggle up. He can give them all of those things."

"Well, shit," I mumbled. "How the hell am I going to work everyday and still make sure he gets enough time with Star? It was different when Koda was a baby because we lived with you guys but now . . ."

"It will taper off gradually. When Star gets a little bigger, he'll back off some, but he'll still check in often just like he does with Koda. And, of course, your siblings will have kids someday that will get the same attention."

200

"We'll have to figure something out."

"She can stay with us while you're working, at least until she gets a little older."

"I can't ask you to do that."

"You didn't ask."

"But you guys are retired. You're supposed to be enjoying yourself and doing all the things that retired people do."

"Baby, that is part of enjoying ourselves and doing what we want now that we're finally retired. Bring her by on your way to work, and we'll either drop her off or you can pick her up when you're done."

"I can do that."

"Now, let's talk about Jovi."

"I was wondering if that subject might come up."

Mom propped her chin in her hand. "She surprised me at the store the other day."

"In a good or bad way?"

"Definitely good. She's got some fire in her. I didn't see it before, but it's there."

"I'm glad she and the girls worked shit out. That could have been very uncomfortable."

"You're right. Has she realized that you're still in love with her yet?"

"She's coming around."

"Look at you learning patience."

"I'm gonna wear her down eventually."

Mom burst out laughing. "Like water dripping on a rock, huh?"

"She's got a lot on her mind right now. She's eager to get back to work, she wants this shit with Rodney over and done with, and then, of course, I'm right there in front of her telling her what I want, which is something she thought was finished years ago."

"Are you taking her to dinner at Gamma's tonight?"

"She doesn't know it yet, but yes."

Mom laughed. "I'm glad you're happy, sweetheart."

"I'm excited. Life has been a whirlwind since I got that call from Cadence but . . ."

"Speaking of whirlwinds, I never thought to ask why she's in jail."

"Welfare fraud and a myriad of drug charges. She's gonna be gone a long time."

"Good." Mom reached out and ran her hand over my hair like she'd been doing since I was a boy and said, "I'm proud of you for stepping up, son. You didn't have to take Star in, but I'd expect nothing less from a man who is so much like his father."

"You think so?"

"You've got all the best parts of him and a bunch of the not-so-good parts too. But it's all wrapped up into one helluva man who makes me proud every single day."

"I love you, Mom."

"Not nearly as much as I love you."

JOVI

"You're clear to come back to work."

"Yes!" I said loudly as I grinned over at True. "I've been going stir-crazy."

"There are some restrictions, but we can work around them."

"Okay. Whatever they are, I'll agree with them. Just get me out of the house."

"I'll still want to check your burns often for a while, and I want you to keep with the treatment we've been doing. Even the worst areas are healing nicely now. They're going to scar but . . ."

"I don't care."

"You say that now, Tori, but you might change your mind once they're healed. I think you should see a plastic surgeon . . . even if it's just for a consultation."

"Okay. I'll talk to whoever you think is best."

"Now for the rest of it. Your body is healing, but how is your head?"

"I'm focused. I think that's the best description. Vengeful might be better but . . ."

"Now you're speaking my language," Jewel purred. "Do tell. Is that sister of mine enjoying herself?"

"She is. Rodney is reeling at this point, and I'm worried that he might do something stupid."

"More stupid than yanking you around by the hair?" Jewel asked with a scowl.

"Well, no. But he was able to get his car out of impound and somehow convinced the accounts manager at the bank to call me and set up a meeting to get everything settled. When I asked if he was going to be there, she hemmed and hawed until I finally asked if she was told not to tell me. She seemed kind of relieved that I'd figured it out, so, of course, I told her I would be there."

"You're not going alone. Let me . . ."

"I'm not going at all. Petra is."

Jewel burst out laughing. "Oh shit!"

"She seemed very eager. I *almost* feel bad for Rodney at this point."

"Get over it," Jewel said firmly. "Well, that settles it then. You're back at work tomorrow."

I pointed to the backpack I'd brought in with me and said, "I brought my scrubs."

"Of course you did."

"What is wrong with me? I only worked half a day, and I'm exhausted."

True pulled a new box of sterile gloves out of the cabinet and took off toward one of the exam rooms as she said, "Some people don't understand how we can be so tired even though we aren't carrying heavy things around or doing manual labor."

"In 2022, there was a study published in *Current Biology* that showed mental fatigue is associated with the accumulation of glutamate in the prefrontal cortex," Terran said without looking up from the laptop on the standing desk in front of him. "That leads to cognitive fatigue which can present some of the same symptoms as physical fatigue."

"My brain is making my body tired?"

"In essence, yes."

"That's good to know."

"How are things with Rodney?" Terran asked, still staring at his computer.

"Quiet, really. Petra is going to a meeting at the bank for me, and he will be there."

"He should have plenty of time to attend meetings since his privileges have been suspended at the hospital."

"What?"

"Rumor has it - and by rumor, I mean my conversation with the head of neurology at Rojo General - that he showed up staggering drunk for a scheduled surgery and then started throwing things at the nurse who refused to bring in the patient from pre-op."

"Oh," I whispered in shock.

"I believe that your pressing charges and bringing his alcoholism to light is going to be the catalyst for Rodney's downfall."

"But I . . ."

"Let me rephrase that," Terran interrupted as he turned around to look at me. "Your bravery in standing up to Rodney is giving the world a glimpse into something that, up until now, they've been oblivious to or simply ignored. Rodney's undoing is no fault of yours."

"Thank you."

Terran ripped a prescription off the pad in front of him and said, "Do me a favor, and get this filled on your way to Gamma's this evening."

I took the paper from him and asked, "Your grandma's house? I'm not going to . . ."

"You'll be having dinner there with Ruf, I'm sure. Make sure you hand the prescription directly to Gamma instead of giving it to Papa. Otherwise, it will end up on the shelf in his garage, and he'll never remember to take it." Terran sighed before he said, "That man is as stubborn as a mule about medications, but if he doesn't start sleeping better, it will begin to affect the rest of his health. I wouldn't be surprised if Gamma brains him with one of her cast iron skillets just to get him unconscious."

I laughed because I could imagine Martha swinging a skillet at someone, although it probably wouldn't be Smokey because she seemed to like him more than she liked anybody else. "I wasn't aware I had been invited to dinner, but I'll make sure she gets this."

"Thank you. And I wouldn't mind if you brought me a plate of leftovers for lunch tomorrow." Terran looked me directly in the eye and said, "That wasn't just a hint. That was me begging."

I burst out laughing and said, "I'll make sure and tell Martha that you requested one."

"How are you adjusting to living with Koda and the
206

new baby?" Terran asked.

"It's fine. Koda's adorable, of course, and the baby is very sweet."

Terran studied my face for a few seconds before he said, "You're not attached at all?"

"Should I be?"

"What do you feel when you look at the baby? Star, isn't it?"

"Yes."

"What does she make you feel?"

"Um . . ." I thought about how much I yearned to pick her up when she cried and how hard it was to resist not touching her when she was nearby. Even when she was sleeping, I wanted to pick her up and hold her close, so much so that sometimes it was almost impossible to resist, and I had to go to my room to get away. Without thinking, I blurted, "It scares me how much I want to hold her."

"It shouldn't."

"I love babies - I always have - but she's not mine."

"Humans are social creatures and have taken care of one another's children as part of their community throughout history. That increased the likelihood of survival if something were to happen to the birth mother. We naturally feel a pull to love and protect infants and children."

"When I look at her, I feel warm inside. I'm afraid that if I start to love her and then something happens, it will rip me apart. I don't think I could survive that."

"You're healing from not just physical trauma, Jovi,

207

but emotional trauma too. Your life is in an uproar, and it seems that rather than take the natural comfort one feels when there is an infant nearby, you're fighting it. Why is that?"

"I've got a lot going on, and she's so . . . Even Koda is so innocent and sweet that it feels like I'm just sucking all the energy out of the room with my shit."

"I've worked closely enough with you to understand that you're naturally a very caring person, Jovi. That's part of what makes you such a good nurse. However, you're denying your true self when you're around Ruf's children. You don't feel that you're worthy because of the decisions you've made that got you to this day."

It was so strange to be talking to Dr. Parker about such personal issues, considering he was usually very aloof and detached. However, he seemed interested in what was going on, and I couldn't stop myself from blurting out, "Ruf said that he never stopped loving me and wants to rekindle what we had years ago. As much as I want that, it scares me . . . almost as much as falling in love with his children only to have to let them go."

"It might take you a little while to find your footing in this new life because you were cemented into your old one - by choice or just from fear of the unknown. I've known Ruf his entire life, and I've looked up to his parents since I first met them. Ruf is like his father in that he'd never let anyone or anything endanger the people he loves. If he says he loves you and always has, I can't imagine how difficult it must have been for him to watch you from afar, feeling that the life you were living should have included him as the main character rather than Rodney. Now that you are free from the albatross around your neck, Ruf can see his chance at the future he's been dreaming of. If that's something you've wondered about, too, it would only make sense that you take the chance. That includes his children and the rest of his family - which I consider myself a part of. It's up to you to decide if you're ready for this, but the fact that it's so hard for you to resist the pull of falling into that role is very telling."

"I don't understand what you mean."

"Fear of failure can be just as debilitating as failure itself. However, you're a strong woman with a huge heart. If you open up and let Ruf and his children in, they will help you find solid ground again after all the turmoil you went through with Rodney."

"So, you think I should just let go?"

"I think that's a great idea. The dopamine hit that you'll get when you finally open your heart and mind will do wonders not just your mental health, but your physical healing too. It may even open the door for the other possibilities."

"I thought I lost the chance to be with Ruf, and now that it's there, I'm afraid to take it."

"It might take you some time to find the woman you were before you settled, but those dreams you had when you were younger are still within reach. All you have to do is put your hand out and grab them. If you don't, it's as if you're letting Rodney hold you back all over again."

"I think you're right."

"I'm always right," Terran said without an ounce of humility. "If you listen to your heart rather than your fears, you'll see that."

"Thank you, Terran."

"You're welcome. To repay me for that sage advice, I'll need two servings of dessert."

"I'll see what I can do."

Terran smiled as he rubbed his stomach in anticipation and then turned back to his computer. I grabbed the supplies I needed to restock an exam room and got back to work, trying very hard not to be nervous about Ruf making plans for me to join his family for dinner tonight without getting any input from me first.

If he thought that blindsiding me was the way to get in my good graces, the man was going to be sorely surprised, and to drive that point home, I might just go ahead and borrow one of Martha's skillets. That would certainly help explain just how *not okay* I felt about the situation.

However, the fact that Ruf was trying so hard to include me in his family did mean a lot, so I wasn't really that upset. If anything, it gave me even more to think about.

"And that's how I'm going to end up in prison."

Tori

JOVI

"Jovi! You're home!"

I had to take a step back so I didn't fall when Koda slammed into me, but that didn't stop me from hugging him back just as tightly.

"Hello to you, too, handsome. How was your day?"

"It was *great!* Our teacher took us outside and let us play for hours. We even got to eat our food outside."

"Picnics are awesome," I agreed as he let me go and turned so he could walk beside me up the sidewalk. "Do you like your summer program?"

"I do. Mostly."

"What's not to like?"

Koda sighed before he said, "Some of the kids aren't very nice to me and Scoot sometimes. It's not their fault, though. They're not allowed to play with us. Their moms work in the school lunchroom and treat us like we're bad."

"Oh, really?" I asked, hoping for more information. I'd spent the last week with Koda as my almost constant companion, and in that time, I had come to love him so much that the thought of anyone being mean to him filled me with a rage that I'd never felt before.

Of course I loved Scoot - she was my niece and an absolute joy to be around, but she was the only child I'd ever been close to before now. Unfortunately, I hadn't been able to spend nearly as much time with her as I'd have liked. Ripley was understandably protective of his daughter, although, from what I understood, he'd been loosening the reins lately. I hoped that meant I could get to know her better, but only time would tell.

One of the many good things about living in Ruf's house meant I saw my niece much more than I ever had before since she and my brother, and now my brother's girlfriend, lived just a few doors down. It also helped that the sweet boy with such a sad expression just happened to be my niece's half-brother, just like Star was her half-sister.

"Talk to me, little man. Tell me about these not-so-nice ladies."

"They're my friends' moms. Well, they aren't supposed to be my friends because I'm a monster and not the fun kind."

"There are fun kinds of monsters? I think if you were really a monster, you'd be the fun kind."

"Liam's mom said that I was a bad boy because my mom didn't love me and that Scoot can't hear because she didn't love her either."

Somehow, my heart had stopped while blood was violently rushing through my body, setting every nerve on fire instantly. I had absolutely no idea what to say in this situation, but I knew I needed to find a way to correct Koda's misconceptions. My bloodlust for the woman who put such an idea into his head would have to wait.

"Koda, sit with me for a minute, okay?" I said as I

tugged on his hand and pulled him toward the porch steps. "I need to explain some things."

"My dad says that I'm a wild boy because God has a sense of humor."

"Well, God does have a sense of humor. Elephants, ostriches, kangaroos, platypuses . . . platypi . . . platy . . . I don't know what the plural word is for them, but have you ever seen an axolotl?"

"A what?"

"An axolotl. It's this fish lizard thing that's kind of creepy and really adorable . . . in a weird sort of way."

"You're bullshittin' me." When I raised my eyebrows, he winced and said, "Sorry. It's been a rough day."

I burst out laughing and then apologized, "I'm sorry. I don't mean to laugh at you, Koda, but you looked just like your daddy when you said that."

"I've heard that before."

"Now, back to what we were talking about. You know everyone's different, right? Not just the way they look or the way they act, but on the inside too."

"Yeah."

"Some people love everyone they meet. Other people don't like anybody."

"My friend Ruthie loves *everybody*. My Lettuce, not so much."

I laughed because he was right about Kale. The man could be a bit prickly at times. "The saddest people are the

213

ones who are so caught up in themselves that they can't appreciate everything around them. I think your mother was that kind of person. I never met her, so I'm not sure, but from what I've heard, she just doesn't have it in her to love anyone as much as she loves herself. That's very sad because she didn't recognize the gifts she was given - gifts that so many other people wish for with all their heart."

"Who gave her a gift?"

"*You* are the gift, Koda. You and Celia and Star are the best gifts that God put on this earth, and your dad and Ripley are lucky enough to have you in their lives forever. I'm lucky too. I'm Scoot's aunt, but I think I'm your friend, and that's just as cool."

"You're gonna be my mom." My heart started racing, and I opened my mouth to argue, but Koda shook his head. "I listen to people when they think I'm just being wild and crazy. I hear things. I hear even more when they think I'm sleeping."

I'd have to file that away and remember it because, apparently, this kid didn't miss a thing, but I had to ask, "Like what?"

"My dad told my Stache and my aunties that he'd never stopped loving you even when you were far apart."

"I love your dad the same way," I admitted.

"So, you should marry us," Koda said with a shrug. "Simple as that."

"It's not really that simple."

"But Dad kissed you in the rain, so it is that simple." Koda shrugged as if the idea were perfectly acceptable. "I heard Dad say that you wanted to have babies before you got old. Do you still want to or can you pretend that me and Star are your babies?"

"Sweetheart, I'd be the luckiest woman on earth if I could call you my son."

"Then do it."

"It's not that simple," I said again. Koda frowned at me, and once again, he looked so much like his father that I couldn't resist putting my arm around his shoulder and pulling him closer for a hug. "How about we take things a little slower than warp speed and just say that I love you?"

"I think I love you too."

"You just love my cooking."

"That helps."

"Speaking of cooking, Terran told me that we're having dinner with your grandparents tonight."

"We are. I'm going to have three plates full. Papa says I have a hollow leg, but Gamma says that I eat like that because I need fuel like a race car that never stops moving."

"I would have to say that I agree with your gamma. You are a whirlwind, my friend."

"But you love me?"

"I do."

"Good. Now all I have to do is get my dad to get off his ass . . . his *butt* . . . and marry you so you can't run away like that woman in the movie Aunt Rylee watches."

"I don't know which movie you're talking about."

"How do you like your eggs, Jovi?"

I had spent enough time with Koda that the abrupt change of topic didn't even phase me. "Scrambled with bacon, mushrooms, onions, and jalapenos."

"It's good that you know that."

Koda took off into the house and left my mind was reeling, not just from the strange egg conversation we'd just had but from all of the other stuff . . . the fact that he'd heard Ruf say he never stopped loving me, he wanted me to be his mom, and that there were two catty, heartless bitches out there somewhere who needed their jaws broken for talking shit about two innocent kids that I loved with all my heart.

It was easier to focus on how I was going to find them and then stay out of prison once I'd taught them a lesson than it was to focus on any of that other stuff, so I pulled my phone out and called my friend Merida, the woman who just happened to run the daycare Koda and my niece attended and who I was almost certain would know how I could find Liam's mom and her catty little friend.

I could think about everything else later because right now, I was on a mission.

"Are you still mad that I dragged you to dinner?" Ruf asked as he leaned over Star's car seat to unbuckle her.

"Irritated, not mad. And it's not that I don't want to visit your grandparents because honestly who wouldn't want to hang out with them? What *irritated* me was that you made plans without telling me, probably because you thought I'd try to find a way to get out of them."

"That's exactly why," Ruf said with a grin. "You get it."

"Aargh! You're insane."

"My parents invited you over for dinner, and you wouldn't go. My sister invited you for dinner, and you wouldn't go. My . . ."

"They invited *you* and the kids, Ruf. Not me."

"Bullshit," Ruf said simply as he lifted Star out of her seat. "Where I go, you go."

"Since when?"

"Bonbon, I've been carrying you around in my heart since I was sixteen fucking years old. It wouldn't know how to beat without you in it, and now that you're here with me, I'm not sure I'd want it to if you were gone again."

Ruf's unblinking gaze held mine as I told him, "You've gotta quit saying stuff like that because it makes me feel like the last years of my life were wasted."

"They were a learning experience for both of us. I've got skills now that I didn't have back then, and you're going to be reaping the benefits of my knowledge for years to come."

Ruf shut the door and turned to greet Ripley and Tori who had just driven up with Koda and Scoot, leaving me a little bit disgusted at the thought of what knowledge he was referencing and how he gained it. I really had no desire to think about how many women he'd practiced with since we broke up.

Not my business. Water under the bridge. You broke up with him, Jovi. It's not like you've been celibate this entire time. Remember that, I thought to myself before I opened the door and slid down. I greeted Tori and then scooped my niece up for a hug.

217

Celia's usually too-loud voice was a little softer today, and I smiled when she said, "Missed you, Jovi!"

"It's only been a day or two since I've seen you, but I missed you too."

"Spend the night."

"You want to spend the night with me? I'm not sure if . . ."

"It's like she's trying to make up for lost time," Ripley grumbled as he got closer to me.

"She and Koda are spending the night here," Tori explained. "Martha called earlier and asked if it would be okay."

"Like I'm gonna say no," Ruf said with a laugh as he passed Star to Ripley. Without a word, Ripley walked off with the baby in his arms, and I smiled when I saw him gazing down at her with an expression I recognized from when Scoot was an infant.

"Go see Papa," Scoot said as she started to squirm. I set her on her feet, and she waved as she yelled, "Bye!"

"She's just talking like it's nothing at all. Three months ago, I'd barely heard her say ten words. Maybe twenty. And now . . ."

"It's amazing, isn't it?" Ruf said as he watched Koda and Scoot run past Ripley into the house. "We better get in there, or Gamma's gonna lose her shit."

"What's wrong?" Tori asked.

"They haven't met Star yet. When she came home with me, Gamma and Papa were in Colorado. They came back a few days later, but by that time, Papa had the sniffles.

It turned into a full-on cold, and then Gamma got it too," Ruf explained. "We've FaceTimed a few times, but it's not the same."

Ruf walked off to get the baby from Ripley, and by the time he had her in his arms, Martha Forrester was standing in the doorway, watching him with tears in her eyes. Ruf walked up the steps to greet her, and she looked at the baby before looking up at his face. The tears streaming down her face didn't dim her smile, and when she reached up and cupped his cheek and said something too quietly for us to hear, Ruf got just as emotional.

"The first time I met her was in the grocery store with Scoot and Koda. I went crossways with some mouthy bitch who said something shitty and then turned around to find Martha and Terra standing there watching me. I didn't realize who they were and said something snippy. Talk about one helluva way to meet the family matriarch."

"I've lived in her orbit my entire life, and I'm sure we'd spoken before, but the first time I remember her talking to me directly was when she caught me and Ruf making out right over there," I said as I pointed to a copse of trees on the other side of the driveway. "It was mortifying."

"I can imagine."

"Even after Ruf and I broke up, she was nothing but nice to me," I admitted as I watched Martha take the baby from Ruf's arms. "I kind of avoided her, though, especially since his sisters wanted me dead."

"That's so crazy to me. Ruf's sisters have been so nice the few times I've met them."

"Yeah, don't break Ripley's heart, and y'all should be fine."

"What do they think about you and Ruf getting back together?"

"How did you know we'd been talking about that?" I asked in shock.

"Koda was talking to Scoot on the drive over. Told me all about dancing in the rain and what that means."

"What it means?"

Tori tilted her head and smiled at my confusion before she said, "You have no idea what you've gotten yourself into, do you?"

I ignored her question and asked one of my own. "Has Scoot mentioned any kids at school excluding her and Koda?"

"My goddaughter Ruthie mentioned that. Scoot told me that some little boy named Liam won't be her friend because she's deaf. Koda did tell me about two . . ."

"Two ladies who work at the school during lunch?" I interrupted.

"Yes!"

"Apparently, they said Koda was a monster and Scoot was deaf because their mother doesn't love them."

"And that's how I'm going to end up in prison."

"I called my friend Merida . . ."

"The daycare administrator?"

"Yes. She knew exactly who I was talking about. Said they get together and have a little hen party once a week to talk shit about everyone else's kids."

"Bitches."

"I was thinking that we should have a hen party of our own at the same time, same place."

"Look at you becoming one of my favorite people," Tori joked.

"I thought we could make it a bonding experience. Invite all the women who love Scoot and Koda."

"There's not a restaurant big enough to hold that many women at one time."

"True, but we could narrow down the guest list to just include the two of us along with my sister and Ruf's sisters."

"Yeah. We're definitely gonna end up in cuffs, but I think it would be a whole lot of fun getting there."

"Come on, ladies," Ripley called from the porch. "Yap yap yap yap. Food's waiting!"

"Sometimes, I want to poke him with something sharp. Maybe a pickaxe. Possibly a harpoon."

"Hold that thought. I'll take out my frustrations on Ruf, and you take out yours on Rip, and we can just add to the charges after our luncheon."

"I'm not sure I can wait that long."

I burst out laughing and then hooked my arm in Tori's as I said, "I think you and I are going to get along just fine. Welcome to the family."

Once we were inside, Martha directed everyone to their places around the table and then sat in her own seat and held the baby while we served ourselves. I thought it was the sweetest thing I'd ever seen when Smokey filled a plate for Martha and then set it in front of her before he kissed her cheek and kissed Star on the top of her head. He murmured something that I couldn't hear that made Martha smile, and I thought how wonderful it must be to love someone so much.

As if it were a movie playing in my mind, I saw Ruf and I in that same position - a little older, a little grayer, but just as happy. When I glanced over at Ruf, I saw him smiling at them, too, and wondered if he was thinking the same thing. I realized he was when he turned to look at me and gave me the same smile Smokey had just given Martha.

"I'm gonna eat all the food, Papa, and then I'm gonna eat all the banana pudding too!" Koda boasted as he scooted closer to the table and looked down at his plate. "My Jovi can cook, but she's never made banana pudding for me."

"I didn't know you liked banana pudding," I said with a grin, loving that he referred to me as his. "I might have to get your gamma's recipe so I can make it since that's your favorite."

"Gamma doesn't give her recipes out to anyone," Ruf said, shaking his head as he lifted a fork full of mashed potatoes.

"I've been known to share one or two on occasion," Martha said without looking up. "After dinner, I'll tell you how I make it so you can treat the boys now and then."

When I looked up from my plate, I realized Ruf was staring at me. I tilted my head in question as I mouthed, "What?"

"Gamma, I know I'm supposed to tell you when someone is mean to me, but I told Jovi instead, okay?" Koda asked. As usual, his abrupt change of topic shocked all of us when he said, "Me and Scoot are gonna move to California so I can be a stuntman. She'll be a stunt girl. That's a thing, right?"

"A stuntwoman is definitely a thing, but how are you two going to do that?" Smokey asked.

Koda answered Smokey and then Ruf and Ripley joined their conversation. I was smiling at their banter when I felt a hand on my arm.

"What did Koda mean? Who has been ugly to him?" I looked over at Martha as she sat back in her chair and readjusted the baby in her arms. "Is it those same children?"

"There are some kids from school who go to the same daycare now that it's summer, and they're not allowed to play with him and Scoot because of something their mothers told them."

Martha's eyes narrowed and that got worse when Tori said, "Jovi and I were just discussing that outside."

"He said that they called him a monster and said Scoot was special because their mother made them that way," I informed her. "I called Merida and found out who the mothers are, and now I'm trying to decide what to do about it."

"What do you think our options are?"

"Well, my first thought was that they wouldn't be able to talk shit about little children if their jaws were wired shut, but now I'm considering things that are longer lasting."

"I like your thought process, but what are you considering now?" Martha asked.

"I know that ruining their lives might be a little extreme, so I thought I might confront them about their bullshit and see what their reaction is before I burn their world down around them."

"That sounds reasonable."

"We're going to see if Rain, Rylee, and Trinity would like to join us for lunch at the same time those two women and their little group meet every week. Give them a dose of their own medicine."

"That sounds like a plan. If they aren't suitably apologetic, you bring it to me," Martha said firmly, her eyes alight with anger. "I'll take care of it."

"Yes, ma'am," I replied with a nod.

Star had been squirming for the last few minutes while we were talking, and it was killing me not to reach over to try to soothe her. It wasn't that Martha didn't know what she was doing, I didn't even consider that since she'd helped raise almost everyone I knew, but Star was starting to get worked up and I wanted to do what I could before she became too upset. I resisted, though, and watched as Martha lifted her up to her shoulder and patted her back as Star's cries just got louder.

"There she goes again," Koda said worriedly. "She's broken, Dad. You need to get her fixed."

"She can't use words yet, so that's what she does to tell us something's wrong," Ruf explained calmly as he watched Martha who was trying to soothe the baby.

Koda put his fork down and started using sign language at the same time he said, "Star Baby, that's enough screaming."

"Use words," Scoot added, also signing while she spoke to the baby. "Words are good. Make sense."

"Gonna need you to dial that down a bit," Koda said as Star started screaming. He looked at Ripley and asked, "How do I sign that?"

Ripley propped his elbow on the table and stared at his plate, trying very hard not to laugh. Smokey didn't have that much control and cracked up, but when Martha scowled at him, he cleared his throat and picked up his glass for a long drink.

"Jovi knows how to fix her," Koda announced. "Gamma, you should let Jovi try."

"Gamma knows what she's doing, bud," Ruf chided. "Eat your dinner, and let her take care of Star."

"Oh, sweet girl," Martha mumbled as she patted the squirming baby's back. She stood up and walked toward the living room, and I was surprised when she called out over her shoulder, "Jovi, honey, come in here, would you?"

I put my napkin on the table and stood up, shooting a worried glance at Ruf. I did not want to step on his grandmother's toes, but I was almost sure I could give Star some relief. What I wasn't sure about was my place in this scene. I felt like I was walking on thin ice that could crack if I stepped wrong.

I followed Martha into the living room and then down a long hall and was surprised when we walked into the master bedroom.

"Now, sweetie, that's enough," Martha murmured in a soothing voice. Suddenly, she held her out to me and said, "I could tell it was killing you not to snatch her up and make it better."

"Oh! Um . . . I wasn't trying to . . ." Star stopped screaming the second I put her against my chest, and I completely forgot what I was about to say. Instead, I rubbed my cheek against Star's head and started bouncing her just the way she liked. She might have been quieter now, but she was still squirming, so I walked over to the bed and laid her down and worked her legs like before. She tooted twice and then sighed loudly. Without thinking, I said, "This is turning into a pattern. I'm not sure if it's the type of formula or if she's drinking too much between burps. It might be the bottles Ruf is using. I found some online that say they don't let any air in, but if it's the amount she's eating . . . I just don't know." I picked Star back up and held her on my arm with her legs hanging off my hand and patted her back a few times before I looked at Martha. "I have absolutely no idea if this is normal or what. I'm not sure what to try first"

Martha ignored everything I'd just said and sat down on the edge of the bed so that she was eye to eye with Star. She reached out and ran her hands over her soft hair as she said, "I was worried that this would be too much too soon, especially when Terra said you don't seem to have a connection with Star yet, but I think she's wrong."

"You and Terra talked about me?"

Martha looked up and met my eyes as she said, "Of course we did. You're living with some of our very favorite people."

I decided to confide in Martha because I knew that she had more life experience than I ever would and everyone that knew her relished her sage advice. "I'm afraid to get too attached to Star because she's everything I've ever wanted. I don't know how I could live if I ever lost her. I feel the same way about Koda, but he's impossible to avoid."

"If everything you've ever wanted is right within your grasp, why wouldn't you reach out and pull it close so it can't get away?"

"I've got a lot going on with my ex. I feel like I'm coming into this with so much baggage that there will be no way to unpack it all without making a huge mess."

"You take one step at a time, Jovi. That's how you conquer a mountain. You can't just jump to the top; you have to go step by step, and lucky for you, there are people who love you holding their hands out to help you on your way. Take what they offer. By the time you get to the top and see the other side, you'll be surrounded by love and your biggest supporters, and that will make the view even better."

"I've never stopped loving Ruf, Martha."

"And he has always carried a torch for you, but your time apart will just make everything sweeter. You guys were so young back then - full of passion and fire along with your hopes and dreams, but there was a lot of work to be done. You've both grown and matured in the time you spent apart and can use everything you've learned to make the future even brighter than you imagined in the first place."

Star started squirming, so I lifted her up and kissed her cheek before I handed her back to Martha. "Here you go. Take her back and give her lots of love. I can get my snuggles when we get back to Ruf's."

"Ruf is your home, sweetheart. You know that in your heart."

"I do."

"I knew that when I met my Smokey, but I tried to resist just like you're doing now."

"It seems like everything worked out," I joked.

"We climbed our mountains together, hand in hand, and watched the world unfold in front of us to include more family than we could have imagined," Martha said as she rubbed her hand up and down Star's back. "I'm glad you're ready to come back, Jovi."

"It means a lot to know you're okay with me and Ruf after what happened before."

"You gave him up to let him spread his wings, and I have always thought you should be commended for that."

"Thank you."

"Now things have come full circle, and you can fly together."

"I hope so."

"Do better than hope, Jovi. Make it happen."

"Yes, ma'am."

FIFTEEN

"No matter what was going on in my life, I never stopped dreaming of you."

Ruf

RUF

"Can I ask you a favor?" I asked as I walked out onto the patio.

"The backhoe is out of commission, but I've got shovels," my grandfather answered with a grin. Ripley and I laughed at his response, and then he asked, "What's up?"

"Can I borrow one of your bikes?"

"Yours still giving you fits?"

"I've got it in the shop right now. Ransome offered to overhaul it for me while I was home with Star, so I haven't ridden in a while."

"You know where the keys are, son," Papa said before he took a sip of his beer. "We'll watch the kids for you."

"I was just telling your grandpa goodbye. Tori and I are going to the bookstore, which means I'm about to be broke, but since they're keeping Scoot tonight, I *might* be able to get out of there with at least the shirt on my back."

"You read more than any man I know," I told him with a grin. "You'll spend a fair amount on books for

229

yourself, I'm sure."

"We're not talking about that," Ripley mumbled before he shook my grandfather's hand. "Thanks for dinner."

"I'm going to sweep Jovi away for a ride if you don't think Gamma would mind . . ."

"Shut up and go," Papa said with a mock frown. "Take your girl for a ride, and make it a long one. Me and Gamma have time to make up for with that sweet baby."

"Thanks, Papa." I walked back through the house, following behind Ripley as he said his goodbyes to my Gamma and laughed when Scoot waved him off like it was nothing for him to leave her somewhere for the night. He grumbled all the way to the front door but left her here, which was a big step for him even though he knew she'd be perfectly safe and content. Once they were gone, I held my hand out to Jovi, who was sitting on the couch watching Gamma feed Star, and said, "Take a ride with me?"

"Right now?"

"Yeah."

When Jovi looked at Gamma, she motioned toward the door and said, "You kids go have some time to yourselves while I enjoy this sweet little girl."

"Come on, Bonbon. Let's go," I said as I reached for her hand and pulled her off the couch. "We can ride around just like old times."

I saw Jovi's eyes widen at that implication and grinned at her as I took off toward the front door.

"I thought your bike was in the shop," she said as we walked down the porch steps.

"It is, but there's a whole garage of bikes out here, so Papa said I could take one of his."

We were halfway down the driveway when I pulled her off the concrete into the grass. "I thought the garage was over . . ." Jovi's voice trailed off when I stopped in front of the big tree where we'd been caught making out years ago. She gasped when she saw what I was pointing at and then smiled as she traced our initials I'd carved into the bark. "I can't believe you did that!"

"I carved it the year after we broke up. I had just found out that Koda was on his way and my life was going to change forever. I was positive there was no way you'd ever be in it again, especially since you were making sure our dreams came true even if I wasn't part of them anymore."

"That's not how it was, Ruf. I . . ."

"I got fucking hammered down at the clubhouse and started pouring my heart out. Luckily, only Hawk, Crow, Phoenix, Jonas, and Lawson were there at the time, and none of them have mentioned it still to this day. They listened to me ramble on about how fucking stupid I was to have let you go and then stood here with me in the middle of the night while I defaced Papa and Gamma's tree. A few of them were even nice enough to hold their phones up to give me some light so I could see well enough to carve our initials without cutting my hand off in the process. "

"That's sweet in a sad and almost disturbing way," Jovi said with an uncomfortable laugh. "Kind of like a wake to mourn our relationship. It's a lot more entertaining than how I got through it."

I was almost afraid to ask, but I did anyway. "How did you grieve?"

"Blue Bell ice cream. Every flavor. I didn't discriminate. I had a couple of drunken nights where I cried on True's shoulder, but I mostly just ate my feelings and watched true crime documentaries and romantic comedies that made me cry. It's not very original, but after about two years, it got a little easier."

"No matter what was going on in my life, I never stopped dreaming of you."

"Do you know how crazy this is? Really?"

"I know doing crazy things is more my style than yours, but maybe you can bend a little on this," I suggested as I took a step closer. I took another until her chest was touching mine, and she had to tip her head back to maintain eye contact. I reached up and put my hand on the back of her head when I took another step and pushed her against our tree.

Our bodies were pressed together now, and I could tell by her breathing that she was as excited as I felt. "It's been killing me to be so close to you and not pull you into my arms. That night when you laid in the hospital bed with me might have been the worst night of your life, but it was one of the best of mine because I knew it meant that if I worked hard enough, you'd be my girl again someday."

"I've always been your girl, Ruf," Jovi whispered before she laid her lips on mine.

The first kiss was soft, the second a little more intense, but when she pulled away to take a breath, I wasn't finished and pressed against her, being careful of her burns that still gave her some pain even after all this time. With my hands in her hair, I fit her lips just right with mine and kissed her with a passion that I had never felt for anyone other than her. The memory of her lips had lain dormant since the last kiss we shared, but it sprang to life in an instant and reminded me just how well we fit together.

The loud pipes of motorcycles pulling into the drive behind me brought me to my senses, but by then, Jovi was in my arms with her legs wrapped around my waist. When I lifted my head to see who had arrived, Jovi fell back against the tree and sighed.

Without opening her eyes, she said, "Kill whoever just interrupted us. I'll wait right here."

"Not that I'm completely against that idea, but there are a few issues with it."

"Name three."

"Mom's sort of attached to the boys, so she might get irritated if they disappear. If I turn around, they're gonna see just exactly how excited you make me - and considering they're my little brothers, that would be uncomfortable for all of us."

Jovi sighed and opened her eyes before she smiled and gave me something else to think about, like she'd done a thousand times before when we were interrupted and needed to join the land of the living before we were finished with each other. "Imagine Miss Murphy teaching economics class in a thong bikini while Mr. Martinez watches in a bright yellow Speedo."

"Fuck, that's rough," I groaned. When we graduated, Miss Murphy was at least seventy and bore a striking resemblance to Olive Oyl from the Popeye cartoon. Mr. Martinez was probably close to Miss Murphy in age, and he was a large man, not so much in height as in width. But worse than that, he had so much body hair that the thought of him in a Speedo was almost nauseating. "How do you always think of the worst things imaginable so quickly? It's not right, Bonbon."

"It's a talent," Jovi said before she gave me a peck on the lips. "Some things never change."

"How much I want you sure as hell hasn't," I assured her before I closed my eyes and willed my cock to deflate. Sadly enough, the image that she'd given me with just a few words really helped, and soon, I was presentable again and could turn and face my family.

"It's about damn time," my brother Ransome said with a grin as he threw his leg over his bike to stand. He rushed across the driveway and pulled Jovi into his arms, and I knew someone had told him about her burns when he held her carefully instead of squeezing her tightly. He looked down at her and smiled as he said, "I guess this means I can't steal you away, huh?"

"You're a little young for me, don't you think?"

"Age is just a number, sweetheart."

"Whatever," Jovi said with a grin. "You've missed your chance. Ruf's a persistent guy, and I've fallen into his trap."

"Damn. Big brother wins again," Ransome teased.

My youngest brother was just eleven when Jovi and I got together and made no effort to hide that she was his first major crush. Just a few years ago, he laughingly admitted that he kept in touch with her after we broke up in the hopes that someday she'd see him as more than just my kid brother and more like the love of her life. Luckily, his crush had faded over time, but the two had remained friends, so I knew that he would be happy to see us back together.

Suddenly, it struck me - Jovi had just admitted out loud that we were together again.

The look on my face must have shown my shock because I heard Rocky snicker, and I looked over to find him laughing at me.

"You look like you just got struck by lightning."

"I think I did." Ransome stepped away from Jovi, and she turned so that she was by my side again, close enough for our arms to touch. I took a chance and brushed my hand over hers and felt my heart start to race when she took hold of it as she kept talking to Ransome. "What are y'all doing here?"

Rocky explained, "We were going to take a little ride and stop at Spokes for some patio time, but we saw your truck, so we thought we'd drop by and say hello."

"That sounds like fun," Jovi said cheerfully. She looked over at me and asked, "Do you think we have enough time to go up to Spokes? I haven't been there in ages."

"You know Gamma's not going to argue about watching the baby for any length of time, so I think we can stop for a beer."

"You go get the bike, and I'll make sure it's okay with her," Jovi suggested. "I've gotta remind her to make Terran a plate with two desserts too. I can't forget those."

"Sounds good," I said before I squeezed her hand and pulled her close. I dropped a quick kiss on her lips and smiled at her. "Thanks, Bonbon."

Jovi took off for the house, and as I watched her walk away, Rocky asked, "So, it's official?"

Ransome laughed. "It sure as hell seems like it."

I couldn't contain my excitement when I grinned at

my brothers and said, "I'd say it's about damn time."

JOVI

It had been years since I'd been on the back of a motorcycle - as a matter of fact, it had been nine years. I'd never ridden with anyone other than Ruf. It was still just as exhilarating as it had always been. I loved having my arms around him with my hands flat on his stomach.

The motorcycle he'd chosen to ride this evening was different from his, and it was much more comfortable than I remembered. The seat beneath me was well-padded and wider than the one on Ruf's motorcycle, and with my legs hooked over the hard saddlebags on either side of the bike, I felt more stable and didn't fear falling off the back. Of course, that meant I could loosen my hold on Ruf, but I didn't, enjoying the feel of his hard abdomen beneath my hands, wishing I could feel his bare skin.

I decided to make my own wish come true, and as we flew down the backroad that would lead us into town, I lifted his shirt and slipped one hand beneath it before I did the same with the other. His muscles clenched as I rubbed my hand over him, going from the waistband of his jeans up to his pecs and then down again.

Since his brothers were riding ahead of us, I decided to take things a step further and let my hands trail down below the waistband and found his cock hard enough to pound nails. I laughed out loud, and even though the wind carried away the sound, I knew Ruf had felt the vibrations against his back when he shook his head. I took a chance and unzipped his jeans and then slid my hand through the opening I'd made so that I could cup his erection.

The bike slowed down, making more space between us and the other Forresters, and I took that opportunity to rub up and down Ruf's hard length as I kissed and nibbled his neck where it met his shoulder. We were getting closer to town, and I knew there was a stop sign coming up soon, so I slowly zipped up his jeans. I gave his crotch a light tap and then moved my hand back up to his abdomen before I bit his neck and kissed the pain away.

"One of these days, we're gonna revisit that situation," I promised as we slowed to a stop behind Rocky and Ransome. "And when we do, I won't stop until you're done."

Ruf shivered, and I laughed out loud, knowing exactly how he felt since I was the same after our interrupted moment at the tree earlier. Ruf turned his head and stared down at my face in shock. I smiled up at him before I used the foot pedals to push myself up just enough so that I could lean over his shoulder and give him a kiss.

"Are we really doing this, Bonbon?"

"Isn't this what you want? Me and you together?"

"It's not just a want, baby, it's something I've dreamed about since I lost you."

"Well, obviously, I'm back," I said sarcastically.

"It's about fucking time."

The traffic cleared, and we pulled out onto the busier road behind Ruf's brothers, and within just a minute, we passed the city limit sign announcing that we were officially back in Rojo. Soon, we started passing clusters of houses until we were finally in the middle of town and turning down the street that would take us to Spokes, one of the bars Ruf's family owned that was run by his cousin Lark.

I was watching the buildings as we passed, thinking about what was going to happen when we went home tonight. Ruf's house had quickly become my home whether I wanted to admit it or not, and I was excited about the prospect of making it permanent even though we hadn't discussed that quite yet. Somehow, I knew it was inevitable, and the thought made my heart race even though my brain was screaming for me to take it slow.

We pulled to a stop at a red light, and Ruf let go of the handlebars and rested his arms on my thighs as he turned to smile at me again. "This is just like old times, isn't it?"

"It is," I agreed. "I still love riding with you. I had no idea how much I missed this."

"I missed it, too, Bonbon."

I propped my chin on his shoulder and squeezed him a little tighter before I said, "I want to do this all the time."

"As soon as I get my bike back, we can start. I'll have to get Koda out too. He's used to riding with me and has been eager to get back to it."

The light turned green, and we started moving again. Before long, we were slowing to turn into Spokes. Ruf followed his brothers as they weaved through the parking lot to find the designated parking area for motorcycles that was right next to the patio. Once he'd turned the motorcycle off, he patted my leg just like he used to. I hopped off the back and then waited for him to join me next to the bike.

I was just about to turn to see who was on the patio when he pulled me into his arms and gave me a lingering kiss that left me breathless.

"Thanks for giving me a chance, Jovi," Ruf said as he pulled back just far enough to look into my eyes. "This is everything I've dreamed of all this time."

"Me too."

"I can't wait to get you home alone tonight."

"Why? What do you have planned for me after we get there?"

"All sorts of filthy things."

"Funny enough, I've been plotting things like that out too," I admitted with a grin.

"Dammit," Ruf said as he let his head fall forward until our foreheads were touching. "I've really gotta learn to control myself around you."

When I heard a crowd of people hooting and hollering, I remembered that we weren't alone and most likely had an audience. I looked over at the patio to find at least a dozen people cheering us on. There were people I'd gone to school with along with some others who were related to Ruf in one way or another. And, as bikers were known to do, they were loud and proud about seeing Ruf and I together again.

Ruf, ever the smartass, turned toward them and took a bow. And even though I hated having all the attention on me, I couldn't resist doing the same thing. When the cheers just got louder, Ruf turned his head to grin at me and said, "Looks like they've been waiting for this to happen."

"I guess we all were."

"I love you, Bonbon."

SIXTEEN

"Scars are points on a map that show the adventures and hardships you've experienced in life."

Lana Tempest

RUF

"I'll get her changed while you heat her bottle," Jovi said as she unbuckled the straps of Star's car seat. She held her against her chest as she set the seat in the coat closet. When she turned around, she furrowed her brow and said, "Chop chop, Forrester. She's gonna start wailing any minute now."

"You're taking charge."

Jovi softly asked, "Is that a bad thing?"

"Absolutely not!" I said as I hurried toward the kitchen to make a bottle.

Instead of going to the nursery, Jovi followed me into the kitchen and asked, "What did you mean?"

I pulled a bottle from the cabinet and started mixing the formula as I answered, "I was just shocked because this is the first time you've ever taken the initiative in helping with Star. Before, you only offered to step in if I was at the end of my rope and . . ."

"Two reasons," Jovi said. She held up one finger and

said, "I didn't know what my place was in your life, but now I do. The second reason is because I talked to your grandmother, and she gave me some advice. Since she's probably the wisest person we know, I'm going to take it."

"What was her advice?" I asked as I dropped the bottle into the warmer and then leaned against the counter while I waited for it to finish.

"She told me that the only way to conquer a mountain is one step at a time and that I should take what I want and hold it close to me."

"Okay."

"I'm holding her close, and when she's settled, I'm going to do the same thing with you."

I burst out laughing at the earnest expression on her face and said, "I like that idea."

"Good because you know how I get when I've got a mission to accomplish."

"And getting me naked is part of that mission?"

"Absolutely."

"Well, let's get started," I said with a chuckle before I pulled off my shirt and tossed it aside. I unbuckled my belt and started to take off my pants. Jovi burst out laughing.

"Hold that thought until we get the baby down."

The bottle warmer beeped, and I groaned. "Now I know why Mom and Dad used to send us outside to play so often."

"It's gonna be a while before she's ready for that," Jovi said as she walked toward the Star's room.

241

I followed her and said, "If she's anything like Koda, that's never going to happen. Things can get out of hand really quickly if he's unsupervised."

"He's so much fun," Jovi said with a giggle. "I love spending time with him."

"Good because he's as addicted to you as I am."

I watched as Jovi laid Star down on the changing pad I'd moved to the top of the dresser she and Koda had painted and smiled when she started talking to Star as she changed her diaper and got her into pajamas. Once Jovi was done, she walked across the room and handed her to me. Before she walked away, she gave Star a kiss on the cheek and ran her hand over her hair as she murmured, "Love you, sweet girl."

"Where are you going?" I asked as I walked to the rocking chair she'd placed in the corner near the window.

"I am going to shower and get ready for bed." I felt my heart drop and knew she read it on my face when she said, "I should be finished by the time you get her to sleep, so I'll see you in just a bit."

"Thank God," I whispered as I sat down and got settled with Star in the crook of my arm. She started to squirm, one of her early warning signals, so I popped the nipple in her mouth and then smiled up at Jovi. "I can't wait."

Jovi walked out of the nursery, and I heard her feet on the stairs as she went up to her room. My phone buzzed, and I leaned to the side so I could pull it out of my pocket and got a frown from Star when I jostled her.

"You're gonna have to get over that attitude, little Star," I said as I smiled down at her. "I'm not sure how you got the idea that you run this place, but I'm here to tell you that I'm the one in charge."

In answer, Star gave me a very impressive side-eye and then farted so loud, it vibrated the diaper in my hand.

I was still laughing when I answered the phone, and Jonas asked, "What's got you in such a good mood?"

"This girl farts like she gets paid good money to do it," I said as I leaned down to kiss her forehead. "She cracks me up."

"Please tell me you're not talking about Jovi," Jonas whined.

I couldn't help but laugh again as I assured him, "I'm talking about Star. She rivals Koda in the gas department."

"Speaking of gas, I'm staring at Dr. Dumbass who just happens to be pumping gas right now."

"Okay. Why is that important enough for you to call me about it?"

"Because I followed him here from my house."

"That motherfucker," I mumbled and then winced when I glanced down at Star. It wasn't like she wouldn't hear that word more than a few times in her life. If she was anything like her brother, something a lot like it would probably be her first word, but I was still trying to curb my tongue around her. "He's still looking for her."

"Obviously. He was parked down the street. My usual truck is in the shop, so I'm driving one of my dad's until tomorrow. That's why he didn't spot me, I guess."

"See where he goes."

"I will, but I wanted to give you a heads up that he's

nosing around."

"I'm awfully tempted to pay that son of a bitch a visit," I said through gritted teeth. "He's lucky I haven't already, but if he keeps fucking around, it's gonna happen."

"I'm down for that. So, how is your little Bonbon?"

"Great."

"Heard y'all rode up to Spokes and caused a scene."

"Not a scene so much as a . . . Okay, yeah, maybe a little," I admitted with a laugh.

"Are you ready for us to bring all of her shit to you?" Jonas asked. "She's got boxes stacked in my garage."

"I'm perfectly ready, but I'm not gonna push her just yet."

"Well, they're not bothering me, so she can keep them there as long as she wants, but when she's ready, I'll gather the guys up, and we'll make a day of it. We'll even let you feed us dinner as long as you're not the one cooking."

"I'm sure that can be arranged. I'll get back to you about it."

"Well, Dr. Dipshit is finished getting his gas, so I'm gonna trail him and see where he goes next."

"Thanks, man."

"I swear, if he camps out in front of my house all night, I'm probably going to beat the brakes off of him."

"Wouldn't the cops be a little bit suspicious if there were someone watching one of their houses?" I asked.

"I'm sure they would, but he's watching my . . . Oh!

You're right. He's probably watching Lawson's house for some reason."

"Well, they are connected," I said drolly.

"I'm gonna have to make a phone call. Concerned citizen and all that."

"Well, I suppose if he does get busted watching your house, that would probably go against the restraining order Jovi has on him too."

"Look at the big brain on the Forrester," Jonas teased.

"I'm not just a pretty face, you know."

"Like the south end of a northbound rhino."

"Whatever, asshole," I said as I got up out of the chair and walked over to the crib. "I've gotta let you go so I can get Star settled in for the night. Let me know what happens."

"Will do."

"And if you decide to rearrange Dickbrain's face, I've got your bail money."

"Good to know. I don't have any big plans tonight, so I might just do that."

Once we said goodbye, I set the phone aside and settled Star on my shoulder to burp, wondering if Jovi had made it back downstairs yet. Considering how long I'd known her and what we'd shared back in the day, it felt crazy to be this nervous, but for some reason, I couldn't help myself. Tonight was a new beginning, and I wanted more than anything to make it memorable for both of us.

And I was more than ready to do just that.

JOVI

"What are you doing?" True asked. "Did you call me from the shower?"

"I'm sitting on the edge of the bathtub shaving my legs."

"Why don't you just shave in the shower?"

"I can't stay in there longer than I have to because of the bandages, so I've been shaving on the side of the tub before I shower."

"Oh. That makes sense."

"I'm going to sleep with Ruf."

"It's about damn time! While you're in the tub, you should make sure and rinse the cobwebs out of there in case he decides to get an up close and personal look at the goods."

"You secretly have a penis, don't you? I swear if you got any more filthy, we'd have to hose you off out back every day."

"It's a gift."

"Well, your gift isn't really helping me. I should have called Lana."

"Let's do that. Give me a second," True said. A few seconds later, I heard our friend Lana's voice, and True got her up to speed. "Now, Lana, Jovi is shaving her legs because she's about to bump uglies with your cousin."

"Well, that's a disturbing thought," Lana mumbled.

"He's delicious. You just can't see it because you share a bloodline," True said cheerfully because she knew how grossed out Lana got when anyone talked about the men in her family. "He looks like his father, who is hot in his own right, but he's nowhere near as good looking as your brother Brandt, who looks just like Fain with his . . ."

"Why do I answer when you call?" Lana grumbled.

"Can we focus on my drama right now instead of trying to make Lana throw up?" I asked in irritation as I got out of the tub and walked toward the vanity. "I'm having a meltdown here, ladies."

"No offense, sweetheart, but it's not like you haven't seen the man naked before," Lana reminded me.

"Technically, the last time they were together, he had the body of a man . . . well, the beginning of one because even I can admit that he's filled out over the years."

"Ain't that the damn truth?" I asked as I remembered all that skin I'd been privy to when Ruf walked around the house without a shirt on, and, of course, how it felt underneath my hands when we were on the motorcycle earlier. "He's definitely matured."

"And I'm gonna go out on a limb here and assume he hasn't exactly been a saint since y'all broke up. There's a very high probability that he's learned a thing or two while you've been apart."

"I know," I grumbled. "I'm different, too, but not in any good ways."

"What the hell does that mean?" True asked, annoyed at the thought of me putting myself down.

"He's covered in tattoos, and I'm covered in burns

that are still healing and a whole bunch of scars. It looks like I've got pink patches all over me from the new skin that's . . ."

"Scars are points on a map that show the adventures and hardships you've experienced," Lana said sagely.

"Shit," True said in awe. "That needs to be on a coffee mug."

"If I knew how to cross-stitch, I'd put it on a pillow," I teased.

"Fuck you both," Lana said through her laughter.

"You could get that as a tattoo," True suggested.

"Mass market keychains, bumper stickers, all the . . ."

"I'm assuming you're about to bang my cousin and you called us for emotional support," Lana interrupted, getting us back on track. "I'm on a date right now, and my food is getting cold on the table."

"You're on a date? Why did you even answer the phone?" I asked.

"Because I needed some intelligent conversation before I fell asleep from sheer boredom. But enough about my pitiful dating choices. Let's get this rolling. Do we need to talk you out of this, cheer you on, boost your ego, or drive over there and drag you out of the house?" Lana asked.

"What if it's not as good as I remember? What if I've forgotten how to . . . Well, I haven't had an orgasm that included outside help in so long that I'm not sure I'll even enjoy myself. I guess it's really about the connection and intimacy but . . ."

"I just threw up a little bit," True interrupted.

"It's been, what? Six months since you and Rodney had sex, right? It hasn't been that long," Lana pointed out.

"Well, true, but Rodney didn't exactly pass out orgasms like a Pez dispenser or anything."

"Oh, sweet baby Harambe," True mumbled. "Put on some sexy underwear . . . No, scratch that. Walk out of the bathroom naked as a jaybird and . . ."

"She can't risk Koda seeing all of that."

"Koda is staying at your grandparent's house," I told Lana.

"In that case, I triple dog dare you to walk your naked ass downstairs and let nature take its course," Lana said.

"No. There's something to be said for pretty underwear. It's like wrapping up a gift you want the man to open with his teeth."

"All the underwear I have came in six-packs from Walmart."

"Good grief," True mumbled.

"Naked, Jovi. You said you were worried about your scars, and I think you should wear them like a badge of honor. He wants you and always has, so it's not going to matter to him if you've got a few more fault lines on your road map. He's going to worship you like the goddess you are, and underwear is just going to get in the way."

"What she said," True cheered. "You go out there and watch him trip all over himself when he sees you, and you'll know he doesn't give a shit about the burns."

"As disgusting as it sounds to me, considering the man is my cousin, I have to say that if he does things right, she won't even remember she's got scars."

"Hallelujah!"

"I'm gonna do it!" I said as I put the cap back on the lotion I'd used on my legs. I looked at my reflection in the mirror and admitted, "But if I'm going, I better do it right now because the longer I stand here and look at my reflection, the more I think . . ."

"Stop thinking!" True yelled. "We'll see you at work tomorrow."

"Get out of your head, Jovi! The man is in love with you. Now, walk out of that bathroom with your head held high and enjoy yourself."

"Thanks for the pep talk, ladies."

The girls hung up, and I sighed as I took one last glance in the mirror. The scars were a myriad of pinks and reds, still tender because of the soft skin that I massaged burn cream into a few times a day. I still had a few bandages - one on the inside of my right elbow, another on my bicep, and one more beneath my breast that wrapped around my ribs.

The urge to pull on a T-shirt and keep it on no matter what was almost overwhelming, but I knew in my heart that Ruf would want to see all of me, regardless of the burns. I decided to take True's suggestion and walk downstairs naked. Ruf said that he still loved me, and I believed him, but that meant I couldn't - and shouldn't - hide anything from him.

The good, the bad, and the ugly should go right along with the wonderful, the fantastic, and the love.

I spun around and left the bathroom and then rushed down the hall before I lost my nerve. This was the future I had dreamed about, and I was going to embrace it with everything I had. I knew without a doubt that I was going to enjoy every single second of it - unless I overthought things and ran back into my room to get dressed.

"I do not prance, woman."

Ruf

JOVI

"You can do this! It's Ruf, not Henry Cavill, although there are some comparisons with the . . . Shit, Jovi. What are you doing?" I mumbled to myself as I stopped in the middle of the hallway, trying not to make a hasty retreat.

"I'm not Henry Cavill, but I am right here," Ruf said from behind me. I spun around and found him leaning against the doorframe of Star's nursery and wondered how in the world I'd missed the fact that he was inside on my way to his room. His eyes roamed down my body as a smile slowly spread across his face before he said, "But right now, looking at you naked in my hallway, I can honestly say that parts of me are *definitely* turning into the Man of Steel."

"That was so cheesy," I said without thinking. I suddenly remembered that I was buck naked and lifted my arm to cover my breasts as my other hand moved to cover my bottom half. I felt my face getting red with embarrassment beneath Ruf's heated gaze and started to rush past him, wondering what in the hell I'd been thinking.

Ruf stepped in front of me to block my way, and his hands came up to rest on my shoulders as he stared down into my face. "I've dreamed of this more than I'd care to admit. It went a lot of ways, but this is better than I could

252

have imagined."

"Peer pressure!"

"What now?"

"True and Lana thought this was a good idea and . . ."

"They'll have my eternal thanks," Ruf mumbled as he turned me so my back was against the wall. "This is one of the scenarios I imagined, but it wasn't how I thought tonight was going to go."

"Me naked in your hall?"

"That's definitely a dream come true," Ruf said as he fit his body against mine, pressing me against the wall. "However, I thought that our first time would be sweet and gentle. I'd lay you down on my bed and worship you with my mouth while I told you how beautiful you are."

"That sounds like a plan," I said breathlessly just a second before Ruf's lips touched mine.

He kissed me long and hard before his lips worked their way along my jaw to my ear. He nipped at my earlobe with his teeth and then asked, "How careful do I need to be?"

"I've got an IUD," I said as I tipped my head to the side to give him better access to my neck.

Ruf's deep chuckle vibrated my entire body and gave me goosebumps that only got worse when he lifted one hand to tug at my hair and ran the other over my hip. "That's good to know, Bonbon, but I was talking about those bandages you're wearing."

"Just don't poke them or anything, and I should be

fine."

Ruf laughed again, but I didn't have time for another round of goosebumps because the hand on my hip scooped down beneath my ass at the same time the other left my hair and went down my other side. My hands were on his biceps, and I felt the muscles bunch and grow before he lifted me up so that we were eye to eye. My legs went around his waist of their own volition, and I gasped when Ruf pressed me back against the wall.

I could feel the length of his erection against my clit and moved my hips to get the friction I needed there as he pushed us away from the wall and started walking. I remembered the first time he'd tried to do this years ago - walk with me in his arms when his mind was definitely on other things - and I started to laugh.

"If you're going to say something about the time I dropped you, I'll do it again but on purpose," Ruf growled as he came to a stop in his bedroom. I smiled, and he said, "Most embarrassing moment of . . . . Okay not the *most* embarrassing, but it ranks right up there."

I forgot what I was laughing about and my own damn name when he bent forward and laid me down on his bed. My legs were still wrapped around his waist, and I wasn't about to let him go, so he followed me down and rested his weight on his hands that he placed on either side of my head. My hands ran up and down his muscular back as he kissed me again. I took the opportunity to push his shorts down over his hips since his hands were busy. He knew what I was doing and lifted up just a fraction so I could get my hand between us, and then he hissed when I wrapped my hand around his cock.

"Shit! Your hands are cold!" I laughed again because I'd heard him say that at least a hundred times over the years, but his initial irritation didn't last long as I ran my hand up and down his length. "We've gotta slow this down, Bonbon."

"No sense in that."

"I've got plans for you."

"I've got plans for you too," I said as I angled my hips just right and touched the tip of his cock to my clit. I swirled it around and bit back a groan as Ruf lost the battle and made a sound that was long and low. "I know you want the sweet and romance and all that, and I appreciate it, but you've been running around shirtless for too long. Do you know how hard it is . . . ."

"Oh, I know exactly how hard it is," Ruf interrupted.

"To concentrate when there's all *that* prancing around . . . ."

Ruf groaned again as I ran my hand up and down his cock but had enough control to say, "I do not prance, woman."

I lifted my head and gave him a kiss and then finished, "With you *prancing* around without your shirt and those shorts holding onto your hips with just a wish and a prayer, a girl's gonna think naughty thoughts, Ruf."

Ruf bit my neck and then asked, "How naughty?"

"That if you don't fuck me so hard I see stars, there's not a . . . ." I let out a yelp when he pushed all the way into me in one thrust, his cock filling me like no other ever had. He stilled deep inside me, giving me time to adjust, and then he was moving his hips in a way that let me know my first orgasm was just seconds away, and there would definitely be a second, and maybe even a third.

In a way, our joining was like reliving an old memory, but things were different now and that somehow made it even better. When we were together before, we were so young . . . each other's firsts in so many ways. We explored each other every chance we got. Tonight's exploration was different - more intense because we were well aware of all the time we had lost and what we'd found again.

Our breath mingled between kisses and murmured words as Ruf made slow love to me, his hips moving almost leisurely until he felt the first stirrings of my orgasm and pumped harder until I was screaming his name with every breath. I was still trying to catch my breath when Ruf suddenly pushed up with his arms and left my body, but before I could ask what was wrong, he lifted my legs and spread them wide. In the next second, his mouth was on me, and my brain short-circuited when he hummed against my clit.

Ruf worshiped me with his mouth and fingers for what seemed like decades until I finally came again with a shout. I couldn't imagine what I looked like at this point - sweaty, mindless, my hair knotted around my face from moving it back and forth on the pillow, but I didn't care. My entire body was singing after two mind-blowing orgasms. The only thing I could think to do was to make him feel as good as he'd made me feel.

I used the grip I'd found in his hair to pull his mouth off of me and tugged at him to pull him back up my body. Ruf followed my lead and kissed his way up my stomach and then caught my nipple in his mouth while his fingers tweaked the other. As much as I loved the feel of his mouth on me, I pushed him away and smiled when he looked at me in question.

"My turn," I said as I pushed him to lay on his back.

He laughed and let me move him, but then his laughter turned into a loud shout when I took him into my mouth and did my very best to make him feel just as out of control as he'd made me. I remembered exactly what he liked when we were younger and worked him into a frenzy, loving the way he chanted my name between moans and groans as he held my hair in his hands.

When I knew he was so close that his own orgasm was inevitable, I reared up and threw my leg over his hips and sank down onto him. His hands came up to my breasts as I ran my own hands up the hard planes of his stomach and his chest until I rested them on either side of his head and gave him a long kiss as I slowly worked my hips up and down on his cock.

"Killing me," Ruf moaned between kisses. He panted as I slowly brought him back to the pinnacle, and when I knew he couldn't take much more, I pushed myself up and took him deep within me. I watched his face as I rode him to orgasm and found myself following along with him one more time.

By the time I collapsed against his chest, we were both exhausted and sweaty, and I fought back a yawn as Ruf ran his hands up and down my back. His hands slowed, and right before his breathing evened out in a sated sleep, he murmured, "Love you, my Bonbon."

It felt like coming home.

I tapped on my sister's office door and waited for her to hang up the phone before I walked inside and sat in the chair in front of her desk.

"Hey. I'm glad you could make it on such short notice," Trinity said as she leaned back to relax in her chair.

"It helps that my attorney didn't call to tell me she needed to see me; Petra sent it via text in their family thread and *three* of my bosses told me I needed to leave work early to meet with her."

"That's convenient, I suppose. You don't have to try and explain why you need to cut out early."

"I guess Petra's still with another client, but I'm glad we get to chat," I told my sister.

"Me too. How are you doing?"

"I'm in love."

"I'm not sure you ever stopped loving each other," Trinity said with a sly smile.

"You already heard that Ruf and I are together?"

"Of course."

"Well, so much for breaking the big news. But I do have something else to talk to you about."

"Oh, no you don't. Can't just gloss over the good stuff. Tell me how you're dealing with suddenly becoming the mother figure to a wild little hellion and a sweet baby who will probably end up a wild little hellion."

"Koda isn't a hellion! He's a sweetheart."

"You really are all in. You already have the mom blinders on and everything," Trinity teased.

"He's a little wild, but he's got a heart of gold. I'm head over heels for that boy."

"Good. I adore him too. And Star is just a squishy little bundle of goodness, so who wouldn't be in love with her?"

"Exactly."

"I was there when Ruf met with Cadence."

"You were?"

"Yeah. He called to see who could come help him, and I answered. When I found out that it involved Ripley, I made some excuse about being a witness or taking notes - I can't remember which - and they took me with them."

"How did it go?"

"Well, none of us are in prison for choking the life out of that worthless bag of blood and bones, and Ruf has a beautiful daughter, so I'd say it went well."

"There's also the fact that she's going to be gone for a very long time."

"I've been tracking her case. She signed a plea agreement for thirty years on the state charges. The others are federal, and she hasn't been to trial for them yet."

"Good. Maybe she'll die in prison."

"One can dream, can't they?"

"That was a horrible thing for me to say out loud," I admitted.

"But we were both thinking about it."

"Since we're both feeling a little feisty, do you want to go to lunch with me and be a mean girl?"

"Do you have a target in mind, or are we talking in general?" Trinity asked with a grin.

I explained what Koda had heard and my conversation with Tori and Martha, and Trinity was immediately all in. "Are we going to eat lunch *while* we torture them or after?"

I burst out laughing and said, "I thought we'd multitask and do both at the same time. Apparently, they belong to a group of friends that meet for lunch now and then, and I just so happen to know when that next get-together is going to be. I'm going to invite Rain and Rylee to come with us."

"If that's the case, then we're definitely going to need legal representation," Trinity said with a bark of laughter. "Good thing you've already got an attorney and I just so happen to be good friends with her too."

"I'm usually not much for drama, but I think these women should understand that talking shit about children is unacceptable."

"Remember that time Mom went toe-to-toe with my band director for talking shit about me?" Trinity asked.

"I do. That was the first time I saw Mom lose her shit. She poked that woman in the chest so hard she's probably still got a bruise."

"And just think - now you're gonna be the mom and have to deal with things like that."

"Koda is definitely going to give us all a run for our money, that's for sure."

"But you'll have the Forresters at your back, so you're set if you have to go to war for him."

"True."

"Petra is ready for you, Jovi," Ebbie Conner said from the doorway.

"Thanks, Ebbie," I said as I stood up. I smiled at my sister and said, "Wish me luck."

"It's going to be okay," Trinity said with a frown.

I didn't take time to ask her what she meant because I knew it wasn't her place to tell me. Instead, I said, "I'll let you know when we're going to meet for lunch."

"Sounds like a plan," Trinity said as I walked out.

I turned to the right and walked down to Petra's office and then tapped on the doorframe when I found her looking down at her phone. She smiled and waved me inside as she asked, "Will you shut the door behind you, please?"

"I'm worried," I said as I pushed the door closed and then walked over to sit in the chair in front of Petra's desk. "What's going on?"

"Rodney's attorney contacted me this morning and proposed a settlement."

"And?"

"I'm going to present it to you and go forward however you choose."

"What's the proposal?"

"He's offering a large sum of money and the house, free and clear."

"No."

"The amount he's . . ."

"No."

"Even if you just get the house, it would . . ."

"No, Petra. No money. No house. No smile and sweep this under the rug bullshit. I want my day in court, I want this to be on his record, and then I never want to see or hear from him again."

"That's my girl," Petra said with a grin.

"What happens now?"

"I call his attorney back with your response, and then we wait for your day in court."

"Do you need me to do anything in the meantime?"

"No. Just keep being you and living your life."

"I can finally say it's my best life," I admitted. "I'm living the dream."

"Good for you, Jovi. I'm happy to see you smiling, but I'm even happier to see the fire in your eyes. Life with Ruf is good for you."

"Better than you can even imagine."

EIGHTEEN

"There are *so many buttons!*"

Koda

RUF

"This is harder than it looks," I heard my son say as I walked through the front door. "No! Don't look at me while you're talking! You're gonna huff and puff, and my card tower will fall down!"

"Okay, I ordered what we'll need to . . ."

"Well, shit!" Koda yelled as I walked around the corner. He slapped the table as the playing cards scattered and said, "Son of a bitch!"

"Boy, what have I told you about that mouth?"

Koda sighed and then frowned at me. "That I'm not gonna get another warning."

"Class A misdemeanor," I said as I dropped a kiss on Jovi's cheek and patted her ass with my free hand. I set the car seat on the table, and Jovi smiled up at me before she started unstrapping Star from her car seat. "No bike ride, buddy."

"But, Dad! It's been so long, and I . . ."

"Them's the rules, player. You gotta learn to control that mouth."

"You just got the bike back, and it's been forever!"

263

"And you've been cussing like a sailor all week. Merida put you in the naughty spot three times, and I've gotten onto you at least four. Enough is enough."

"But, Dad . . ."

"I wanted to take a ride just as much as you did, so we're both being punished for your language. Think about that," I said as I pulled my phone to text my brothers. I heard motorcycles outside and realized it was too late to cancel and glanced toward the front door.

"You should still go for a ride with the guys," Jovi encouraged. "You finally got your bike back, and I know you've missed it."

"I don't want to leave you here alone with both kids, Bonbon."

"Are we doing this or not because taking care of both kids is what I signed up for," Jovi said with a pointed look.

The past two weeks had been blissful since Jovi and I had rekindled our relationship, and I knew she was probably as exhausted as I was. We had easily fallen into a pattern that was the kind of domestic bliss I'd never even aspired to and reminded me a lot of what my parents had together.

Every morning while she was in the shower, I'd get up and feed Star and then make a pot of coffee while Jovi got ready for her day at work. After a few cups of coffee while we entertained Star, who was growing by leaps and bounds and much more alert and aware now, Jovi would make breakfast while I got Koda up and ready for daycare. Once she was ready to leave, I got a kiss from my woman before I kissed my little girl goodbye for the day. Jovi would drop Star off at my parents' house on the way to work. After I saw Koda off, I would do my morning routine and then go to work. Afternoons were the opposite, and I picked up Star on my way home while Jovi started dinner and got Koda settled after his day away from home. After dinner, we worked together to clean the kitchen and take care of other household chores while we took turns caring for Star and spending time with Koda.

Last weekend had been a whirlwind of activity with a family dinner at my parents on Friday and then a cookout at the clubhouse on Saturday. Sunday was one of the best days I'd had in years, spent at home relaxing with Jovi and the kids while we got ready to do it all again this week.

Even as much as I had enjoyed the last two weeks with Jovi, I had been looking forward to today because I finally had my motorcycle back and was dying to take a long ride. Since Koda had missed it almost as much as I had, we'd planned to go for a ride together, but now that wasn't going to happen, and I was almost as upset about it as my son.

"Are you sure you don't mind?"

"Honey, you need time alone to recharge. Take that time this evening and hang out with the guys. I'm going to have my time with True and Lana tomorrow afternoon while you're here with the kids."

"And then tomorrow night will be me and you," I reminded her as I pulled her into my arms with Star between us.

"Exactly," Jovi said with a wicked grin. "Tori is way too excited about keeping Star overnight. I think it's making my brother paranoid."

"Why?"

"She's got baby fever."

"Oh shit!" I laughed and said, "It's a good thing you don't have that. I'm not sure how we'd handle having you pregnant while Star's this young."

"I'll have them remove my IUD when she's a year-and-a-half old so I can hopefully get pregnant and have a baby by the time she's three." I felt my heart begin to beat so fast it made me dizzy. Jovi burst out laughing before she said, "God, if you could see your face right now! That's hilarious."

I watched Jovi strap Star into her bouncy seat that we'd left on the table after our coffee this morning and realized that watching Jovi kiss Star made my heart slow to a steady rhythm. The little girl who had surprised me by taking over my heart had done the same for Jovi. Watching Jovi interact with Koda and Star warmed my heart, but the thought of her doing the same thing with a baby that was a little bit me and a little bit her made it race.

That was crazy since a month ago I was wondering how in the hell I would be able to handle having two children. Now I was excited to imagine having even more.

"I missed you, sweet girl," Jovi said as she smiled down at Star who was staring up at her with wide eyes. "Who's my sweet baby?" Jovi made kissing noises as she toyed with Star's foot and then said, "I love you so much."

"How much do you love me?" Koda asked quietly. He still had a frown on his face from the upset of missing his bike ride but couldn't resist the game he and Jovi had started playing soon after she moved in.

"I love you more than I love Hershey's syrup on vanilla ice cream."

"I love you more than . . . noodles in my spaghetti."

"I love *you* more than the center of a cinnamon roll."

266

"Ooh. Cinnamon rolls," Koda mumbled dreamily.

Jovi walked around the table and leaned over the back of Koda's chair. She wrapped her arms around him and leaned down to kiss him on the cheek before she asked, "Want me to make you cinnamon rolls for breakfast on Sunday morning?"

"I want some for dinner!"

"They take too much time to have them for dinner, and we've got breakfast at the diner in the morning, so I'll put them together tomorrow evening for you to have on Sunday morning as we start our lazy day."

"You're my number one mama, Jovi," Koda said sweetly.

I saw tears fill Jovi's eyes before she reached out and ruffled his hair. "I'm the luckiest woman on earth to have you in my life, Koda Bear. You're my number one sweetheart."

There was a knock on the door, and the sweet moment was interrupted when Jovi looked my way. "I bet those are your friends here to see if you can go outside and play."

Just then, the front door opened and Jonas called out, "Honey, I'm home!"

Jovi laughed and called back, "You've got the wrong house!"

"No, I don't. It smells so good, I think I'm going to move in," Lawson said as he walked through the doorway. "Koda, are you ready to ride?"

"I can't," Koda said petulantly. "I'm on house

arrest."

"Misdemeanor or felony?"

"Misdemeanor," Koda said before he sighed. "Stache kept saying my mouth was gonna get me in trouble someday. I guess she was right."

"Cussing?" Jonas asked. When Koda nodded, Jonas shook his head and said, "That sucks, little dude. Do better."

"Your brothers stopped at Brawley's to see if he can join us," Lawson explained.

"Y'all have fun. I'm making chicken and dumplings for dinner, and it'll be ready when you come back."

"When you get sick of this clown, you're welcome to move back in with me," Jonas said as he threw his arm over Jovi's shoulder. "I do love your cooking."

"She's our Jovi now, and you can't have her back!" Koda said with a glare. He looked at me with wide eyes and motioned toward Jonas, as if asking me to jump in as backup before he said, "Right, Dad?"

"Never gonna happen, Jonas. I'm sort of attached to this crew," Jovi said as she rested her hand on Koda's back. "I'm not going anywhere."

Koda looked relieved and then raised his eyebrows at Jonas causing all of us to laugh.

"You're sure you don't want me to stay?" I asked.

Koda gave me a pleading look as he begged, "Please let me go, Dad. I promise I'll do better."

"Can't do it, son. You had more than enough warnings this week and I told you this was gonna happen if you didn't watch out." Koda hopped up from the table and walked out of the room with a huff. "Don't leave it like this."

"Sorry," Koda said before he turned around and gave me a hug. "Love you. Ride safe."

As Koda walked out of the kitchen, I said, "Love you, too, bud."

I pulled Jovi into my arms and gave her a kiss. "He'll be fine. I'll go check on him in a few minutes."

"I know you will." I kissed her again and then smiled down at her. "Call if you need me, and I'll pull over and call you back."

"Love you."

"Love you, too, Bonbon."

JOVI

"Look at you being all domestic and shit," True said with a grin. She lifted Star up to her shoulder to burp her and patted her on the back as she said, "You're definitely in your element."

"I feel like it."

"You're happier than I've seen you in years."

"I am. It feels right, you know?" I pulled another of Star's blankets out of the basket and folded it before I added it to the growing pile on the kitchen table. "Koda insists that I'm his mom now, and every time he says that, it makes my heart feel ready to burst with happiness."

"Speaking of Koda, when do you think he's gonna get over his snit?"

"I don't know," I said as I glanced toward the doorway. Koda had been angry after he watched Ruf and the guys ride away and stomped around the house until I told him he should go think about why he was in trouble and make a plan to change things so it didn't happen again. "I should go check on him. He's been in his room a while."

"Did you ever think this was how our Friday nights would be?" True asked. She burst out laughing and said, "Don't answer that. Of course you did, you just didn't think this was the path that would get you there. You've always dreamed of being a domestic goddess mama bear and here you are."

"Domestic goddess mama bear. I need that on a shirt," I said with a laugh as I stacked the folded laundry back into the basket. "I'm gonna go put this stuff in the nursery and then check on Koda. I'll be right back."

"She's snoozing, so I'll follow you in and lay her down."

I walked into the nursery and put away clean laundry while True patted Star's back to get her settled in her crib. I nodded at my friend before I left the room to see about Koda, but she didn't see me because she was staring dreamily down at the sleeping baby.

It looked like I wasn't the only one with fantasies of motherhood, but there was no way I'd voice that out loud to True because she'd just argue. Instead, I went upstairs and tapped on Koda's door. When he didn't answer, I took a chance and opened the door, guessing that he had either fallen asleep or turned his snit into the silent treatment.

I was shocked when I found the room empty. I

walked to the top of the stairs and called his name and then waited patiently for him to answer. When he didn't, my heart started racing as I spun around to check the other bedrooms. I glanced into the bathroom, the room I had used when I first moved in, and then the weight room that Ruf used every morning.

Koda wasn't upstairs, so I jogged down the stairs and almost bumped into True at the bottom. "Koda's not in his room."

"Where did he go?"

I shrugged and called his name again. When he didn't answer, True said, "I'll check the rooms down here."

"I'll go outside."

I went out back and looked around as I called his name. I even squatted down so I could see into the house he and the other kids had been building together. When there was no sign of him in the backyard, I ran through the house and met up with True in the living room.

"He's not anywhere down here."

"He's not out back. Double-check upstairs while I look out front. If he's not there, I'll go to Ripley's and get them to start helping me search."

"We should call 911."

"Let me check Rip's first," I called out as I jogged down the front steps.

I started calling his name, my voice frantic with fear, and I heard Tori, my brother's girlfriend, yell, "What's wrong?"

"Koda's missing!"

"Shit. Did you call 911?"

"He's not with Scoot?"

"She's staying with your parents tonight." Tori jogged down the stairs and said, "I'll check Sadie's and see if he went to visit Ruthie."

"I'll go down to Brighten's and check with Griff."

"He's not in the house!" True called out from behind me as I started running toward Brighten's.

"Call 911! He must have run away!" When I got to Brighten's, I rang the bell and banged on the door, but no one answered, so I went next door to Crow's and did the same. Crow's cranky neighbor walked out onto her porch and watched me, so I jogged across the grass and asked, "Have you seen a little boy? His name is Koda, and he's missing."

"The Forrester boy?" the woman asked.

"Yes. I can't find him and . . ."

"Let me check my backyard and then I'll go down that street, door to door. You can go down that one and come up the other side."

"Okay," I said as I changed course and ran across the street. I banged on Jason and Stone Marks' door, and when Jason answered, he instantly knew that something was wrong. "Koda's missing."

"Shit. I'll take the other side of the street, you go down this one." Over his shoulder, he called out to his brother, "Spawn is missing. Come on!"

I heard Stone's voice behind me as I sprinted across

272

the grass to the neighbor's. No one answered, so I kept going until I found another neighbor and then another. I could hear sirens in the distance when Ruf's cousin Roar Forrester opened his door. I told him what was going on and asked him to call Ruf as I kept going from neighbor to neighbor.

He picked his daughter up and hurried down the stairs beside me with his phone to his ear as he said, "We'll check the park."

As two police cars passed me on the street, I heard Rain Forrester calling my name from the other end of the block.

"Did you check behind the garage?"

"What?" I asked.

"In the backyard!"

"I looked in the yard. I even looked in his house."

"Behind the garage!" Rain said before she took off running toward Ruf's with Lucky right behind her.

I'd been running so long that I had a stitch in my side and couldn't catch my breath, but I powered through and ran as fast as I could to catch up with Rain. I could see True standing on Ruf's porch with Star in her arms as she talked to two officers I didn't recognize and watched as Rain turned left along the side of the house toward the fence. I was crossing the grass, wondering why in the world she didn't go through the house when she put her hands at the top of the picket fence and scaled it as if she'd done it a million times before.

I knew I couldn't do that even if I had a ladder and a trampoline, so I ran past the police officers into the house with True calling my name behind me. I had just run through the back door and onto the patio when Rain appeared from around the back of the garage with Koda sleeping in her arms.

"Oh my God!" I yelled as I burst into tears. Without even thinking, I took him out of her arms and clutched him to me before I fell to my knees in the grass.

"I'll go tell everyone we found him," Rain said, patting my shoulder as she passed me.

"What's wrong, Jovi?" Koda mumbled before he rubbed his eyes. "Why are you crying?"

"I thought I lost you."

"I was playing with my trucks."

"I thought you ran away. I looked everywhere," I said through my tears.

"I can't leave the yard unless I tell my dad first," Koda said as he reached up and wiped the tears off my cheeks. He held his hands there and stared up at me as he said, "I'd never leave you, Jovi. You're my new mama."

I heard motorcycles out front and then Ruf's voice in the house, but I didn't have the strength to turn around and look. I still hadn't caught my breath from my sprint around the neighborhood, and my heart was racing from the terror I'd felt at the thought of losing Koda.

"Please don't cry, Jovi. I'm sorry."

"You didn't do anything wrong, bud," I heard Ruf say from behind me. I looked up as he dropped to his knees in front of me on the grass, and when he smiled at me, I sobbed. He quietly tried to soothe me by saying, "It's okay, Bonbon. Koda's right here."

"I thought I lost him, and it scared me to death!" I wailed.

By now, Koda was crying, too, probably just because I was so emotional. Ruf pulled us both into his arms, murmuring that everything was going to be okay as he tried to get us to calm down.

After a few minutes, my breathing slowed, and I was finally able to calm down. I leaned back so I could look at Ruf and said, "I looked everywhere but never thought about going behind the garage!" I looked at Koda and asked, "Didn't you hear us calling for you?"

Koda shook his head as Ruf said, "He falls asleep in random places all the time, Bonbon, and he can sleep through anything. I'm sorry, but I thought you knew that."

"That's why he makes me take a shower because he's afraid I'll fall asleep and drown in the bath." Ruf shrugged, and Koda rolled his eyes and said, "I'm not gonna do that."

"I feel like an idiot," I muttered.

"Don't. There's no reason to beat yourself up about it. When he was a toddler, I lost him behind the damn couch of all places. My mom couldn't find him once, and he was sleeping underneath her bed, and Gamma found him sleeping in her pantry one afternoon."

"That's why Dad lets me stay up as late as I want to on the weekends. I sleep when I'm tired."

"And I know that he's gonna pass out somewhere in the house when he gets tired enough," Ruf said with a shrug. "That's just his thing."

"I'm sorry I scared you, Jovi."

"It's not your fault, Koda Bear. I'm sorry I freaked out."

"Let me go deal with the cops," Ruf said as he stood up.

"You called the cops on me?" Koda asked in outrage. When I nodded, he looked up at Ruf in horror. "Code Blue, Dad!"

"Come on, bud. Maybe they're newbies and they'll let you see the inside of their car."

"Newbies?"

"The ones who've met him won't let him anywhere near their patrol cars," Ruf explained.

"There are *so many buttons!*" Koda said as he bounced up and down in excitement. He reached for my hand and tried to pull me up off the grass as he said, "C'mon. Let's go!"

"I'm not sure my heart can handle much more of this parenting thing," I admitted as I followed Koda into the house.

"You reacted like any parent would, Bonbon."

"I don't think I'm very good at this. What's gonna happen when Star gets older or we have kids of our own and there's more than one to keep track of?"

"Jovi, you've been living in a house with Grade A Forrester spawn for a month now. If you can handle Koda adventures, you're a gold star veteran. Ask anybody."

NINETEEN

"Oh, damn. Did I do that?"

Jonas

JOVI

"I bet you really needed this after what happened last night," Lana said as she adjusted the massage chair next to mine. I looked down at the tub where my feet were soaking in blissfully warm water and nodded at the aesthetician when she asked if it was okay, before Lana asked, "Have you recovered yet?"

"I thought I was gonna have a heart attack. I lost him, Lana."

"You didn't really lose him. The boy is a wild one, but he obeys the rules . . ."

"Most of the time," True interrupted from my other side.

"I was terrified."

"I can imagine," Lana commiserated. "It's okay, though. Now you know another of his random places."

"When I was talking to Rain last night, she said he fell asleep in her bathtub once. Thank God the water wasn't on."

"Is he narcoleptic?" True asked.

"I don't think so. He just goes to sleep when he's tired, and it doesn't matter where. When I talked to Martha at the diner this morning, she told me that he was playing hide-and-seek with Smokey and fell asleep in the pantry. Scared the shit out of them." The three of us laughed, and I added, "Now that I think about it, I've noticed him disappearing before but didn't think much of it because if I asked where he was, Ruf would just tell me he was napping."

"Well, now you know to look *everywhere*, especially where you think it would be crazy to fall asleep."

"Watching him fluster those police officers yesterday was hilarious. He pushed so many buttons that they couldn't figure out how to turn everything off for at least ten minutes."

"I bet that was funny," Lana mused.

"Brawley had been riding with the guys and didn't warn them that was going to happen. I guess they're new."

"He said it's a rite of passage for every cop that meets Koda," True added with a laugh. "Poor guys."

"Well, it's been two weeks now. What's the update on where this is going?"

"Where what is going? Me and Ruf?"

"Yeah," Lana said with a nod. "Forever, right?"

"Yes," I said firmly. Then I admitted, "Although I'm terrified of being a parent, I think that has more to do with walking into an established relationship between Ruf and Koda. I'm not nearly as afraid of taking care of Star."

"Because she's new. She'll never remember a time when she didn't know you as her mom."

"That's what you're going to be," True said knowingly. "When you're all in about something, you're *all in,* Jovi. Whether it's your plans to go to school and become a nurse practitioner or becoming the best mom on the planet, I've got faith that you'll succeed."

"I do too," Lana assured me.

Suddenly, I became choked up and had to sniff back tears as I admitted, "I missed y'all so much."

"We missed you too," True said sadly. "Even though we saw each other every day in the office, it wasn't the same as before you met Rodney."

"It happened so gradually that I just woke up one day and realized that I hadn't spent any time with you in months. I had no idea how to fix it."

"It was up to me to fix it, Lana."

"And how is that going?"

"I had another meeting with Petra yesterday because Rodney's attorney sent over another offer, which I declined. I want this to go to court and Petra said his attorney is running scared because he knows we're going to win."

"Good. Did you hear what Jewel did?"

"No, what?" I asked Lana.

"She had Connie reschedule all of the appointments so we can all be there on your day in court."

"You're kidding!"

"Nope," True said with a grin. When Petra was in the office the other day, I heard Terran tell her to find a reason to put him and Spruce on the stand so they could defend your honor. She said she had it all planned out. Jewel's going to get up and speak too."

"So are Amy and Roscoe," Lana added. "My mom wants to testify too."

"That way it won't just be a nurse against a surgeon. It will be *multiple* doctors standing up for the nurse against the surgeon."

"Holy shit," I whispered. "I had no idea."

Lana laughed as she told me, "Spruce walked out of his office with banana bread crumbs all over his shirt, pointed at Petra and said, 'Do whatever nefarious shit you have to and win Jovi's case because she *finally* started baking again now that she's happy.'"

"Yesterday, he got onto me for baking so often and told me I was bad for his health," I said through my laughter. "Of course, he said that right before he walked off carrying a handful of cookies . . ."

"Gamma told my mom that you are the best thing that's ever happened to Koda and Ruf. She swears Koda has grown an inch since you moved in, and she's positive it's because they've finally got someone cooking them decent food."

"The freezer is full of frozen meals she's been sending him for God knows how long!"

True scoffed, "Take that compliment and run with it, honey. That's the Gamma stamp of approval, and believe me, those don't come easy for outsiders."

Lana laughed before she said, "She's not an outsider anymore. She's family."

The thought of that made me happier than I could

have ever thought possible. I had a family of my own with a gorgeous, wonderful man, a little boy who held my heart in his hands, and a baby girl I couldn't live without.

Life was good.

"I promise I won't move anything too heavy, but I want to go through some of the boxes and make a pile for donations. We don't need duplicates of things you already have, and there's no sense in moving it twice when we can drop the donations off as we're on the way home."

"I love that you call it 'home' now," Ruf said through the car speakers as I pulled into Jonas' driveway. "I just left Mom and Dad's, and I'm going to run home and get my bike before I come to help, okay?"

"Do we get to go for a ride today?"

"Yeah, the guys asked if we wanted to join them on a run around the lake, but you and I are going to break off later and go for a ride alone."

"And why is that?"

"I haven't been able to think of anything else since you promised we were going to revisit that situation, Bonbon."

"You want me to give you a handjob while we're riding? Do you think that's safe?"

"I don't know. I'm getting kind of dizzy just thinking about it. It might make me pass out, and then what?"

"Why don't we go for a ride and find a deserted road out in the country, and I'll do one better and give you a mind-altering blowjob instead?"

"God, I love you."

"We'll see if you still feel that way after you move the picnic bench out onto the patio so we can put the new table me and the girls picked out in the kitchen."

"I just got over the three million pillows you insist need to go on the bed every morning, Bonbon. What are you doing to me?"

"I compromised on the dining room, Ruf," I reminded him.

"I know," he mumbled. "Okay, I'm pulling up to the house, and the guys are already waiting for me. I'll see you in just a bit. Love you."

"Love you too."

I found my earbuds and then left my purse in the passenger seat when I got out of the car. Once I had them in my ears, I turned on my favorite podcast and then slipped my phone into my back pocket. The codes to the gate and garage door were simple, so it didn't take long to get inside and start sorting through the boxes of my things that I had taken way too long to deal with.

Within just a few minutes, I was engrossed in the true crime story I'd been waiting for all week. It didn't take me long to sort through the first box and get to work on the next one. I started piles for donation, put a few things aside that I would want in storage, and was holding up a throw blanket when I got a peculiar feeling that I was being watched. I shook the feeling off, blaming it on the creepy podcast, but then felt the sensation again just as I got a faint whiff of whiskey.

I spun around and came face to face with Rodney. Before I could scream, he wrapped me into the blanket I'd been holding, leaving my arms useless so that I couldn't defend myself. For the first few seconds, I was paralyzed with fear, which put me at a disadvantage, but then I was engulfed by a rage so powerful that it gave me a strength I had no idea I possessed.

I leaned my head back to look into Rodney's face and was shocked by his sneer. It made me wonder how I'd spent so long with a man who was nothing more than a selfish monster who always had to get his way. I set that thought aside to ponder later, and without hesitating, slammed my forehead into his face. I felt the cartilage in his nose crunch right before I was sprayed with blood that burned my eyes and had me reeling as he suddenly let go of me.

The blanket fell away, and I was able to wipe my eyes just enough to see Rodney bent over with his hands on his face. I used my back foot to push off from the ground and jammed my knee upward, catching his face again and causing him to rear up with a shout. I stepped back and pushed off again, but this time, I kicked and let out a roar as my foot landed right in Rodney's groin.

He sucked in a deep breath as he jackknifed forward and started choking on the blood streaming down his face. I kicked once more and got him in the side of the head this time. I was trying to catch my balance when I heard the roar of a motorcycle nearby. In the split second I took my eyes off of Rodney to glance out at the driveway, he swung wildly and landed a punch on the side of my face. My cheek exploded with pain, and I spun around. I wasn't able to get my arms out in time to stop myself from slamming into the tool bench beside me.

I heard a loud roar right before there was a sharp pain

on the side of my head and everything went black.

I followed Jonas around the corner and looked to the side when he motioned toward a sedan that was parked in front of his neighbor's house. I couldn't hear him over the pipes, but I knew exactly what he was trying to tell me by the look on his face. I shot ahead of him and turned into the driveway, but before I had a chance to engage the brake to look around, I saw Jovi go flying and then collapse on the ground.

Without thinking, I twisted the throttle and aimed my bike at the son of a bitch who had just hit my woman. He had just enough time to spin around and look at me before I pulled the brake and yanked the handlebars to the side, a move I knew would make my rear tire spin on the gravel and swing around dangerously.

Rodney flew to the side, propelled by my motorcycle. It sputtered out right before I ended up facing the mouth of the driveway and my brothers and friends who were all jumping off their own motorcycles. I put my boot on the ground and felt something soft beneath it and looked down to see Rodney's hand beneath my heel. I suddenly realized that he was pinned between my motorcycle and the frame of the garage door, and rather than drop the kickstand, I stood up and swung my leg over the back of the bike as I pushed it away from me so that it would fall on him.

Rodney let out an agonized scream and then sucked in a breath and screamed again as he pushed at the motorcycle to get it off his chest.

"Does that burn, motherfucker?" I growled before I turned and went to check on Jovi. Ransome was already on

284

his knees beside her, and as I dropped down beside him, Jovi's eyes fluttered open. Her entire body tensed, and she tried to scoot away, but I put my hands on her shoulders and leaned over her. "It's okay, Bonbon. I'm here. It's okay."

"Rodney . . ." Jovi's eyes got wide when Rodney screamed again, and she tried to look around me to see what was going on, but I blocked her view.

"I guess we oughta get that off him," Ransome said as he took in the scene behind us.

"Don't try too hard," I ordered.

"Didn't plan on it," Ransome said before he patted Jovi on the arm and stood up.

"Let me up," Jovi said before she swallowed hard. She took a deep breath before she said, "Please, Ruf, help me . . ."

"I don't know how you're injured, Bonbon. You're covered in blood. Be still until the paramedics get here."

"I don't think it's my blood," Jovi said as she grabbed my arm and pulled herself up.

I realized that Rodney had stopped screaming and glanced over my shoulder to find Jonas, Lawson, and my brothers pulling the bike off of him. Ransome saw me watching and said, "He's out."

"Dead?" I asked.

Ransome sighed heavily and shook his head before he said, "No."

I wanted to get up and make that happen, but I knew I couldn't do anything with Jovi sitting here, so I filed it away for another day and turned back to her. She was sitting in front of me, using the tips of her fingers to gently touch her cheek. She wiggled her jaw and whispered, "Not broken. Just bruised."

I moved her hair back from her face and said, "You've got a goose egg on your temple."

"Hit the tool bench," Jovi muttered as she tilted her head to the left and then right. "Probably a concussion."

"Lay down, and we'll get the paramedics to take you to the ER so they can . . ."

"Where's Rodney?"

"I hit him with my bike," I said without any remorse.

"You . . . hit him?"

"Yep."

"Is he dead?"

"Hopefully," I muttered as I turned my head to see what progress the guys had made. I could tell by Rodney's color that he was still alive and saw his eyes open and then close again. "No. He's alive."

"Are they . . ." I felt Jovi move, and by the time I turned back to look at her, she was peering around me. "What is that . . . His shirt is . . . Is he burned?"

"Tailpipes."

"Oh shit," Jovi whispered. She chuckled for a second and then said, "That's fucking ironic, isn't it?" She started to get up, but I held her still until she shook her head. "Let me up, Ruf. I need to check on him."

"The hell you do! He hurt you!"

"This time, he didn't hurt me nearly as much as I hurt him," Jovi mumbled before she scrambled toward Rodney. I sat there in shock as she reached out and felt for his pulse and then started to assess his wounds.

"You're gonna fucking help him?" Jonas yelled.

Jovi said something that made him throw his head back with a bark of laughter, and I saw my brothers start grinning.

"What did she say?" I asked as I started their way.

"I said that living with burns like this makes you want to die, and I want him to experience every goddamn second of it!" After a few seconds, she asked, "Did anyone call 911?"

"Shit. One of us should do that," Rocky said with a shrug.

"Yeah. One of us should get right on that," Ransome said as he nodded and looked around at the group of men. "You want to Jonas?"

"Nah. My phone's in my pocket."

"So is mine."

"Hell, I'll do it," Rocky said as he pulled his phone out. "What's the number again?"

Jonas burst out laughing, and Jovi glared at him before she yelled, "Call 911 right now, Rocky!"

"Yes, ma'am," Rocky said with a grin before he dialed and put the phone up to his ear.

"You fucked your bike up, brother," Ransome said with a sigh when I stepped up next to him. "Engine's probably fine, but we're gonna have to shine up the chrome. Probably has a few scratches too."

"Well, shit," I muttered as I looked at my motorcycle that was laying on its side in the middle of the garage. "I've been thinking about a new paint job, though, so I guess this is as good a time as any."

"What color are you thinking?"

"Are you fucking kidding right now?" Jovi snapped.

"Bonbon, you've got a much bigger heart than any of us, so I'm not exactly sure what you expect right now."

"At least pretend you give a shit if he lives or dies. That's gonna go a long way when the cops get here and start questioning you."

"She has a point there," Jonas said as he looked down at Rodney. "Is he right-handed?"

"What?" Jovi asked.

"Is he right- or left-handed?"

"Right."

"That sucks. I think his hand might be broken," Jonas said before he stomped on Rodney's hand that was lying next to his boot. I saw him grind his heel down before he said, "Damn. Did I do that?"

Jovi looked up at him and bit back a grin before she said, "That wasn't very nice, Jonas Dean."

"Oops," he said with a shrug before he glanced at Rodney's hand and winced. "That's gonna leave a mark."

"Not as much as those burns on his chest," Ransome said with a grin. "Did you know that a hot tailpipe can range from 700 to 1400 degrees?"

"I didn't, but now he does," I said honestly. "I wonder how hot boiling noodles get."

"A rolling boil for water is 212 degrees," Jonas answered.

"How the hell do you know that?" Jovi asked.

"Hank got me hooked on Jeopardy as a kid."

"You still watch that?" I asked as an ambulance stopped at the end of the driveway. "I guess Rocky finally remembered how to use his phone."

"I've kind of got a thing for Amy Farrah Fowler," Jonas said with a shrug.

"Put your game faces on, boys," Jovi said and promptly burst into tears. I could barely understand her through her sobs as she explained what had happened to the officer that rushed up the driveway with the paramedics. I reached out to help her up and then tucked her under my arm as she said, "I don't know what would have happened if they hadn't gotten here when they did."

I turned her to face me so she could sob into my chest and made sure the officer could see how distraught I was at the horrible thing that had just happened, which was difficult to do since I was trying very hard not to smile.

TWENTY

> "Someday when I'm really old, I'll find a girl that loves Legos and motorcycles and can cook as good as my Gamma. I'll dance with her in the rain, and we'll be married."

Koda

JOVI

"You're off work for a week, and then I'll reassess," Terran said as he put his penlight back in his shirt pocket. "Call the office and make an appointment for next Monday, and make sure you bring a loaf of banana bread for me, please."

"But I . . ."

"I'm not going to share with my brother because he tears off chunks like the caveman that he is instead of using a knife like a normal human being."

"That's true," Jewel agreed from the other side of the bed.

"I can work, though," I argued.

"You look like you got hit in the face," Terran said.

"I did get hit in the face!"

"Exactly."

"What does that . . ." I looked over at Ruf and found

him grinning, so I glared at him and grumbled, "Fine, but I don't know if I have what I need to make banana bread."

"I said you couldn't come to work, but I didn't say you weren't allowed to go to the grocery store," Terran said as he walked toward the door. "I'll get the paperwork started for your release."

"And people say he has no bedside manner," Jewel mused with a smile as she watched her brother leave the room. "I can't imagine why."

"Do I really have to take another week off? The girls are going to hate me for leaving them high and dry."

"Bullshit," Jewel snapped before she shook her head. "They know exactly why you're off and when you'll be back. It's fine."

"Have you talked to Petra?"

"I have. She's on her way here to see you now," Jewel told me before she looked over at Ruf. "And she's going to want to talk to you, too, I'm sure."

I squeezed Ruf's hand, and he smiled at me before he said, "It's going to be okay, Jovi."

"I don't want you to get in any trouble because of me."

"He violated a protective order and assaulted you and a trespass order when he went onto a police officer's property. The DA now realizes they made quite the mistake not pressing charges on the first assault and have decided to reopen the case." I looked up and found Petra smiling as she walked into the room. As she neared Ruf, she put her fist out. Ruf bumped knuckles with her, and she said, "Good job aiming your bike at the guy. When I told my dad about it, he said that your family gives new meaning to the old saying 'drive it like you stole it.'"

Ruf chuckled and said, "I guess all those times me and the guys practiced spinning out on our dirt bikes came in handy."

"Have you heard anything about how Rodney's doing?"

"Not well," Jewel said with an exaggerated wince. "Somehow, his hand was crushed in the *accident,* he's got a broken nose, broken ribs, and severe burns all along his torso and thighs."

"That's gotta hurt," Petra said sarcastically.

"Oh. And one of his testicles ruptured. I don't know how that . . ."

I gasped and said, "I kicked him in the junk!"

"Is that a medical term, Nurse Jovi?" Petra asked through her laughter. "'The junk.' I love it."

Jewel gave Ruf a knowing look and said, "I'd make sure you don't piss this woman off. When she gets to the end of her rope and starts fighting back, she's gonna go for broke."

"Noted," Ruf said with a grin. "I'll make sure I mind my p's and q's."

"You better," I tried to give him a stern look, but it turned into a smile. "I'd never hurt you, Ruf. You're my hero."

"Nah, baby. I just helped. You were doing a fine job of saving yourself when I got there."

"You know the routine, Jovi. Take it easy and give

me a call if you develop any vision problems or dizziness. Be sure to ice it to keep the swelling down and . . ."

I waved my hand and said, "I know."

Jewel turned to Ruf and said, "Walk with me to the nurses' station, and I'll give you a printout of what to do since we've already established that nurses are horrible patients and the absolute worst at taking directions when it comes to caring for themselves."

"Yes, ma'am," Ruf said before he squeezed my hand and followed Jewel out of the room. Over his shoulder, he called out, "You're in trouble now, Bonbon. I get to play doctor."

"Blech," Petra said with a disgusted sneer. She shrugged and said, "Although, I have to admit that he's turned into quite a handsome guy."

"I think so."

"Well, let's get down to business. Do you still want to take Rodney to court, or would you like to hold off and see what happens with the prosecutor?"

"Let's wait and see if he has to pay that way. If not . . ."

"If you don't get justice that way, we'll put things in motion again," Petra promised. "Although, from what I've heard about his injuries, he's feeling that 'eye for an eye' kind of justice right now."

"Will Ruf get in trouble?"

"I'll make sure he doesn't," Petra assured me. "As far as I can tell, they're considering what he did with the motorcycle a measure of defense for you. If they decide to take it another direction, I'll counteract whatever they come up with. Just rest assured that there will be no Forresters paying for the sins of that douchebag."

"Thank you, Petra."

"Are you okay with how things went down this afternoon?"

"Oddly enough, I am. It's hard for me to rationalize how little sympathy I feel for him because at one point, I loved him with all my heart, but looking back, I see that I gave up on him long ago. I was just existing in limbo until he forced my hand."

"Your burns are healed now?"

"They are. Of course, the new skin is very tender, and I have to take special care of it, but I'm going to be fine. Jewel had me visit a plastic surgeon just to get his opinion, but I'm okay with them. They're not really visible outside of my regular clothes." I saw Petra look down at my arm where the skin on the inside of my elbow was pink and new. "That's really the only one you can see, and I'm sort of . . . I don't want to say proud of it, but that's kind of how I feel."

"You went through a dark time and came out a warrior on the other side."

"I did, and now I have the life I always dreamed of."

"Good for you, Jovi. The road took some twists, but you're right where you were meant to be."

"I am."

RUF

"When we have more children, we're going to have to get a bigger bed," Jovi said as she ran her hand over Koda's hair. "I like the snuggles."

"When you wake up in about an hour and feel like you're sleeping in an oven, you'll change your mind," I warned her. "When that happens, I'll carry him to his bedroom."

"No, I'll be fine. He was really upset when he saw my face, and I think he just wants to make sure I'm okay." Jovi took her hand off of Koda and rubbed it over Star's belly. "And then there's this girl who has no idea yet just how lucky she is to have such a great big brother."

"Your brother was pissed when he came over earlier. If Rodney wasn't already going through so much, I think Ripley would have put the hurt on him. He still might."

"That's so weird to me. Rip and I have never been all that close, but he's been different lately."

"Love will do that to a man."

"Thanks for being so understanding with Mom and Dad when they were here. They've both lived through the same sort of thing that Rodney put me through, and I know seeing me in this situation brings back a lot of memories that they've tried their hardest to get past."

"Your sister scared me a little," I admitted.

"Really? How?"

"The way she laughed when she found out about Rodney's balls made the hair on the back of my neck stand up. I've got zero sympathy for that bastard, but I've got balls, and I cringe every time I think of how much that shit must hurt." Jovi giggled, and I winced. "There goes that tingle down my spine again. I didn't realize you could be so vindictive."

"What goes around comes around."

I rubbed my wrist against Jovi's hip when it itched, and she looked down at it before she grabbed it to stare at the tattoo there.

"What's wrong?"

"I probably don't want to know, but whose lips are those?"

I glanced at the tattoo there and smiled at her. "Does that tattoo bother you?"

"No. Yes. Maybe a little. No." I laughed at her indecision and then pulled her hand toward my mouth so I could kiss her knuckles. When I got out of bed, she asked, "Where are you going? I didn't mean to upset you."

"You didn't," I assured her as I walked into the closet and flipped the light on. I pulled a shoe box off the top shelf and sorted through it until I found what I was looking for and then carried the card I'd found over to the bed. I turned on the lamp beside the bed before I handed it to her. "This is what I used for that tattoo."

Jovi took the card from me, and I could see the shock on her face. When she opened it, tears filled her eyes and she said, "Those are my lips."

"Yep. That's the birthday card you gave me right before we broke up. I had Uncle Fain ink your kiss on my wrist so any time I thought of you, I could just look down and remember how it felt when you kissed me."

"That's so sweet, Ruf."

"You thought it was another woman's lips, didn't you?"

"Maybe."

"My girl is jealous," I teased as I took the card back to put it away. I turned the light off and laid back down in bed, snuggling Star close to me when she started wiggling. "No need to be jealous. I'm yours and always have been, even when we were apart."

"I love you, Ruf."

"I love you, too, Bonbon."

"Do you want to go to Scoot's?" Jovi asked Koda as they walked out onto the porch. "You guys can play in the rain together. Maybe she'll even dance with you like I did."

"That's gross!" Koda said in disgust.

"It's just a dance, Koda. You can dance with your sister." Jovi sat on the other end of the porch swing, and Koda climbed up to sit between us and then scooted as close to her as possible.

Since we picked him up from my parents' last night on our way home from the hospital, he'd been glued to Jovi's side. The second he saw the bruise on her face, he burst into tears at the thought of someone hurting his Jovi. No matter how much I assured him that 'the bad man' would never hurt her again, he didn't seem to believe me. I knew it would take a little time, but he'd relax someday, hopefully soon because I really wanted to get close to Jovi and couldn't do that since he'd attached himself to her like a barnacle.

"I'm not gonna marry my sister."

"What does dancing in the rain have to do with marriage?" Jovi asked with a laugh. "I don't get your thought process."

"You only dance in the rain with someone you're going to love forever."

"Oh, really?"

"Yeah. That's what it means. My Stache loves the rain, so my Lettuce makes sure to take her out dancing in it every chance he gets. That's how they got married. They were in the forest in Alaska, and Lettuce danced with her in the rain so they could live happily ever after."

"That's why you were so excited when I was dancing with your father," Jovi said quietly as she looked over at me in shock. "I didn't understand why it was so important or why both of you were so intense about it."

"I've never danced in the rain with anyone but you."

"That's so sweet."

"Someday when I'm really old, I'll find a girl that loves Legos and motorcycles and can cook as good as my gamma. I'll dance with her in the rain, and we'll be married."

"Does this mean we're married?" Jovi asked Koda.

"Not to me, goofball. I danced with you because I'm going to love you forever. You're married to my dad."

"Dance with me, Jovi," I said as I stood up from the swing and held my hand out toward her.

Jovi put her hand in mine and let me pull her out of the swing, and I winked at my son as she walked past me.

"Are you gonna do it?" Koda whispered. When I nodded, his eyes got wide and he started bouncing up and down in excitement. "Holy shit!"

I couldn't even get onto him for his language because that was exactly what was going through my mind right now too. I followed Jovi down the steps and laughed when she tilted her head back and let the rain fall on her face.

"It's beautiful!"

"You're beautiful," I said as I pulled her into my arms.

We danced together for a few minutes as Koda watched us from the porch, and finally, I spun Jovi around and pulled her into my arms. I dipped her back and kissed her before I asked, "Will you marry me, Bonbon?"

Jovi's eyes gleamed, and she nodded, so I kissed her again as I pulled her up to stand. Once she was settled on her feet, I reached into my pocket and pulled out the ring I'd gotten from my mom and then got down on one knee.

"Oh, Ruf," I whispered. "It's beautiful."

"I love you, Jovi. I've always loved you and always will. Will you do me the honor of becoming my wife and the mother to my children?"

"Yes!"

I slipped the ring on her finger and then kissed her knuckles before I stood and pulled her back into my arms.

Jovi rested her hands on my cheeks and stared into my eyes for a second before she said, "You've been my dream man since I was just a kid, and now my dreams are finally coming true."

"Woohoo!" Koda screamed right before he plowed into us and wrapped his arms around my waist. "You're gonna be my mama!"

"I am," Jovi said happily as she let me go and leaned down to hug my son. "And I'm going to love you forever and ever too."

It felt like the piece of me that had been missing for years slipped into place and made me whole again, and I owed it all to the woman who was smiling down at my son with her heart in her eyes. Years apart hadn't dimmed my love for Jovi, and I knew that it hadn't lessened how she felt about me either.

Some things were meant to be, you just had to wait for the right time for dreams to come true.

EPILOGUE

RUF

"Hey, Dad. Where is everybody?" I asked as I walked into the living room. I looked around and realized that someone, probably my mom and sisters, had picked up around the house. I took a deep breath and smelled one of my favorite dishes my gamma made and knew it was probably simmering on the stove. I couldn't wait to get a taste of it. Dad sniffed and then wiggled his nose, but when he tried to lift his hand to scratch it, Star squirmed, so he put it back down. "Do you want me to take one of the kids so you can at least move your arm?"

Dad shook his head as his big hand covered my two-week-old son's back, and then I watched as he kissed the curls on the top of his head.

"You leave them be. You know how I feel about nap time," Dad said with a frown. "Let us sleep."

"Is Jovi in bed?"

"Let her sleep too."

"I'm gonna go take a nap with her," I said as I walked past him. I reached down and ran my hand over Koda's hair and then touched Star's cheek before I rested my hand on Remy's head. I tugged on my dad's beard and said, "Wake me up if you need me."

"Been taking care of babies since before you were even a twinkle in your mom's eye, son. I think I've got this.

Besides, your mom will be back soon. She went down to visit with your sister."

"Thanks for helping out."

"Wouldn't want to be anywhere else."

I left Dad and the kids in the recliner and made my way to the bedroom, taking care to be quiet. I pushed the door open and saw that Jovi was sleeping, so I carefully shut it behind me and then kicked off my shoes and crawled into bed with her.

"Hey, baby," Jovi said sleepily as she moved closer to me. "Is it finished?"

"It's all done. If we keep having kids, I'm gonna run out of skin to tattoo."

"At least one more," she mumbled against my chest.

"In two years?"

"Yeah. Koda will be ten, Star will be four, and Remy will be two."

"You're crazy, woman."

"You knew that when you married me."

"I knew that when we were teenagers and you told me you wanted four children."

"It's best to have a plan."

"Always the planner."

"But you love me anyway."

"Always have and I always will."

Check out Cee Bowerman on Facebook. You can also find information about the author and her books on www.ceebowermanbooks.com.

COMING SOON

LUCA RUSSO, FOUR FAMILIES, BOOK 3
COMING JUNE 15TH, 2024!

A favor for a friend took Luca on the adventure of a lifetime and changed his life in a way that he never expected. When he met Tabby, he wasn't sure he should trust her but knew instantly that she was the one for him. No matter how hard he resisted the pull, he couldn't help but fall for her and make her his own. A twisted tale of secrets and half-truths wasn't exactly the way to start a lasting relationship, but that was the foundation they had to start with. Luca had no choice but to play the hand he was dealt - and to do that successfully, he needed to get a ring on her finger sooner rather than later.

Tabitha was thrust into a whole new world when she came to New York from her small hometown. With barely a dime to her name and the help of new friends that she couldn't live without, she had carved out a life for herself and her daughter that had ups and downs she wasn't sure how to navigate. A secret sent her running back into the arms of her chosen family and would ultimately put her in the path of a man she couldn't resist.

Join Cee Bowerman as she explores the world of the New York mafia in the Four Families series, and fall in love with Luca and Tabby - a couple who were destined to be together from the start.

Please take just a few minutes to leave a review of this book on Amazon and feel free to share the link with your friends. I enjoy discussing my books and characters and would love to hear from you.

About the Author

Cee Bowerman is proud, lifelong resident of Texas. She is married to her own long-haired, tattooed biker and is the proud mom to three mostly adult kids - a daughter and two sons. She believes in love, second chances, rescue dogs, and happily ever after.

Cee received her first romance novel along with a bag of other books from her granny when she was recovering from surgery at 15. She has been hooked on reading romances ever since. For years, she had a dream of writing her own series of stories, but motherhood and all the other grown up responsibilities kept getting in the way. Luckily, with the support of her family and the encouragement of her son, she purchased a computer and let her dreams become a reality.

Made in the USA
Columbia, SC
21 January 2025

51459807R00167